THE MISFORTUNE OF
MARION PALM

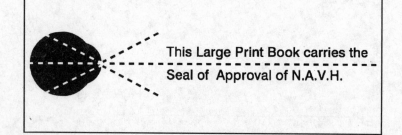

This Large Print Book carries the
Seal of Approval of N.A.V.H.

THE MISFORTUNE OF MARION PALM

EMILY CULLITON

THORNDIKE PRESS
A part of Gale, a Cengage Company

Farmington Hills, Mich • San Francisco • New York • Waterville, Maine
Meriden, Conn • Mason, Ohio • Chicago

Copyright © 2017 by Emily Culliton.
Thorndike Press, a part of Gale, a Cengage Company.

Thorndike Press® Large Print Basic.
The text of this Large Print edition is unabridged.
Other aspects of the book may vary from the original edition.
Set in 16 pt. Plantin.

LIBRARY OF CONGRESS CIP DATA ON FILE.
CATALOGUING IN PUBLICATION FOR THIS BOOK
IS AVAILABLE FROM THE LIBRARY OF CONGRESS

ISBN-13: 978-1-4328-4639-8 (hardcover)
ISBN-10: 1-4328-4639-6 (hardcover)

Published in 2018 by arrangement with Alfred A. Knopf, a division of Penguin Random House LLC

Printed in the United States of America
1 2 3 4 5 6 7 22 21 20 19 18

For my sister, Kate

In Upper Flatbush, already two miles deep inland from the bridges, a young woman of Manhattan asked a druggist how she might get into certain territory well south of there. Without thought of irony he began, "Oh. You want to go to Brooklyn."

— James Agee, *Brooklyn Is: Southeast of the Island: Travel Notes*

CONTENTS

9

Marion Palm is on the lam.

A blue JanSport knapsack filled with $40,000 rests between her ankles. She's taking a train to a midwestern city. She'll buy the ticket under an assumed name. She said goodbye to her two daughters an hour ago and lied about where she was going. She did not say goodbye to her husband. He'll need to figure this one out on his own.

Marion Palm took her daughters to a Greek diner on Montague to say goodbye. She and her youngest agree: the cheeseburgers have a palliative texture because the meat, cheese, and bun present similarly. Her oldest has never cared for hamburgers and french fries but appeases her mother when she can.

Marion Palm ran out on the check because it was cash only and her cash was in the knapsack, organized with rubber bands. The rubber bands are multicolored and from her desk at work. She keeps them in a tray meant for rubber bands, paper clips, and loose change. Opening the knapsack at the diner would mean her daughters might see all the cash, and they would tell. Better to run from the $27 check.

Marion's train moves up a line on the clicking timetable, and Marion taps the toe of her left shoe. She's mimicking a woman ten feet away who is not on the lam. Police with German shepherds stroll through the crowd. Marion wants to smile at the police and say, *Hi, officer!* She wants to pet the dogs.

A homely woman is an invisible thing. This is her and her disguise. Her heart recognizes that she is on the lam and beats harder for her. This is a natural progression of criminal behavior. She is wrathful and sad that she must go on the lam. She will miss her daughters.

The money does not belong to her. There is no honest reason why she should have it.

A man stops in front of her to rattle coins in a creased paper cup. He wears filthy sweatpants, a parka, and a bag shaped like a tennis racket. He smells like urine. He bows to Marion.

"Spare change?" he asks.

"Haven't got any," Marion says. All the

cash is needed, and she left her coin purse behind in the basement of her brownstone, along with her credit cards, Social Security card, passport, driver's license, and cell phone.

The man intuits the woman's fixedness. He moves on.

Her train rises up once more, and Marion knows she must purchase her ticket soon. She closes her eyes to stem her panic.

THE WALL, OR PROGRESS

Nathan Palm doesn't know he's alone in the house. He thinks his wife is downstairs because he hasn't heard her leave. In his office on the third floor, he looks at a legal pad on his dark wooden desk. There's a pen next to it. He can't make any decisions because he thinks he may have done something terrible.

He writes half a line, but rather than finish the thought, he relives his morning, which was fine and normal until he opened his mouth. He stands to call out for his wife. He'll ask her about their plans for the weekend. How about an excursion, a family excursion? He'll plan it, he'll say. He'll do anything. He must fix this before he can write. He bellows her name and jogs down the stairs with his head still on the legal pad but also on the morning and now on the weekend. If he can just see her face and locate within her face that all is well, he'll

18

be allowed to keep writing. He looks into the bedroom, the living room. He pauses and listens to the house. The creaks and moans of the stairs and uneven hardwood floors give up occupants' locations; the house is quiet. "Marion?" he asks. He has a first line, it could be a way in, but Marion hasn't answered, and without that answer from Marion he'll never write the second line. He checks his watch. The line in is never good, but he knows he has to write it. The doorbell rings.

The line isn't it, but he won't find it with the doorbell going. He waits for Marion to spring up from wherever she is and answer. The air is unsettled by the doorbell, but nothing moves.

Nathan opens the front door and discovers his daughters out there on the stoop, eight and thirteen, and they look abandoned. Their coats are zipped, but his youngest shivers. At this time of day his children should not belong to him; they belong to school.

"What are you doing here?"

His youngest wails that she is sorry. She is really sorry. When his daughter wails, she is usually wailing that she is sorry.

"Mom signed us out. We had cheeseburgers and then she said she was going to visit

Shelley for a week."

This is his oldest, Ginny. She is good with details but has a capacity for cruelty. Nathan Palm relates more to his younger daughter than to his older daughter.

"What?"

"Shelley."

His youngest is now in the doorway with Nathan, wrapping her arm around his thigh and crying. When Nathan kneels to look her in the eye, she gives up his thigh in favor of his neck.

"Why is Jane so upset? Why didn't your mom bring you home? Why did she take you out of school?"

His oldest frowns and shrugs.

"Don't know. Dad, do we need to go back?"

Nathan pictures his work on the third floor. There's that half line, which could be a full line, and now he believes it might be good. He imagines the book the poem would be included in; he conjures up the spine of the book, found on an old crowded bookshelf. His success is something past. The work is finished and he is content. His daydream is to be home again, but he has never commuted. He once sledgehammered away a low ten-foot-long concrete wall. When they bought the house, this wall

20

bifurcated the backyard. Marion wanted to hire someone, but Nathan, inspired, bought a sledgehammer at the hardware store. It was a good purchase to make. He learned how to wind the sledgehammer behind him and up, over, and down into the wall. He repeated the action until the concrete fractured; then he focused on the fracture until he could dislodge a piece of the wall. The wall became less. There was movement. There was a display of accountability. When the wall was gone, he missed it. He would lose that line. It seemed good only on the first floor. It would sour on the third.

"No. Let's watch some television and drink juice."

The Palm girls watch a rerun in the den and sip cranberry cocktail. Nathan stands in the kitchen to phone his missing wife. He thinks of the terrible mistake he made that morning. As the phone rings, he lives his morning again but chooses not to see his wife in her nightgown, rotating her wrists, and because he does not see her, this wiser and ideal version of Nathan never says a word.

WOMEN WHO EMBEZZLE

Marion Palm is an expert on women who embezzle. She does not think of women as embezzlers. Embezzlers are men; for women, embezzlement is a practice.

Women who embezzle do not live lavishly. The reason for the practice has nothing to do with status. It has to do with justice and enforced reciprocity. Women who embezzle will save the money, pay some bills, and then buy a Jet Ski for their family. Women who embezzle will bid extraordinary amounts on rare Victorian dolls on eBay.

Women who embezzle are not apologetic, but they may cry when caught. When women who embezzle embezzle from churches, they fall to their knees and pray. They do not pray for forgiveness. They pray for safety and protection. Women who embezzle from offices do not cry but cross their arms and stiffly smile, as if to say, *What did you expect?* They've worked at the office for twenty years and are seen as a piece of furniture. A filing cabinet. They may be eager to be caught. They may want credit for their greed and ingenuity.

Marion Palm has embezzled $180,000 over the years from her daughters' private school in Brooklyn, where she works part-time in the development office. Her daughters' quarterly tuition payments are paid by her husband's family trust. She's never seen his money and so it does not exist. It's explained to be the interest from Great-Grandfather Henry Palm's fortune. The money is now represented as a series of digits online, in unending transit through international wires.

She's spent some of the money she embezzled on appliances, exercise equipment, and several family trips to Europe. Her husband, a writer of difficult fiction and terse prose poems, receives a monthly allowance from the trust and believes it is enough for a family of four because he does not know what things cost. He does not know how to worry about money, and Marion has never asked him to. He enjoys the Sub-Zero refrigerator, an environmentally friendly boiler, a state-of-the-art elliptical machine, and a new patio. He believes these are things all families deserve.

Marion Palm has embezzled $180,000, spent most of it on her family, but saved $40,000 in cash for herself. It was hidden in the basement of the brownstone. She collected it this morning after she read an email from her supervisor informing her that the school was about to be audited by the IRS. Her supervisor was panicking, because Marion has been, in essence, doing her supervisor's job while the supervisor suffers a glacially slow mental breakdown. *What should I do?* the supervisor asked. *The board keeps asking me questions about the books and I don't know any of the answers. When are you getting here? As you well know, these stress situations trigger my fight-or-flight. Come to my office immediately. Did you inform me that you would be late?* Marion deleted the email.

Marion has saved the knapsack for an occasion like this.

SHELLEY

Marion isn't picking up. Daniel, her office-mate at the school, hasn't seen her. Neither has the hall master nor Marion's supervisor. There was a meeting Marion missed, and Daniel reports to Nathan the meeting agenda. Daniel is another father and unpleasant. Marion sits across a desk from Daniel, and Nathan doesn't understand how Marion can tolerate Daniel and why she bothers to try. Daniel air-quotes incorrectly. Nathan feels him air-quote over the phone.

"I haven't seen her 'per se,' but if you do see her, please remind her that Deb needs to speak to her. She said it was urgent. We need to discuss the Pumpkin Patch vis-à-vis logistics and also, of course, marketing 'strategy' for the Wing Initiative."

Nathan wonders if these words mean anything, and despairs for his wife.

"So you haven't seen Marion today?"

"No, as I said —"

"Thank you. My wife is missing." Next Nathan must call his wife's closest friend, Shelley, another Brooklyn mother. This one divorced her husband to move to the Hudson Valley to ride horses and sculpt and sleep with mountain men, or so Nathan hopes. He likes Shelley and was bored by her lawyer husband. When they divorced, he wished Shelley well. Marion hasn't spoken to Shelley much since she moved, but now the girls say their mother has hopped on the Hudson Line to visit her.

He should have called Shelley first, but hoped the girls were confused and Marion was sitting at her desk listening to the terrible Daniel. If his wife left him, she would go to Shelley.

He calls Shelley and leaves a message. It's a strange message to leave. He imagines his wife and Shelley hiking cathartically, discussing or not discussing him. Perhaps the girls know more than they say. But in terms of trauma for children, abandonment must rank high, so he sits on the couch with his daughters to watch television.

Two episodes pass and Jane is asleep, curled into her father; she's the type who misses nap time.

Nathan runs his fingers over Jane's braids

and asks Ginny what she thinks may have happened to her mother.

Ginny is wedged into the other end of the couch, as far as possible from her father and her sister, long legs tucked. When her body acts teenish, when she needs this physical distance between herself and her family, Ginny is disquieted. She feels as if her center of gravity has moved.

"Your mom is visiting Shelley?"

"That's what she told us."

Ginny's waiting to tell how they didn't pay for their cheeseburgers. It was odd, her mother's behavior. When they finished eating, Marion told Ginny and Jane she would meet them outside on the sidewalk and left the diner alone. They were to sit for two minutes more at the table and then follow. After doing as they were told, Ginny and Jane found their mother hiding in a de-phoned phone booth at the end of the block. She told her daughters to run, and she ran faster than them. Her blue knapsack was particularly unsettling, the way it bounced on her back. Ginny wants to understand her mother's actions before she tells her father.

"I thought Mom was mad at Shelley," Ginny says.

She was, Nathan thinks, but still took her

27

calls during dinner. When Shelley started dating and painting and discovering and visualizing the self ("I allow myself to love myself," "I allow myself to feel beautiful"), Marion said she was disgusted. Her friend's self-absorption nauseated her, but she wouldn't tell Shelley how she felt. Marion said to admit that anger would demand a scene, and the scene was impossible, because it would require from her more involvement, more patience, more listening. She said she would end up comforting Shelley, and it would still be only about Shelley, thereby giving Shelley exactly what she wanted: attention. Better to fade angrily away. Nathan feels women are more burdened by obligation than men. So Marion may be, at last, doing her duty by visiting, then confronting, then comforting. But though this is all possible, Nathan still believes his wife has left him.

The last time he saw Marion was their encounter this morning. The girls had left for school. He was reading the *Times* at the kitchen counter and drinking coffee. He looked to his left, and there was Marion in her nightgown, standing in the door frame. Bare feet. She stared at him and let her fingers curl up. Nathan looked at his wife's feet; her toes curled down. She must be angry, Nathan thought at the time, and before he fully investigated that thought, considered what could have made his wife angry, he said, "I've got a thing in Dumbo today," and Marion didn't say, "Fine." Didn't say, "Till when?" She said none of the things she usually said when he said he had a thing to do. Instead she stood in the door frame and made and unmade fists.

He'll avoid talking about Marion to his daughters until he receives verification that he's been left. He won't bring her up until he has some idea how long this punishment will last. He'll pretend that this is normal.

Poor girls, he thinks. Poor women.

MIDWESTERN CITY

The departure will draw attention, but Marion decided when she began embezzling that she would not be waiting for the police when caught. She prizes her own ability to coordinate, once wasted on PTA functions and her husband's literary readings. Now she is coordinating her own getaway and she is and will continue to be magnificent.

Marion Palm hoists the $40,000 up and takes her new driver's license from the front pocket of her knapsack. She sent away for the fake ID and it cost her $300. She bought this fake ID after purchasing a previous one on West Eighth for $70. She'd overheard the high schoolers discussing the operation. However, once she was in the basement of the store, which sold skateboards and bongs, she realized it was a scam for the underaged of Brooklyn, Manhattan, and New Jersey. The lamination of the West Eighth Street ID curled up and the watermark too boldly announced itself. Marion won't make that mistake again. When it comes to a new identity, it's best not to go with the bargain.

She still needs to buy her ticket to the midwestern city. She estimates it will be a fifty-hour trip. She chose where she would run away to as she would choose a destination for a family vacation. She read articles in *The New York Times* travel section and pictured herself at various restaurants, museums, and landmarks. She felt she made a good decision, and she made it sitting at her desk at work.

Marion remembers a movie as she approaches the ticket counter. Cary Grant tries to buy a train ticket from New York to Chicago, and the man behind the counter hesitates to look at a HAVE YOU SEEN THIS MAN? photo of Cary Grant. He's twisted charmingly to the camera and holds a long knife with an odd grip. Cary Grant must flee the ticket counter and stow himself away on a train, and lucky him, because he gets to have dinner with Eva Marie Saint.

Hitchcock shot the scene at Grand Central. Marion would much prefer to make her escape from that location. She wants to be romantic about it. She wants to wear tortoiseshell sunglasses like Cary Grant and

31

have that be, as a disguise, both sufficient and necessary. Alas, this is not a movie; Grand Central serves only the commuter rail now and so Marion must spend her time in Penn Station. Low-ceilinged, fast-food-smelling, spirit-crushing. It's a structure seemingly built to make its current occupants question their significant life decisions.

There's no line at the ticket counter, and only one barred window is marked as open for business. Marion looks into the office behind the window. Two women and a man chat in swivel chairs facing inward. Marion must knock on the Plexiglas behind the bars with her knuckles to get their attention. They all swivel to look at her, and stare. Eventually one of the women rises.

"Can I help you?" she asks.

"Yes, I need to buy a train ticket," Marion says.

"You can do that at the ticket machine," the woman says, gesturing vaguely to the great beyond behind Marion.

"Yes, but I'd like to use cash," Marion says.

"Cash," the woman says.

"Yes, cash," Marion says. She pauses. "I left my credit cards at home. By accident."

"Okay, fine. Hang on." The woman taps

the keyboard next to her and waits, eyes focused on the monitor. Marion believes she's turning the computer on for the first time that day. The two other Amtrak employees are staring at the interaction in wonder. There is no WANTED picture of Marion; she has not maybe killed a diplomat like Cary Grant. Detectives in fedoras may never ask questions about her whereabouts, but what if they do? There is a whole lot of other people's money resting between Marion's calves and ankles. She's making an impression on the woman behind the counter as well as her friends in the back. She interrupted them, demanded something of them that was unusual. She imagines them describing to the police a nervous, frumpy woman who had $500 in cash but no credit cards, no bank cards, and a dubious ID. They would give a good description of her; there might even be security footage, and a computer record of her destination. The police would be waiting for her train at the midwestern station, ready to read her her rights, put her in handcuffs, and return her to New York City for prosecution, possibly on the same train she came in on. This ticket would be a waste of money.

"Wait," Marion says. "I just found my card. It was in my pocket." The woman stops looking at the computer. "I can buy my ticket at the machine."

The woman throws up her hands in annoyance and returns to her swivel-chair group. Marion stands with her hands flat on the grimy white counter, then looks for her daughters on either side of her. She remembers that they are in Brooklyn while she is in Manhattan. She removes her hands from the counter.

JUST PLAY

Nathan orders a pizza when he notices the hours have passed and Marion still hasn't called or texted. When Jane asks in the middle of dinner if she can play outside — a request frequently made at this time and usually denied — Nathan says yes, fine, and she leaves with her half-eaten slice in hand; Ginny, surprisingly, follows. Jane works on her slice of pizza, then forgets she holds the slice and carries it like a sheet of paper. Ginny reminds her sister that the slice is her dinner, but Jane is not hungry. The day is now gray and wet, the yellow and orange leaves slick, vibrant, and flat. The leaves adhere to the girls' shoes and socks. The tree that deposited the leaves stands in the far corner of the backyard, which is long and rectangular and filled with strange unkempt vegetation. When parents and babysitters aren't looking, the Palm girls climb the tree to peer into their neighbors' yards for stray cats and other children.

They haven't climbed the tree today because it's damp and their father could be watching from the kitchen.

Jane is more imaginative than her sister, and likes that she is. She easily creates worlds, whereas Ginny gets hung up on the details or, worse, demands realism.

"Pretend we're escaping from prison," Jane poses.

"Are we criminals?"

"Yeah, but we were right. We live in a police state. You be the secret police. I'll be the underground."

If Nathan were paying attention to his daughters in the backyard, he would be proud. He would talk about it at dinner parties to charm the wives of his friends.

Ginny interrogates various characters played by Jane. Ginny demands to know where the criminal is hiding. Is she in the attic? Is she in the basement? Jane's characters clutch babushkas and wipe brows. The pizza slice is in the dirt. Jane climbs the tree, despite its dampness, to escape Ginny. Ginny marches. Jane swings.

Ginny was embarrassed by her mother at school and later at the diner. She'll be required to explain to her teachers why her mother is gone. She'll tell the truth, but it will look like she's lying, so she'll need her father's confirmation, and it will be difficult to reach him on the phone.

Ginny believes her mother is in some great trouble, so she's playing with her sister, even though she is too old for it. Her mother and her father have both lied to her today. Her parents have lied to her before, but she thought those lies were purposefully designed. The randomness of the day makes Ginny think of disease, even though no one is sick.

Inside the house, Nathan's back on the phone. He dials and redials his wife's cell. Marion's voice tells him repeatedly to leave a message, and he leaves several. The messages escalate, and this is the last one:

"Where the fuck are you? Why didn't you tell me you were visiting Shelley? I'm sorry. Okay. Is this you leaving me? Is it real this time? Did you forget to tell me? Are you insane? I'm sorry. Are you angry? Who does this? I don't understand."

HOMELESS AT PENN STATION

There is an area devoted to waiting for Amtrak trains at Penn Station, and one must have a ticket to enter it. Or so the signs claim. Marion passes the guard without a problem. She believes that the required ticket is a legal way to keep the homeless men and women away from the seats, where they could really set up camp. The gentleman who asked for Marion's spare change, for instance, is barred from this central waiting area.

The waiting area is not conducive to waiting for a train. There are no timetables within most lines of sight, and the announcements on the loudspeaker, while frequent, are often unintelligible, and so a train could arrive and depart without one's having been informed. There are televisions, and they perhaps once displayed track information, but these screens are now devoted to safety videos. They instruct the waiting on how to react to a terrorist attack or a lone shooter. Actors mime various scenarios, such as dialing 911 and correctly hiding behind a large pillar or a fern. The final scenario instructs individuals on how to engage with the terrorist, but this is advisable only if one's death is imminent. It is suggested that by engaging with the terrorist, one will probably die but may save others in the process. Again, Amtrak does not want one to lose one's life, but it feels it has to mention the possibility.

The best way to wait for a train at Penn Station is to stand in the central atrium and watch the flicking timetable with one's luggage resting between one's feet. One must be prepared to run when the track number is announced; one must be prepared to elbow fellow passengers — it's the only way to get a window seat. Marion's taking a break from waiting correctly. Besides, she was only pretending to wait for a train, too frightened to pick one. Her feet hurt from standing, and she kept finding her children in her peripheral vision. She kept extending her hand, expecting Jane to reach up and take it.

She wonders if she should buy a train ticket to a closer city. She could buy a ticket to New Jersey with cash without arousing suspicion. Once there, she could buy another, and see the country for a while; there is no need to arrive at a destination. But the knapsack is heavy, and with every interaction there is the chance of being found out.

She's also too organized for that kind of unfocused escape. She wanted to buy the ticket to the midwestern city because it seemed like a good solution. She liked the idea of going West as an outlaw. In the abstract, it seemed funny.

She is 6.4 miles away from home. It is 7:04 p.m. She's been at Penn Station for five hours.

She should buy a ticket for the next train no matter where it goes. But the woman behind the ticket counter will absolutely remember her. Buying a ticket from a human and with cash is an obsolete act. She may also remember that Marion looked for daughters who were not there.

Marion puts on the knapsack, heads out of the waiting area, and does not look once more at the timetable. She walks past the ticket kiosk, past the ticketing machines. She's on an escalator, rising back to the street. She's opening a glass door and leaving the dreary station. Hooking her thumbs underneath the straps of her knapsack, she walks confidently into the crowd.

BEDROOMS

Nathan Palm's stomach extends from the pizza and the scotch. He is winded on the stairs, following Ginny and Jane to bed. He finished his voicemails and doesn't know what else to do. Should he call their friends? Should he call the police? But he's not concerned; he's abandoned. And he's been through this before. Police and friends will take the disappearance the wrong way, and he'll appear foolish.

So he'll get domestic. He'll play single dad. He'll get his daughters ready for bed.

Ginny reminds him, not gently, that she is thirteen years old.

Jane, however, is glad when he watches her brush her teeth. He turns down the bedsheet for her, pulls the wrinkles smooth, and she slips in. He offers to tell her a story.

Ginny listens from her bedroom down the hall. It is not comforting. Jane pretends to be younger than she is. Nathan pretends too. They act idyllic to subdue themselves. Ginny must do the dangerous thinking.

She sneaks downstairs to her father and mother's room. The blinds are down. Paperbacks tower. Her mother's jewelry and mail crowd the top of the low bureau. Her father's clothes are on the floor.

She finds his wallet in the pocket of a pair of jeans. There are three twenties in it, and Ginny takes two. She folds the twenties small and goes back up. Her father still murmurs magically. Ginny sits on her made bed, turns off the light, and hides the two twenties under the base of her lamp. She looks out the window at the passing cars and counts the red taillights in the dark.

A Missing Boy

In the middle of Brooklyn, a ghost is in the making. It will happen by accident and because of logic. A small shift to the routine will have unforeseen devastating consequences. It will maim hearts. It begins with an open gate.

A Brooklyn mother delivers her special son to a special school, and it is a morning like every other morning; it must be so, or her son won't budge. On the sidewalk, she adjusts his collar and tries to catch his eye. She accepts this nonacceptance; she recognizes his nonrecognition once more and leads him into the schoolyard. She has a mental catalogue of each of his small affections. The last time he spoke. When he reached for her hand in a shopping mall. Some are real expressions from her son — his intention to connect is clear — and some are surely random and accidental happenings, but she keeps them all the same. She

43

closes the gate of the playground carefully behind her. She hears the gate latch.

At least, she believes she did. She can't remember when asked about it that afternoon. No one can. Everyone believes they latched it, heard it latch, but no one can remember with any certainty because the whine of the gate and the clicking of gears are common daily sounds.

But someone is guilty, because the gate's left open for the Brooklyn mother's son to make his escape. It's not until the students are settled on the rug inside and the teachers are counting the bodies in the circle that they notice their numbers are off. A roll call is taken, and the boy's mother receives a message at work. Her boy has gone missing.

INSPIRATION

Shelley calls when the girls are asleep. Nathan is in the kitchen, implausibly eating more pizza. He's also pouring another drink. When the phone rings, he believes that it is Marion. This night could be over soon.

"Hi? Nathan?"

He recognizes Shelley's voice. She relays his strange message back to him. She hasn't heard from Marion in months, and if Marion is coming to stay with her, it's not a great time.

"I mean, I just started this new woodworking project, it's really exciting, but wood chips everywhere. You know."

"Wood chips? No."

"I mean, a new project. You have to start, you must seize the inspiration, because it doesn't come that often. You know."

"I don't, Shelley. It's never been like that for me."

"But what happened? Where is Marion?"

Nathan looks at the last slice.

"Miscommunication. She's visiting her cousins in Utica. I thought she was going next week, but it turns out it was today, and her cell died."

"Good. I'm so glad. You sounded worried."

"I was, but it's all sorted now."

The two chat about the Hudson Valley and the long winters until one of them can safely make an excuse and get off the phone. Ginny, who has been listening to her father lie from the hallway, now tiptoes back to bed. She is righteous; her suspicions have been confirmed. She is angry; her father should have been honest with her. She is frightened; her mother is missing.

Nathan sits at the desk in the den with his drink. It's Marion's desk, but the ancient desktop computer belongs to the family. The girls sometimes play games on it, and Marion checks her email, but mostly it likes to crash and to be rebooted. Nathan clicks into his wife's email account, but she's signed out. She's also deleted her browser history. Nathan takes a largish sip of scotch, checks his own account, and he has thirty-four new emails. Most are from Daniel. He reads one and then deletes the rest, because they are all the same. The last email is from Marion's supervisor, Deborah. Deborah's tone is fine at the start, professional yet concerned, but it deteriorates, and what's left behind are run-on sentences and a clash of quirky yet oddly suggestive emojis. It ends with two questions rather than a signature: *Where did Marion go? Doesn't she know we need her?* Nathan opens a window to respond, but instead emails the person he was supposed to meet that afternoon but never did. *I'm sorry,* he types.

SHOPPING

Marion looks for a space to be. She's incapable of spending any of her money and she cannot rest. When she needs a bathroom, she panics. She walks into several Starbucks but is frightened away by the baristas or the homeless people who usually use those bathrooms. She walks to the Whole Foods on 59th, and in the bustle of wealthy Manhattanites and the people who work for them she is able to find a bathroom more anonymously. As she pees, she holds her knapsack off the floor, because there isn't a hook and because she can't let go. After, she sits there, still, with her pants around her ankles, until someone pounds on the stall door.

She walks through the grocery store. She goes up and down the aisles. Ginny's in the grains aisle until she turns into a petite woman in yoga pants and pristine running shoes. Marion eats free samples until she

48

notices an aproned man noticing her. It's time to go, and she takes an escalator back to the first floor of the mall. She spends more hours in a kitchen store, in a clothing store, and in a bookstore. There, Nathan hovers over new hardcover nonfiction. Marion blinks. She reaches for her phone in her pocket, but remembers she left it in the basement after she returned it to factory settings and dropped it in a glass of tap water for good measure. Nathan becomes a stranger. She pats her pocket again and again, remembers again and again.

The last store to close is the bookstore, and she is shut out into the street and the night. Central Park is dark except for the yellow glowing air under the streetlights. Male joggers head into the dark park. She finds them foolish. The women will jog in the morning and be sensible, wise, and safe.

She has a home and a bed and she is 7.5 miles away from both.

She edges the park. Doormen watch her as she goes by. Some say goodnight. She's nearing the Plaza Hotel when one calls to her: "It isn't a good idea to be out alone. I know everyone says New York is safe, but we're still very close to the park."

"I'm not a tourist," she says. "I'm from here. I live here."

He apologizes. "It's just that you looked kind of . . ."

When he doesn't finish the thought, Marion walks on. She sees a box of light and it's the Apple Store and she remembers the Apple Store is twenty-four hours. She pretends she has a laptop that just died with her report and it is a very important report on budgets and losses. She makes a mental note: she will not look *kind of* anymore.

ROUGH

Nathan can't sleep, or rather, he is unable to give himself the opportunity to sleep. He sits up with the television. Each episode of something needs to be watched; otherwise he visualizes the morning before. During the commercial breaks, he plays through how it could have gone another way, how he could have said nothing as she stared at him in that flannel nightgown. Instead he had to talk. Something in her eyes made him talk, because he wanted to help, which is not uncharitable. He wants his family to be whole, and yet Marion stares at him in her nightgown, feet bare, the flannel swelling around her stomach and her ass and her knees. She hasn't brushed her teeth. *I have a thing in Dumbo.* He didn't need to tell her, so why did he? Why did he say anything at all?

His eyes must close at some point, because they open again around five with an early-morning talk show. He fumbles upstairs to his bed but never bothers to set an alarm. Ginny wakes him when Jane's school bus is about to arrive. He is still wearing his clothes from the night before. The first morning without Marion will be a rough one.

Both girls are still in their pajamas drinking orange juice when the bus driver honks her horn, and Nathan must go out to the street to explain to the bus driver that he will take Jane to school today. The bus driver is annoyed with him for not calling this in to the dispatcher. It's time wasted on her route.

Nathan won't take Jane to school, Ginny will, but he'll walk his children to the F station, even though Ginny informs him that this is unnecessary. Humiliating, even. Nathan Palm doesn't care and tells her so.

"I am your father. I am not humiliating."

As he walks home, he thinks of his father and how humiliating he could be.

CENTRAL PARK

Spending a night in an Apple Store is not a good idea. Marion is lucky she looks the way she looks: nonviolent. But after three hours the employees are suspicious. They begin to move her from one computer to another, asking questions about her RAM needs and explaining the millions of pixels available to her. As she tries every set of headphones displayed, one persistent employee asks her over and over again what it is she is hoping to accomplish. Marion acts sane until she figures sanity is not an asset. She barks that she is busy, busy, can't he see, and the employee becomes meek and slinks away. After that, no more blue shirts bother her.

As she circles the store, she circles her options. There are not many. She researches the trains that leave New York City, but none of the arrival cities call out to her. The case is the same with the buses. She can't picture herself on the streets of these places. She dislikes the architecture of most midwestern cities. Perfect sidewalks and parks without life. She considers Philadelphia for an hour: it seems affordable, and the red brick structures are attractively run-down, but at the end of the hour she finds a reason why it wouldn't work. An hour after that, she can't remember the reason but feels certain it was a good one. Vermont is briefly her new home around 4:30, but then she knows too many Brooklynites who often speak of moving to a farmhouse and tapping their own maple syrup. Who knows? One of them might actually do it.

She's stumbling on the logistics. She would need to buy a car in order to survive in most of these places. She's frightened of driving now, and also, how could she buy a car without a legal identity? Without a credit history and insurance? How could she work? Marion knows she should have considered these questions more completely when she packed the knapsack full of cash and drowned her phone but is glad she didn't. If she had, she might not have been able to leave.

When the sun rises, Marion climbs the glass steps of the store and exits. She heads into Central Park, where there are benches and she can cry safely with her knapsack beside her. The air is sharp and cold, but regardless, she is glad to be out of the fake air of the computer store.

She hasn't slept in twenty-four hours. Neurons fire, instructing her to wake her daughters up for school, to make them breakfast and pack their lunches. She feels like she's left the stove on or a window open during a storm. A bathtub fills with hot water and now spills over the porcelain lip. She considers resting her head on her knapsack but blinks away the idea before it becomes too attractive. She would be nothing without the knapsack.

She closes her eyes and begs for inspiration. She opens her eyes and remembers laughing with Nathan about a melancholy English teacher who had an affair with the rumored gay but hetero-normatively married college counselor. They'd conducted the affair at a Days Inn off Fourth Avenue in Sunset Park, chosen by the adulterers for its acceptance of cash and relative anonymity. It's decided: Marion is heading back to Brooklyn.

CHAPEL

Ginny takes the F train to school and the B57 back home. On the first day of every month she's given a new green MetroCard by the city. She loses it most days and must fly through her backpack and her coat pockets and her books to find it again. She usually does, but hides from her parents her absentmindedness. The MetroCard is symbolic of her new freedom or even a physical manifestation of her freedom, and she knows that her father wishes she did not have one. Given any opportunity, he could take it away from her and she would be back on the school bus with her sister, a foot taller than the other riders. It would be impossible.

Her mother has shrugged her shoulders at Nathan's anxiety about the MetroCard in the past.

"When I was growing up, I had a bike. During the summer, we just took off. We had to be back by dinner. My mother didn't know where I was."

Even Ginny could see that Marion was baiting Nathan.

"How pastoral for you," Nathan said. "The thing is — and I don't want to take anything away from your street smarts — downtown Brooklyn is slightly more dangerous than Sheepshead Bay. And with that fucking thing, she doesn't even have to stay in Brooklyn. She could go to the fucking Bronx and be back by dinner."

"Don't go to the Bronx, honey."

Mother and daughter smiled conspiratorially over the dinner table.

Ginny's backpack is heavy with textbooks, so she walks hunched, her arms swinging front and back. She juts her jaw and clenches her teeth. Her father's twenties are tucked in the front pocket of her jeans, and she periodically checks to make sure they are still there. She ignores Jane, who babbles as they walk from the subway station to the school.

Ginny's head is back with the last time she saw her mother. They ran down Montague toward Court, and then Marion Palm pulled her girls into a CVS. Ginny thought their mother was going to take out some cash from an ATM and go back to the diner to pay, but instead she stopped in the shampoo aisle. That's where she told them that she was going to visit Shelley, and then she left. Marion didn't say anything about going back to school, so her girls didn't. Ginny took Jane home on the bus with her in the middle of the day. Jane didn't have a MetroCard, but the driver was nice and let her ride for free. Ginny wasn't supposed to have Jane there — she should have taken Jane back to school — but she didn't know how to explain where they had been and what they had been doing. When Nathan didn't ask about it, Ginny realized that she had been worried about the wrong stuff.

Still with her mother in the shampoo aisle, Ginny looks up, and she is in the wide arched entryway of her school. She doesn't remember the walk from Jay Street. She pushes Jane in the direction of her classroom, and Jane goes willingly and happily. She waves bye-bye. Ginny looks at the clock; the sisters have been walking slowly, and now she is two minutes late for chapel, and another lateness means another detention, and so she begins to run up the stairs, panting under the weight of her backpack.

"No running," the hall master calls out.

The chapel is on the third floor, and an out-of-breath Ginny pushes the door open.

The eyes of the middle school turn to watch as she slides into the back pew reserved for latecomers. The dean of the middle school pauses his announcement to look over his lectern at her, and then he resumes.

She is embarrassed, of course, and there is the customary longing to disappear, but beneath or above the embarrassment she wonders if the dean looked at her too long, as if he knew that she and her mother and her sister had dined and dashed. She feels other teachers' gazes on her; she is marked today. She must reason with herself: They can't know about the diner. They can't know that her mother didn't come home last night.

Ginny is busy convincing herself that this is true, so she doesn't see her homeroom teacher walk to the back of the chapel and stand behind her. The homeroom teacher has bent forward and rested her forearms on the wooden pew to whisper into Ginny's ear. "See me after chapel," she says, and Ginny manages to nod. It may be her lateness that will be discussed. It may be some other things. Her homeroom teacher wears Bible socks and long dangly earrings and hates cursing. She's never not grinning, and even though Ginny is thirteen, she is taller than her homeroom teacher. It makes it difficult when the homeroom teacher is attempting to discipline her, because Ginny can see her white scalp through her thinning hair.

Ginny closes her eyes again, folds her hands in her lap, and touches her chin to her chest.

"Are you praying?" says the boy next to her.

Ginny opens her eyes, ready to counter the accusation, but the boy is smiling kindly. He is in the eighth grade and Ginny is in seventh, so his speaking to her is extraordinary. She smiles a different smile from her normal smile and coughs a laugh.

"Yeah, I'm praying," she says.

"Okay, I'll pray too," he says, and the two edge forward in their pews, close their eyes, bend their heads, and try not to smile. At the lectern, the dean speaks passionately about the successes and failures of the school's compost heap, and then chapel is over. The boy whispers "Amen" into Ginny's ear and slides away. Ginny is now in love.

She waits in her pew for her homeroom teacher, who will demonstrate Ginny's lack of punctuality and therefore respect by showing her an attendance book, and she will insist that Ginny approve of the punishment meted out to her. Ginny wishes she didn't mind. She objectively understands that the detention is meaningless. There is no permanent record; her mother told her that. But now she is ashamed and in love. When she falls in love, she doesn't understand what's happening, and retreats. She knows girls who keep pictures of famous boys in their lockers, and Ginny finds this practice strange and a little distasteful. Why would anyone casually admit to these feelings? She doesn't understand the girls who want the world to know that they are in love. She suspects that the love isn't real, that these girls are just fans. But still, they go to the same movie over and over to see a large face they like on a screen. Where does that impulse come from? Why does it look to feel so different from what Ginny feels for the boy who shared her pew?

She suspects that he made her feel better about a bad time and she was grateful. But gratitude should not merit love. Gratitude should not get the better of her.

MERCURY

The school is founded for girls. While it is more rigorous than other girls' schools of the time, the focus is still on the more wifely arts: music, dance, painting, and languages. There are sepia photographs of young girls wearing bloomers doing calisthenics. Each day the girls pray to a Protestant god in the chapel.

There's a fire. The well-trained girls rush from the flames; one dies, but the board of trustees chooses to carry on. When the school reopens, boys are allowed in.

The building must be entirely rebuilt. Red brick turrets go up. A cast iron gate surrounds the property: the school and a large courtyard where ginkgo trees will grow and loom. The chapel is redesigned, expanded to include a balcony, and Tiffany stained glass windows are donated. Divided by an aisle, the girls and boys sit in the chapel to pray. Staircases abound and do not complement each other. The board purchases a church on the corner of the block, and there are great plans, but it falls into disrepair from lack of funds and becomes a ghostly storage room. Inventive teaching methods are adopted. New math is inflicted. The school abandons its Protestantism, and the girls and boys no longer pray in the chapel. The chapel is used for community meetings, recitals, and awards ceremonies. When the students meet there, they call it chapel, and this hint of piety is nurtured by the school. Meanwhile, the old church morphs from "storage space" to "structurally unsound liability," and the students sneak in to smoke cigarettes or experiment with each other's bodies.

Brooklyn is changing, transforming, thriving, and now the school is known as a progressive lower and middle school. The high school, however, is different; it is a last chance to graduate for those who have been expelled from schools in Manhattan. These teenagers have brought weapons to their previous schools. They have juvenile records. They have had extended stays in mental institutions. They've overdosed. They've failed. Now they are enrolled in a school across the river from their wealthy parents. Or they are bright, quick, and poor. They've

been offered scholarships for their bright-
ness, and this school is better than the alternative.

The young schoolchildren herald a future
demand for a product: a competitive private
high school education in an outer borough.
These children live in brownstones that are
being renovated. At the end of the school
day, nannies, babysitters, and au pairs wait
in the courtyard to walk the children home.
The administrators of the school look at the
rich children, sense opportunity, and begin
to raise the cost of tuition at a slow but
steady rate. Some of the bright, quick, and
poor are still accepted, but not as many.
Manhattan's fuck-ups are quietly expelled.
A new building is built. A new playground.
Laptops appear. There is a bustle of hope
for a new branch of hierarchy. There is an
endowment.

A science teacher finds a puddle of mercury on the floor of the chemistry lab. The
chapel fills with the new kind of students
to discuss the incident, because mercury is
not a game. The science teacher tearfully
asks the responsible student to step forward
and explain why there is a puddle of mercury on her floor. In this elite culture, the
student should admit wrongdoing. The
student should be eager to confess. Yet no

student rises to the challenge. No student explains. The science teacher casts a final look of disappointment and gives up.

The mystery is solved when a new and larger puddle of mercury is found the next day. It's revealed to be seeping out of the pipes. The young girls in bloomers, when not doing calisthenics, learned rudimentary chemistry and poured mercury down the drains. A hundred years later, the mercury has eaten through the pipes and is depositing itself back into the classroom. The science wing is draped in plastic sheets by genderless people in hazmat suits. The science teacher must undergo testing for possible mercury poisoning. A new fund-raising initiative begins, and the hazardous church will be transformed into a state-of-the-art science wing, a gleaming facility with pristine pipes. A letter from the principal is sent to parents and distinguished alumni to introduce Marion Palm, the development officer at the helm of this auspicious project: the Wing Initiative. Be in touch with Marion Palm. Or, Marion Palm will be in touch with you. The students sit in the stairwell by the old science wing and watch the shadows of the suited people behind the plastic. The students are smug in their innocence.

TACOS

The house without Marion is louder. Radiators clang and bang, the refrigerator hums, and the next-door neighbors' dog barks more often. Nathan sits at his desk on the third floor with his hands folded in his lap. He looks into a notebook. A car alarm goes off.

He rises and pads around the empty house for an hour or so. He listens to the sounds he makes but also tries to think of something to do. His ideas are to clean, to cook, to read, and after that to go back to writing, and these are all good ideas, but he cannot begin any of them. He picks up a dishtowel and puts it back down again. He goes into his younger daughter's room, the most chaotic room of the house, but he feels calm here. Nathan manages to make her bed for her, although Marion would say she should be making it herself. He picks up the dolls from the floor and poses them appealingly on the shelf above his daughter's bed. He is able to do this. Once more fatherhood offers a kind of way out of inertia.

Nathan appreciates the tidy room and feels like a good dad. He walks down the hallway to his older daughter's room and does the same. There are no toys or Barbies, but her clothes are everywhere. He does not want to investigate his daughter's clothes too closely, so he throws them all into a hamper. A new sound is added to the house, the circular sloshing of the washing machine, and Nathan feels productive again. He will plan dinner for his daughters and go shopping for the necessary groceries.

Nathan Palm finds himself weeping in the kitchen. He is not the kind of man to weep. How can he buy groceries weeping? He will frighten the butcher. Marion stands in the doorway in her nightgown, and he tells her once more, *I've got a thing in Dumbo.* Then: *I mean, not like that. I mean. Did the girls get off for school okay?* He leaves his coffee unfinished to escape the kitchen, and as he passes Marion, he smells her morning breath, a hot, foul wave around his neck. He believes she's breathed on his neck for this purpose. He puts together later in the day what this hostile action means: Marion knows.

He opens cupboards. He wants to make the girls hamburgers because he thinks that would be fun, but in the kitchen he finds an old taco set. There are four chicken cutlets in the freezer, and the set contains packages of spices and a sauce for the meat. There is a fresh tomato in the crisper, and some lettuce that's limp but viable, as well as half a block of cheddar cheese. He is relieved that a meal is here, one that he can concoct from his wife's pantry without leaving the house.

Nathan takes the chicken out of the freezer and sets the package in a glass bowl. He runs cold water over the chicken, and the bowl gradually fills, allowing the chicken to buoy itself to the surface. Nathan watches. He no longer weeps.

THE MISSING BOY

The boy likes trains, the mother tells the detectives. He knows every station of every line. He's nonverbal, but it's clear he's memorized the subway map. When a stop is skipped or a train goes from local to express, he throws tantrums. He's agitated when the trains run behind schedule. *The trains are scheduled?* the police ask, making a slight joke of it. The boy's mother nods. Delays are a torment to her son, and therefore a torment to her too.

The boy's picture causes the detectives to pause in their questioning. His eyes look beyond the camera, his jaw hangs a little open, his shirt is neat, pressed, and red. The boy's mother had it taken a year ago, and it was difficult, but she managed. He's sixteen and tall, but very thin. The detectives promise to do everything they can, but don't say *We'll find him.* A boy who likes trains, he could be anywhere.

In the kitchen, the boy's teacher from the school asks, on a loop, to please let her know if there's anything she can do. So far she's only been allowed to pour coffee for the detectives and the boy's mother. *Cream? Sugar?* She tells the detectives it's true about the trains. Whenever the class goes on a field trip, the boy gravitates toward the subway stations. He wants to be under-ground. She vibrates a little, as if she tasted something bitter; she didn't mean that, she didn't mean to leave the latch open, she should have noticed. She pours a coffee for herself, and when she brings it to her lips, it splashes a little over the side and stains her shirt. *Shit. Goddamnit.*

Hang on, a detective says, *you left the gate open? You let the kid wander off?* The teacher says, *No, I don't think so. I should have seen it happen.* The detectives give each other obvious side-eye, meant to unnerve the teacher. The teacher dabs at her shirt with a wet paper towel.

A reporter leans in the hallway outside the mother's apartment. She managed to get herself buzzed into the building, and now she's waiting. Her desk needs a quote from the mother, and from a detective. This is theoretical, because the cops won't talk to her yet. They prefer the big white guys with

70

notepads, not the twentysomethings with iPhones and graduate degrees in journalism. A cop leaves the apartment, and before the door closes behind him the reporter sees a woman; she believes it is the mother, but it is the teacher. The reporter asks the cop her question, and he replies. The reporter taps away on her phone with both thumbs as he speaks. He'll get in trouble, he shouldn't be talking to her, he's just a uniform, but it's an emotional reaction the cop is dictating to the reporter. *The city needs to be on the lookout for this boy. Return this boy back to his mother — it will take a city to find him.* The reporter sends the quote to the desk right away, along with a physical description of the teacher, who she believes is the mother, and a promise of a photo. It's a good story.

PITCHFORKS

Marion is doing the opposite of commuting on an empty N train that is trundling back to Brooklyn. She looks out the window into the darkness and occasionally into packed trains filled with miserable-looking people. Still, they presumably have slept, and she hasn't. She must be more miserable than they are. However, it feels good to be, at last, on a train.

She is about to doze off when she remembers that this train will run under the school, the scene of her crime. In her office she felt the trains rattle by every ten minutes or so. She liked it. But to be so close to the place she has robbed for a decade, she must be vigilant again. What if she sees someone she knows? New York is like that.

She forgets that Brooklyn is large. She's lived in it all her life and yet she fails to remember that parts of it exist. When a forgotten neighborhood looms up, she is bothered because she should have known it was there. It is like expecting another step on a staircase in the dark and instead hitting the floor.

Sunset Park. Where the young teachers of the school live. They are in their late twenties and early thirties, mostly unmarried. They complain about the N and the R. Marion wonders if she should reroute, if she should head deeper into Brooklyn, where not even the poor private-school teachers will go. She holds the knapsack tighter on her lap.

She decides no, it will be fine. The young teachers are far too involved with themselves to notice her. They are slightly hungover.

Besides, it's a Tuesday morning. They are all above her, in the school, pretending to have authority over the privileged young of Brooklyn. The teachers may applaud Marion's actions. They may admire her and decide that they too will embezzle. They will take what should be theirs, after all their hard work. The teachers will think of Marion Palm with affection as a woman who enlightened them to the glorious possibility of their own independence.

What will actually happen: the teachers will only be confused by Marion, and because confusion is uncomfortable for teachers, they will forget her.

There is a group of people who will prosecute, and these are the trustees and the administrators. They will always hate her. And the parents. She imagines pitchforks. She grins to the empty train.

JAYWALKING

Jane is alight with the train ride to school with her sister. They walked through downtown Brooklyn together and unsupervised. Her sister did not wait for the walk sign. Instead they jaywalked between two cars when Ginny said, "C'mon."

Head high, Jane enters her classroom and hopes someone will say, "Where were you?" No one does. The classroom is noisy with projects, and Jane's late, so she collects herself in the cloakroom. The teacher does not even ask where she's been.

Jane deconstructs the walk from the train station to the school once more. Her sister seemed really tall. She's remembering when her sister briefly took her hand to cross the street. She dropped it when they hit the curb, but Jane's in that moment of hand-holding when she notices the silence of the room and looks at her teacher, who is looking at her, along with the rest of the class.

"What?" Jane says.

The class laughs. Jane's cheeks flame up, and the teacher repeats herself pointedly and slowly, as if Jane is too stupid to be in the third grade. The question is about a book they read yesterday, and Jane can't remember the main girl's name, so she says, "The girl," but the teacher catches her, and she must admit to what she does not know.

Jane circles around her error for the rest of the day, and her sublime walk with her sister is gone.

DENISE

Nathan Palm is frightened. Marion, he must remind himself, has done this kind of thing before. She comes back. But this time there is a difference: she's involved the kids. She left them at a CVS. Nathan Palm has considered calling a number of people for help.

He wants to call his wife. It was strange to have a day without her voice. He has written about her voice before, because he says it was the thing that first attracted him to her. This isn't entirely accurate, but he doesn't remember as well as he should. When he first saw her at the café where she worked, he had a hard time not looking at her breasts. It made him focus on the objects behind her. He pictures the young Marion. He sees a foggy mirror behind the bottles, a chalkboard listing specials, a strand of white Christmas lights. He also sees Marion's breasts.

When he looked at the things behind her, he listened to her voice. It sometimes disappointed him when she misused a word or agreed with a wrong opinion, but he eventually understood that Marion was performing for a clientele who did not want a dissenting waitress.

Then Marion would be on the phone, ordering two cases of Sancerre to be delivered by Wednesday, and she would become a different person, an older, capable person. And she would negotiate, she could negotiate! She had a head for details. She was never flustered. She had a smooth, deep, melodic voice; she enunciated her words, except when she didn't. And when she didn't, it was for some reason, he knew. Did she not want to be overheard? Did she want to hide her words from him?

Nathan Palm misses both his wife's voice and her breasts. He has to admit that.

He can't call his wife so he calls Denise, an old friend. He has known Denise (or rather Denise has known him) since he was a baby. Their mothers liked to drink white wine, smoke cigarettes, and listen to classical records together in the afternoons, and he and Denise would play. She was older by two years, and Nathan remembers that Denise always acted uninterested in him but never left his side. More often than not, they didn't talk but played quiet games. The games changed according to age, and when Nathan turned fifteen, the game became sexual. At sixteen, their mothers had a falling-out (Nathan believes there was an infidelity somewhere), but he and Denise kept in touch. Denise is his oldest friend.

"I think my wife left me," he says over the phone.

"You think? Did she take the kids?"

"No. She told them she was visiting her friend Shelley in the Hudson Valley."

"So?"

"So Shelley doesn't know anything about it. And she hasn't shown up there. And it's weird. It's fucking weird. Marion took the kids out of school and left them in a CVS on Montague."

As he tells his story, the story becomes a story and not something that happened. He is aware of choosing the correct details and leaving certain ones out, to best illustrate his point in the shortest amount of time. He does this for everyone, and he supposes that his honed details might be what people like about him. For Denise, however, the abandonment story might not work. Denise considers the workings of upper-middle-class marriages hopelessly boring, and while

79

she appreciates details, they have never impressed her.

"Denise, I don't know what to do."

"What do you think happened?"

"I think Marion left me."

Denise pauses, then: "What did you do?"

"Nothing. Nothing."

The Misfortune of Marion Palm

"That's probably not true."

There is a woman in Dumbo that lately I sometimes sleep with. And I may have told my wife. This is what Nathan thinks. But he asks, "Do you think Marion is unhappy?"

Denise doesn't answer. If she answered, she would say, *If I were Marion, I would be unhappy.* She's expressed this sentiment before.

"Would you come over?" Nathan asks, aware of the tightness in his chest and that if someone isn't in the house with him soon, he may lose it. He cannot ask the woman in Dumbo. He can never see her again. Besides, she'd say no.

"I can't."

"Why?"

Denise says she will come in an hour.

When Nathan Palm hangs up the phone, he does not feel better, as he expected he would. He feels that something needs to be discussed, and that he has done something wrong. He has made another misstep; he is sure of that.

Up Front

The Days Inn is predictably depressing. When Marion pulls open the glass door, a young woman exits, and Marion wonders if the young woman is a prostitute. She chastises herself: she is guiltier and more illegal than the prostitute.

She books a room for two nights and asks boldly if she can pay in cash. The man behind the desk doesn't care, just barks, "Up front." Marion kneels down to the knapsack and opens the zipper three inches. It is the first time she has dared to open the knapsack, and she wishes she didn't have to. She fishes out five $20 bills. It takes a long time, and the man behind the desk grows impatient. She snaps at the man, says she will be one more minute, okay?

Straightening up, she gives the man behind the desk the money, and they glare at each other. He hands her a room key and her change, briefly explains the complimentary breakfast buffet, and gestures to the elevators.

When Marion opens the door of her hotel room and sees the bed, she cries in relief and for her children and for herself, and as she cries, she tucks herself in. Under the comforter and sheets, she takes off her shoes, her pants, her shirt, her bra, her underpants. She's naked with her clothes in a bundle beside her. She holds one of her breasts and goes quickly to sleep.

Board of Trustees

Daniel, during a mild panic attack in the third hour of his first working day without Marion, sends an email to every employee of the school. The email includes a casual yet thorough transcription of Daniel's conversation with Nathan. He explains that Nathan used the word *missing* to describe Marion, but this must be metaphorical or ironic, because how does a woman from Carroll Gardens go missing in this day and age? Daniel asks this, but then writes, *Of course, I may be wrong. Perhaps women do go missing. Perhaps this is my privilege speaking, but we also need to address the fact that Marion has been crucial to Deb, just crucial, and that she's left behind a gaping hole of functionality and competence, not that Deb isn't crucial or competent, but what with her absences and numerous doctor appointments and light sensitivity, it's really Marion who would have been helpful in an auditing-*

type situation. Which is what we are facing now. Today. Not that Deb isn't helpful. Also, has anyone noticed that the petty cash fund is curiously low?

After several reply-alls, which briefly crash the school email server, Daniel receives a text message from Anna Fisher, a member of the board of trustees, inviting Daniel to the founders' conference room later that same day. Daniel is briefly thrilled at the prospect of a one-on-one with such a powerful figure. It is well documented by the staff that Anna Fisher has been essential to the refinement of the school's brand. In fact, she may have been the first person to use the word *brand,* and the school is grateful for her contemporary forward thinking. However, Anna's subsequent texts make it clear that Daniel will be facing the whole board. Also, she adds in the next bubble, if he is to send any emails in the future, they need to be approved by her first.

Even Daniel is able to surmise that this will not be a good meeting for him, so he is early for the meeting as a gesture of his repentance, and is able to help set up the coffee and bagels with the food-services staff.

A group of pleasant-looking people enter the room, all late but with excellent excuses.

Anna is the latest. After pulling off a knit hat and dragging her fingers through her soft blond hair, she leans forward and asks Daniel to summarize his email in a few short words. Daniel speaks until Anna leans forward even farther to interrupt him.

Then you don't know where Marion is?

No, not per se.

And Marion has been filing the school's quarterly tax returns for the past five years.

Well, it has been a group effort, but one that Marion primarily handled. Led.

And there have been accounting discrepancies?

I'm not sure if I'm qualified to call them that, but there do seem to be some . . . well, irregularities, maybe.

Thank you. Have you had a bagel?

Daniel rises and begins to spread cream cheese on half of an everything bagel, but the board is silent and so he decides he should leave. Before he does, he bows to the group, half-smeared bagel in hand, and when the door shuts behind him, the pleasant-looking people laugh.

But seriously. Seriously. Where is Marion?

Has anyone heard from her? No?

What are we going to do without Marion? The lawyers are concerned.

The lawyers are always concerned. A risk-

averse type. I suppose we'll have to find someone to clean up.

I wonder where Marion's gone off to.

Have we reached out to Nathan?

I sent an email, and texted. He didn't get back to me.

We shouldn't pry.

We shouldn't? The lawyers seem to feel that it's important we locate Marion. Something about the audit, something about account-ability and transparency and irregular deduc-tions. I don't know. I stopped listening.

Well, it seems slightly crass. Let's leave Nathan Palm alone.

Of course, there's always the children.

A conversation about their mother could be helpful. A gentle conversation. We are, after all, concerned about their well-being. Right?

Right. Let's check in with the Palm girls. But can we take a different approach from Dan-iel's? Keep this calm and quiet.

And I'm sure we can find someone to step into Marion's shoes until she returns.

I agree. I mean, she is only part-time.

DENISE GETS A TOUR
OF THE BROWNSTONE

Denise has never been to the brownstone before. Nathan had to text her the address. From the living room windows, he watches her approach the house. She holds her phone out, looks up and down, checks the number of each house she passes, and also navigates the buckling sidewalk. There's a cigarette in her right hand, but she flicks it into the gutter before opening the gate to the front yard of the Palm brownstone and slips the phone into her jacket pocket. Nathan opens the front door before she has a chance to ring the doorbell. He's not afraid of seeming eager this time.

Inside, Denise looks at the molding and the stairs, crafted from mahogany and inherently grand. After years of polishing, the wood in the house no longer requires maintenance. It gleams on its own, the rich red banister in particular. The oils from sliding palms have given it a natural sleekness.

There are bay windows in the front of the house, and a smaller bay window in the dining room, and the kitchen, which juts out into the backyard, is bright. The rest of the house is dark. Chandeliers, or the vestiges of chandeliers, ornament the ceiling of each room. Two chimneys run up the east side of the brownstone, and one fireplace still works. Denise asks Nathan questions about wallpaper and renovations. Nathan's surprised; he always is when Denise doesn't act like she's twenty-two. He forgets that she is his age. He forgets that she has some social ability.

There are a few things he really likes about Denise: her thick straight hair, her barefaced distrust of the nuclear family, the way she wears T-shirts, her lack of interest in him, her lack of interest in anything besides Northern Renaissance paintings. He likes her apartment, her flat stomach, her taste in music. He likes that she would never think of going to a gym or running or biking anywhere. She never discusses what she can't eat. She still smokes and has never talked about either her habit or quitting that habit. She just smokes.

She is another trust-fund artist. She never would or could worry about money, and Nathan finds that a rare thing in a person.

It is a strange life in the United States to be absent of motivation. In New York, it is even more difficult to explain, though certainly more common. No one will ever sympathize with them. They understand that, Nathan and Denise, and yet they both wish they had finished college with a degree in economics. They wish they were more needed by their families. Nathan has made the attempt to be needed by having a family of his own, but he's not sure it's working. Denise has never tried.

"It's a nice house," she says. They are in the master bedroom.

"Thank you."

"Where are your kids?"

"School. I don't think they know what's happened. What's happening. I mean, not that I do either."

After a pause, Denise asks, "What did she take?"

"I don't know."

"Let's look."

She walks into the closet. He watches from the doorway as she slides hangers to the left and cocks her head like she's at the sales rack of a department store. He momentarily wants to kick her out of his room, out of his house.

"Jesus," Denise says, and she holds up a

large, shapeless floral dress.

"There's a belt that goes with it — it's not that bad."

"It's that bad."

She opens drawers; she looks for empty spaces, but there are none. Marion's things are all here.

"Does she keep other stuff anywhere? Have you noticed anything else missing?"

Nathan shakes his head, trying to understand what this might mean. If she took most of her clothes, that would mean she's left him. If she took a few things, she is visiting someone. Her leaving behind everything: he can't think about what that means.

"What about the basement?" Denise asks.

This time Nathan follows Denise as she trots casually down the stairs. In the kitchen, she finds the door to the basement and descends. Nathan closes his mouth and breathes through his nose. The previous owners had cats, and the smell lingers on in the poorly ventilated parts of the house.

"Where the fuck is the light?"

"Just wait a fucking second."

Nathan finds the light switch, and Denise is illuminated. Nathan looks at her and then looks around. It takes a moment to register that something is different. He hasn't been down here in a while because of the smell.

Boxes have been sliced open, and their contents spill onto the floor. An old dollhouse of Ginny's has been emptied of its tiny furniture. Cans half full of dried paint have been overturned; one oozes a plastic puddle of pink onto the dirt floor.

"Is it always like this?" Denise asks.

Nathan shakes his head and steps into the mess. He thinks about yesterday morning. He was working on the third floor. He didn't know where Marion was, but now he understands that she was here, making this peculiar mess.

"Is that a door over there?" Denise asks.

"It opens into the front yard."

Denise steps over the mess to the heavy door. "It's unbolted, you know."

Nathan is swiftly furious. Marion left the basement door unlocked. Anyone could have gotten in. Her daughters slept vulnerable, unprotected. The fury feels good. Nathan no longer feels entirely to blame.

"I wonder what she was looking for," Denise says.

MARION AT FOURTEEN

Marion at fourteen is restless. She is one of the poor quick and bright but does not get to go to a private school. Instead she attends a large public school for gifted students in the middle of Brooklyn, but fails after her first year. Her mother slaps her face. Marion transfers.

She graduates from high school eventually, and applies for college. She lives at home. She takes a few courses at Hunter but stops attending early in the semester. Her mother doesn't hit her again, but there is no suggestion that another semester will be paid for. Mother and daughter glare at each other over the dinner table. Each has failed the other. Neither has gone or will go to college. Marion's father chooses to ignore the seething women; instead he tells them how beautiful they are. It is an interruption and a pointless one. It does not make them feel good. Marion and her mother know they are not beautiful. They think they are living with a fool.

Without the pretense of classes to attend, Marion sleeps in. She sees her friends at night, and during the day she drives her father's car. She drives herself to Long Island and back. She enjoys summer places in the winter. She spends time in dive bars near the coast with fishing nets on the walls. The men in the bar stare, but she has a beer and reads. When winter turns into spring, she drives to the beach, the first to brave it. She has a chair and an umbrella and a cooler. She goes to the beach like others go to work. She reads a wide range of genres on the beach, but prefers dystopias. She likes it when everything is going wrong, and ignores the morality lesson she's supposed to be learning.

It is perfect beach weather when Marion finds herself about to be kicked out of her house. Her mother accuses her with test scores, with tales of prodigy-like behavior as a young girl. Marion knows she was no prodigy; she met the other prodigies when she was fourteen and she was not like them at all. Marion was something different.

Marion's bags are packed, and she moves in with another disappointment. They giggle about it over cheap red wine the first night.

Nick has a kitchen table and that's where they sit. He doesn't have much else. Nick was never considered smart, but he has turned out to be gay. Marion holds his hand when they admit to each other how frightened they are. They've made some decision that has landed them in this shitty apartment, but they can't remember when they made it or why. They are both from Sheepshead Bay. Her father works for the MTA. His father is a real estate agent. Her mother gives music lessons. His mother worked until she died of ovarian cancer. They now live in Red Hook, and it is empty but near the water. They both need that. That first night, Nick slides a switchblade to Marion for her walk home from the subway.

Marion at twenty is restless and scared. The apartment costs money and she does not have any. She needs to go out and get some money. Nick works for his open-minded cousin as a man with a van. The cousin can look past Nick's sexuality because of Nick's size. Because Nick is so large, they can now advertise that they move pianos. It's good business.

Marion can't move pianos, but decides that she will find something. She applies to be a waitress at a SoHo café. A small woman with a stutter declares that she will make Marion a better person; she means a better worker. She screams when Marion reaches for a coffee spoon with her right hand instead of her left. This is the small woman's restaurant, and she is bipolar. The other staff scuttle around the room, and they all reach for coffee spoons with their left hands. They all set the table the same way, the most efficient way. They are little robots, and Marion, trying to be a little robot, fails.

But the bipolar woman keeps Marion on in spite of all her flaws as a server, because Marion's cash register is perfect to the cent at the end of the night. The owner quizzes Marion and discovers that the flawed server can calculate difficult equations in her head. The owner's eyes get smaller, and she decides she can trust Marion. It is partly because Marion is white, and the owner holds her racist generalizations close, believes in them like tarot cards, but it's also because of Marion's charmless and robotic way with figures. Marion might save the owner some money.

With a panicked heart, Marion learns to reach for the coffee spoon with her left hand always. She returns home with cash. She dreams about serving brunch. She has a fuzzy sense of purpose. Her chest tightens when she gets off the train at Second Avenue. The customers can destroy her with thoughtlessness when they treat her as less than human. She's good with money. She has that she tells herself when she grips the cash and the knife in her pocket.

GINNY'S DETENTION

Ginny's homeroom teacher informs her of the detention. Three tardies equals one detention. One more tardy will earn her another detention and a call to her parents. Three more tardies after that will mean disciplinary action. Ginny knows better than to argue, but she wishes her homeroom teacher wouldn't repeat this litany and smile. It makes Ginny feel like she should also be smiling, but that would be misread and could earn her another misdemeanor. She tries to look repentant.

Detention will be from 3 p.m. to 4 p.m. Ginny understands.

She calls her father, to let him know that she will be late, but he does not answer the phone. This is normal, but now she's unable to reach either of her parents. In other circumstances, she would go by her mother's office. Sometimes Marion would tell her to go away because she was working, but other times Ginny got a cup of sugary tea. It's a time they shared.

Ginny feels like she should look at her mother's desk. She has ten minutes left of her lunch, and she picks up after herself and goes. Her mother's office is in the basement in the new building with the lower school, and while it's all fluorescent lighting, there is something cheerful and warm about it, a pale pink-and-orange glow, and it's a nice place to be when the weather is cold.

The door to her mother's office is open. Her mother is not at her desk, and this was to be expected, but it still upsets Ginny. She walks behind the desk and sits in her mother's chair. She opens and closes a drawer. She taps the computer keyboard, and the hard drive whirs awake. The monitor blinks on. Ginny taps into her mother's inbox and reads the unread subject lines. *Where are you????* say many of them. One is from Ginny, sent last night from her phone. She thought she should try.

She's investigating the inbox when her own email, remarkably, goes from unread to read. Ginny stands. She pulls her phone out of her back jeans pocket and quickly types another email to her mother's work address. *Mom?* is all it says.

Then her email goes back to unread. Ginny has frightened her own mother away.

"What are you doing?" It is the dreaded Daniel, her mother's officemate, in the doorway.

"My mom asked me to."

"Oh, okay. You've heard from Marion, then? Well, I guess that's okay. You can sit there. I'm very busy, so you'll need to stay quiet and not disturb me. I have some phone calls to make. It's actually very difficult that Marion — your mother — isn't here right now. It's incredibly busy. I mean, it's always busy, but now especially." Daniel has a few odd tics, and Marion is good at imitating them. He has the habit of standing suddenly, and then sitting again, but as he does, he braces himself on the chair arms and thrusts his pelvis out. His son, Ezra, is nine, and Daniel is clear about never wanting Ezra. Ezra was Daniel's wife's idea.

"So do you know where Marion is?" Daniel sits down carefully at his desk. "I mean, of course you do, but more her actual locality?"

"My grandmother is sick. My mom's with her or something."

"Oh, your father didn't mention that."

"It just happened."

"How old is your grandmother? Because

it is complicated as the generation above you, responsible for you, deteriorates, 'declines.' My wife's mother, my mother-in-law, is not a monster but she has glaucoma, and my wife, she does what she can."

"My grandmother had a stroke. She can't read anymore."

"That's terrible. My mother-in-law can't see very well either and —"

"I mean she doesn't know how. We're going to 'need' flash cards."

"Flash cards."

"You know — 'dog,' 'cat,' 'their.' I've got algebra."

Daniel doesn't register that a thirteen-year-old is mocking him with air quotes and rises again, thrusts out his pelvis, sits, and adjusts his tie.

"Of course, yes, yes, go ahead. If you're late, tell your teacher you were speaking to me. And please give your mother my deepest condolences. And also ask her when she is coming back to work. Because there is an extraordinary amount of things that we need to do. I'm very busy."

Ginny is late for algebra and receives another tardy. Daniel sends multiple texts about Ginny's grandmother to Anna Fisher. Anna texts back, *Who is this?* Daniel replies,

Daniel. He adds, *I would have emailed, but you forbade it.*

THE SCHOOL BUS

Jane at eight doesn't have many friends. She used to have a lot, was very popular, always the first request for playdates. Now the requests are fewer and more secretive. Girls ask their mothers to make a playdate with Jane when they want to really get down and *play*. Jane is still the best at *play*. But this kind of play isn't cool anymore, and Jane doesn't understand. She sits by herself on the bus. She doesn't mind; she makes up stories. She does mind when the kids on the bus chant things at her. Then she cries or yells or presses her forehead against the cool window and huffs. They are now chanting, "Jane *fart-ed*! Jane *fart-ed*! Jane *fart-ed*!" The bus driver is trying to make them stop, but she's also navigating Flatbush Avenue. The children go on.

Atticus kneels on his seat backward in order to peer down at Jane; he wants to announce to the bus when she officially starts to cry. Atticus is the initiator of the chant, has claimed to have smelled the offense. Jane stands to face Atticus, draws her arm back, lets it spring forward, and slaps him across the face, and the sound, the crack, reverberates. The bus driver asks, "What happened, what happened?" while Jane watches Atticus's eyes go glassy with tears. Jane says, "Nothing, Phyllis," and Atticus twists away. He can't admit that he is crying.

Jane feels good until she feels terrible. Atticus has a hand print on his cheek. He will inevitably tell, and she will get in trouble. She says, "I'm sorry, I'm sorry." Atticus mumbles back from his seat that it's fine. His words are damp.

Jane at thirty will feel two ways about this memory. First she'll feel pride. The little shit deserved it, and no one helped her, no one cared that she was being tormented every day. Jane at eight doesn't even know the torment is happening, that is how young and naive she is. She is helplessly herself, unable to mask one part of her personality in order to go under the radar. But Jane at thirty will also feel shame. It is the beginning of a certain kind of knowledge about herself. For an eight-year-old girl, Jane is strong. She's been kicking, but the girls and boys dodge that, and she ends up looking foolish. Hitting is more effective. And while Jane feels bad that Atticus is crying and scared that she will be punished, it felt wonderful to hit him. She's satisfied. Jane at thirty will still want to hit and kick.

DAYS INN

Marion sits in bed, watches a sitcom, and eats the best black beans and rice she's ever tasted. She can't concentrate on the show, the beans and rice are so good. She's eating out of a Styrofoam container with a plastic fork, and the fork scrapes the Styrofoam and Marion doesn't care. This is the food she returns to. It's what she lived on when she was first on her own; it's the food she could eat when she was pregnant. It's what she ate when she learned about Denise and the others. It settles her stomach.

She bought it from a taqueria a few blocks away. She was careful to buy it when the teachers were still in meetings, around 3:30 p.m. As soon as she is able, she must find a new neighborhood, because this is not tenable in the long run. The teachers will soon trudge back to their tiny grim apartments, and Marion will need to hide from them. Also, she can hear fucking next door and the carpet is dirty. Still, she's not having a bad time. Marion feels as if she is repairing herself. Her sleep is heavy and sensual. She wakes gradually. Her skin feels good. She administers carefully to her own needs.

Fueled by the black beans and rice, the perfect protein, Marion decides she's headed deeper into Brooklyn. Sunset Park is a helpful indicator of what she needs in a hideout, even if it's not safe. She'll go deeper into Brooklyn, back to where she came from, where no one will notice she's back. Carroll Gardens, Brooklyn Heights, and Park Slope: she couldn't walk a block without an inane conversation with someone she hardly knew. Where Marion's from, neighbors give a halfhearted wave to each other and then go back to minding their own business. They may complain to each other about a shared inconvenience but never the faux but chic suburban small talk with yoga mats and canvas grocery bags and flaxen-haired children. So proud to be acting neighborly in a city. That type of exchange belongs to the delusional rich, Marion believes.

As a precaution, she will change her appearance. Dye her hair, buy some new clothes. It's most likely unnecessary; two children, Nathan, and a decade have altered

Marion on a molecular level. However, she needs confidence. Then she will look for a room. Marion closes her eyes to chew and taste the last bite of her dinner.

GINNY'S DETENTION

In algebra, Ginny daydreams that the boy she prayed with also has detention. In her daydream, she shyly sits next to him, and they whisper to one another, and he is amazed by her, and after detention he walks her to the subway. It's not exciting, but it's what she wants.

Unfortunately, the only other student to have detention is a boy whom Ginny has known since she was four. This boy has a rage problem. He throws chairs. Worse, he wears gray sweatpants and a gray sweatshirt every day, and he tucks the gray sweatshirt into the gray sweatpants. He looks like an anemic boxer from the seventies. He's sitting at a desk, ankles wiggling, and when he hears Ginny come into the room, he swings his head to look at her. His eyes open too wide. He looks like he wants to throw a chair.

Ginny decides no. Can't. Won't. She runs

from detention, down the stairs, and to the front hall. The hall master reminds her not to run, and she's outside, breathing hard, reveling in the glory of her wrongdoing and escape. Her father's twenties are in the front pocket of her jeans, and she checks to make sure they haven't gone missing. She walks on and passes the CVS where her mother left her; it does not bother her as she thought it might. It's hard to attach meaning to a CVS. She continues up Montague. The neighborhood changes from commercial to residential (more trees, fewer banks). Ginny's back at the Greek diner. She's swinging the glass door open. She's feeling short.

The man at the counter doesn't notice her at first. Ginny must be brave to speak to him. He has a thick mustache and an accent and seems to take it personally when he cannot hear someone over the noise of the diner: clanking silverware, dishes being scraped and stacked, the hiss of meat on a gas griddle.

"Yes? Yes?" the man says.

"Me and my mother."

"Yes? What do you want?"

"My mother and me and my sister were here."

"Did you forget something?"

"Something, yeah, well."

And the man is looking at her; he is recalling her and her family, Ginny can tell. He has taken his hands off the cash register and now they rest on his slender hips. He is peering down at her.

"Your mother — she's the one who didn't pay."

Ginny feels her cheeks flush. She blinks away the urge to cry.

"I think she forgot."

Ginny takes the twenties out of her pocket and holds them up to the man. He looks at the money suspiciously and takes it from Ginny. He turns the money upside down and right side up again, as if he is not absolutely sure that this *is* money. He acts like it is something other than money. He eventually gives it back to Ginny, after he's looked at it and maybe figured out what it is.

"No, your mother paid, I forgot. This is yours. She paid."

"But she did not pay," Ginny says. "I'm trying to pay."

"She came back, it's settled. It's fine."

Ginny's hope soars, and briefly this seems like a big understandable misunderstanding. But the cashier's explanation doesn't make sense.

"I don't think so. She was getting on a train."

The man with the mustache leans forward.

"Listen! Don't worry about it. We're not calling the police. Go home." The word *police* stands out, and Ginny must look more worried than ever. "Oh shit," the cashier says. "Shit shit. Sit at the counter. Put your backpack here. We'll make you a burger."

The cashier calls his mother over to man the cash register, and he sits down next to the teen. He sighs and runs his hand over his hair, which is slick and large. Although he appears very old to Ginny, he is only twenty-one. There's a lot that happens in those years between, but also not that much. The cashier is out of his depth but returns to his hair for comfort, confidence, and guidance. After this moment, he tells Ginny the truth.

"Your mother did not pay. Usually we call the police. We run them down. It is a big deal because we are a small restaurant. A small business. But your mother — it seems she was acting a little strange. So I paid for her out of my tips. It's no big deal. But do not say anything to her. And do not say anything to *her*." The second *her* refers to the cashier's mother. "Sometimes mothers, they go a little crazy. Don't worry about it."

"She left," Ginny says. "I don't think she's coming back."

"Would you like a milkshake?" the cashier asks.

"I'm full."

"Okay. Well, thanks for the offer and everything, to pay, but don't worry about it. Just stay cool."

Ginny is now in love with both the cashier and his hair, and blushes again.

JUDGMENT

Nathan paws through his wife's closet. He's left Denise in the basement. She said she was interested in the negative space. Nathan rolled his eyes at her and left her in the cat-piss-smelling basement.

Nothing is unexpected, except, considered all at once as a wardrobe, it's depressing. Skirts with the elastic waistband worn out. Dingy bras and underpants. One blazer from JCPenney. Marion was not a stylish dresser, but Nathan never grasped how collectively cheerless her clothes were. His wife's clothes seem calculatedly unfashionable, a kind of self-punishment. Once again he's sorry for her, and sorry for himself. She's left behind her jewelry. His mother's tennis bracelet is still in the leather case.

He once wrote a poem about her that she disliked intensely. She found a draft on his desk when she was turning out the lights on the third floor. He had written about her at thirty-four as a mother of two. She'd put on weight then, and walked slower, as if the health of her two girls accelerated her un-health, her lack of health. It soon became his responsibility to take them to the park or the zoo. Marion didn't want to be seen around active people or her active daughters. He wrote a poem about his wife standing still as his children grew more epic and tremendous every day. This healthy growth depressed Marion. It weighed her down even more.

Of course he had been angry that she hadn't liked the poem. She should have liked it. She should have been honored by the poem and its honesty.

"You wrote a poem about me getting fat" was what she said, and there was nothing left for him to say. What she said was also true.

Marion once read him a quote, not to him but at him. She did this sometimes. She found quotes about writing to lob at him like a tennis serve.

"Get this, here's what Ibsen says," she'd said in the present tense, as if Ibsen had a weekly column in the *Post*. " 'To live is to war with trolls in the holds of the heart and mind. To write: that is to sit in judgment over one's self.' "

He wondered if she wanted him to explain the quote to her, to speak to the relationship between self and the writer, but saw fury in her brow line. She thought he did not sit in judgment of *his* self; she thought he sat in judgment of *hers.*

It was a simplistic way of looking at his writing, but he could see where Marion was coming from. He couldn't seem to explain, however, that the poems he wrote about her felt more alive than his other work. He liked them more. He thought they were more honest.

Marion was the most honest. The way she had moved in that café had been honest, even when she was lying.

He has been making himself up for years; how can he sit in judgment over something fundamentally unreal?

He sits in the closet, her underwear in his hand, and he thinks of his poems and his house and his being a father. When Marion does come back, she will be an entirely different sort of person. She will be the sort of person who abandons children at a drugstore, and therefore he cannot also be that sort of person. Unless drugs are involved, he thinks, only one person in a marriage with children is allowed to be that sort of person.

Denise is still in the house when Jane comes home from school, but Nathan doesn't need to make excuses for the strange woman in the basement. Jane has an odd look on her face and responds to his questions about school with one-word answers thrown over her shoulder. She indicates that she wants to be alone by dropping her lunchbox on the foyer rug, slipping her backpack off her shoulders, and climbing the stairs. Nathan is inclined to ask her if she has homework to do, but who cares? He watches his daughter's small hand slide up the banister. Jane's backpack stays in the foyer, and the lunchbox will remain unopened. Nathan will forget to refill it with a sandwich, juice box, fruit, and a cookie. Jane's teacher will need to take her to the cafeteria the next day.

An hour and a half later, Ginny comes home. Nathan is sitting in the living room, not reading articles on his iPad, just scrolling down. When he hears Ginny let herself in, he crosses to the front door. He looks with deliberation at his eldest daughter, but Ginny seems unperturbed by his anxiety. When asked where she's been, she replies that she was walking. Nathan knows his daughter is lying, he can feel it. But Denise left an hour ago, and Nathan was careful to close the front door quietly after her in order to conceal her presence from Jane.

The taco dinner he planned falls apart in front of Nathan and his daughters, who are waiting to be·fed. The lettuce is brown. The chicken smells off. The taco shells snap and crack into a cornmeal dust. Nathan throws the entire mess into the garbage and finds old·takeout menus in the den. He wants Chinese, greasy, old-school Chinese, the kind Marion won't eat. He asks Jane what she wants from the menu and she tells him the orange kind. Orange chicken? he asks. No, she says, the other orange kind.

Nathan says okay, and what does Ginny want?

Ginny rolls her eyes. "It all tastes the same."

Perhaps it's now time to discuss Marion, Nathan considers, and where she might be, but he can't make himself do it. Last time she came back. Last time the girls were simply happy to see their mother again. Nathan decides to wait a little longer. Maybe this will sort itself out.

GINGER TEA

Having slept most of the day, Marion finds herself awake at midnight. The sex hotel is alive with the sound of television sets. She doesn't mind, but she doesn't want to be inside either. She throws the papery sheets off her body and dresses herself in the clothes she left in, a pair of black work pants and a blue blouse. The armpits of the blouse are still damp with sweat from her day of homelessness. The pants have lost their shape and bag in the butt and the knees. Marion must buy new clothes at the next opportunity. But now she's in the hallway, slipping the electronic key card into her pocket. She's left the knapsack behind, trusting the motel's promise of peace and privacy to its occupants, but still puts a DO NOT DISTURB sign on the doorknob. To be outside without the knapsack will be liberating. It may also be a mistake. Still, it would be more dangerous to take the knapsack with her at this time of night, and so Marion takes the risk. Down the elevator, through the seedy lobby and the glass doors, unnoticed by the night desk clerk, Marion is on her own in the dark.

Fourth Avenue is refreshingly ugly. She's been too long within the radius of charming Brooklyn, where it's easy to avoid unpleasant sights and smells. Fourth Avenue is separated by a median, and trucks rumble in both directions. The garbage piles up here, and there are no stoops, but there are houses. In the summer Fourth Avenue smells like garbage and shit, but now, in the autumn, it smells like exhaust fumes. On the corner of each block, a bodega or Laundromat. In the middle of the blocks, a Burger King, an urgent-care medical center, a takeout place with illuminated pictures of the food served, a car service where the men sit on folding chairs inside, smoking, watching a game, their tan and black Lincolns parked up and down the street.

Marion walks to a corner store. She wants a Coke, a real Coke, and a bag of sour-cream-and-onion potato chips. The bell chimes when she walks in, and the man behind the counter acknowledges her with a loud hello but doesn't look her in the eye. She's not the only customer; a couple, young and drunk, giggle over the food they should buy to sober themselves. There is a smell to the store, though, different from that of other bodegas, and Marion asks about it.

"Ginger tea," the man behind the counter tells her, pointing a knobby finger at the corner of the store, where there is a hot plate set up with two coffeepots. One is filled with coffee, the other with a light brown liquid in which large chunks of shaved ginger float.

"Can I buy some?"

"Sure," the man says. "It's very spicy, but good for digestion."

Marion makes a noise that means "Oh, wow. I didn't know that."

So she buys a Coke, her chips, and a cup of this spicy tea. She spends her change on lotto tickets. Instead of walking back to the motel with her black plastic bag of goods and her Styrofoam cup of tea, she walks up the hill to the park. She can't remember the name of the park she's looking for but knows it's here somewhere. She thinks there is a view. The houses she passes are small and have aluminum siding, but they have stoops. She can hear the couple down the block, laughing, dropping keys. When they manage to unlock the front door of their building, the street sounds too quiet without them. Marion looks up and down the hill for a new compatriot. No one. In her past life she would have turned around, but now she walks up. It's important that she push at her boundaries. What more can happen to her?

She does not see her daughters or her husband in the shadows. It might be because she's finally gotten some sleep. It might be because this is not a scene they would ever be part of. Although she remembers herself as a teenager, out late like this. Maybe Ginny will be here soon.

Eventually Marion does find the park, but she cannot go in. She cannot enter parks at night alone; her upbringing won't let her. She sits on the concrete border. The tea is too spicy but smells nice, so she removes the lid and sets the cup next to her. She opens her bag of chips and enjoys a fistful. The real Coke afterward is so sugary it coats her teeth, but it rinses away the sour-cream chemicals. She scrapes at her lotto tickets with her thumbnail and looks for a win. She imagines winning.

ACTION

Jane is confused by the disruption of another morning with her mother not there. She must be reminded by her father that her mother is with Shelley. "She'll be back soon," he says with his back to her. She misses another school bus pickup, and so her sister must take her on the subway again. She doesn't want to go to school, she wants to go back home, she wants her mother, but Ginny insists they get on the train when it arrives. Ginny pushes her onto the car and tells her to grow up.

"I don't know when Mom is coming back, but it's *not soon.* You better get used to it."

Jane wants to cry so she pretends to cry, and Ginny squeezes the soft part of her arm, feasibly so she'll stop. This makes Jane cry for real, and no pinching will stop her. She cries loud and hard, and several passengers watch. Ginny notices the looks and Jane does too, but she doesn't care. It seems

123

valid to have an audience. After all, her mother is gone and no one has said when she's coming back. This is terrible, and when terrible things happen, other people should know. They should pity. They should grieve.

When a skinny woman leans over and asks the two girls if anything is wrong, Ginny says no. Jane says, "That is a lie."

The skinny woman makes a face but takes out a copy of *The New Yorker.* Instead of reading the magazine, the woman watches the Palm girls like a babysitter.

Ginny is sick of being watched all the time and blames Jane. She grips Jane's hand the whole walk to school, not in a protective way but because she needs her sister to walk faster. The Palm girls can't be late again. Ginny says, "Retard, come on." Jane twists herself out of Ginny's grasp and walks in a huff ten paces in front of her sister, her arms swinging like mad. Ginny jogs a little to catch up with her, so Jane walks another ten paces in front. Jane is punishing her sister. She should not be treated this way by Ginny.

When it comes time to cross the street, Ginny runs to Jane, takes her by the arm with such a grip that Jane can't escape it. Ginny pulls her across the street, Jane grunting in anger. When Ginny lets go, Jane takes off for the school. She runs in, is admonished by the hall master, but is undaunted. She is going to find her teacher. She's going to tell.

"Ginny says that our mother has abandoned us."

This gets the attention and concern of the third-grade teacher, even though she is busy helping the class deposit their lunchboxes in their cubbies. Jane is taken to the cloakroom for privacy.

"Don't lie to me, Jane. Lying isn't a nice thing to do."

"I'm not lying. Mom is on a train, but she left us at CVS all alone. Daddy says that she is visiting her friend, but Ginny says she's never coming back. Can I go home sick?"

The third-grade teacher has her hand over her mouth and looks beyond Jane at the coats for a solution. This is a correct reaction, Jane feels. Jane is led away from the cloakroom to an office with only grown-ups, and this pleases her. This is not a childish problem. *This is important!* she had wanted to tell Ginny. *Do not tell me that I am not important!*

Jane is told to sit on the rug, and she does, cross-legged. There are three adults on the rug with her, looming large. One wears a long pleated skirt and her glasses on a chain, and the glasses rest on her large breasts as if the breasts are a shelf. The way she sits on the rug seems uncomfortable, her legs swung to the left; she leans heavily on her right hand, and the flesh is getting pink around her wrist.

The second adult is Jane's teacher and she sits cross-legged like Jane. She has one ear pierced and wears one long earring all the time. Jane likes to sit in her lap and wishes she could sit in her lap right now, but when she tried, she was settled elsewhere by the woman in the long skirt. For some reason, this is not the right time to sit in her teacher's lap.

The other adult is a man in a suit who does not seem happy at all to be sitting on the floor. He has gray hair that does not cover his head. He does not remind her of her father, or of any of the adult men she knows. The adult men she knows like to perform for her, speak to her in funny voices, and usually encourage her to perform right back. These are the friends of her father and her mother, and she has received only encouragement from them. This man in front of her is distracted. She has not pleased him in any manner so far, and feels she needs to. She remembers him now: he's her mother's boss, the one who speaks at the winter celebrations and the raffles.

"So you said your mommy left?" the woman with the glasses and the breasts says.

Jane confirms.

"When did your mommy leave?"

"Not yesterday, but . . ."

"Two days ago. She took Jane out of class," the teacher says to the man on the floor.

"Did your mommy say where she was going?"

Jane shakes her head again.

"Eugene, may I speak to you outside?" the teacher says to the man.

"One minute. Jane, pay attention. Did your mother say where she was going?"

Jane looks out the window. They are in the basement, but some sunshine beams through the grate, and she hears a pigeon making its noise. As an adult, she will associate this school with her mother's embezzlement and with the throaty call of pigeons.

Jane understands that she is being interrogated. The man adjusts his tie and looks at her without kindness. She looks at her teacher and then back at the man. Her teacher is concerned for her; the man is just concerned. The man is not trying to return Jane's mother to her. Jane thinks of the game she played in the backyard with her sister, and appreciates her sister's instinct for secrecy. The Palm girls have something to hide.

"I'd like to see my sister, please."

"Her sister is in the seventh grade."

"She's in class right now, honey," the child therapist says, for that is what she is, the woman with the breasts. She is meant to give Jane a sense of security and has done precisely the opposite.

"I don't care. I won't say one word without her. I need Ginny."

The man gets onto all fours, and Jane thinks he's about to lunge at her, but he is just trying to find his way up off the rug. His back seems to be giving him some trouble, he cannot lift himself upright, and so Jane is in an excellent position to stare down her interrogator, finally eye to eye.

RECOVERY

It isn't necessary to invite Denise over the third morning. The doorbell rings at 10:30, and Denise is on the stoop with a cup of coffee and two bagels. In the kitchen, she begins the business of the bagels, slicing, toasting, spreading cream cheese. She's familiar with the kitchen now, after her snooping. Nathan feels intruded upon. He must remind himself that he said, "Come by tomorrow. Come by every day."

She sits at the kitchen table, chews on her bagel, and leafs through *The New York Times.* After breakfast she wants to go to the basement and Nathan wants to go upstairs to have sex and then sleep. He tries to initiate this scenario, but Denise is uncomfortable. "What about Marion?" she says, but not in a sexy, breathy way; she's looking down at her knees and at Nathan's hand, which is attempting to smoothly creep up her thigh. He says into her ear, "Fuck her — don't worry about her. You never did before." Denise can't explain, but this is different, so instead of going upstairs to the bedroom they end up fumbling in the kitchen like teenagers. Nathan tries to unbutton Denise's jeans, but she swats him away. She opens his fly instead and performs an awkwardly angled hand job under the kitchen table. After, Denise heads down to the basement and Nathan goes to his room to sleep alone. He doesn't want to hear Denise sifting through his family's belongings — the old clothes, toys, games that lost some pieces or were just boring. Jane still plays down there when it's raining outside.

Nathan feels calmer now, but also less alive. He wants Denise in his house and he wants her out of his house. It's not enough, either way.

THE MISSING BOY

The reporter's paper with the boy's picture on front sells 700,000 copies. It's a daily rag but the first with the story. No one expected a missing kid from the middle of Brooklyn to matter. The story's picked up by the *Times,* and the police commissioner is forced to publicly agree with the empathetic young cop. The city should be on the lookout for this poor boy. *Yes,* he says to the mother, *the city will help.* The police commissioner looks baffled to be at this press conference, but the NYPD PR rep says, *Actually, this is a great opportunity. So long as we find the kid.*

MISSING posters are taped up in every subway station in the city. The kid's pixelated face looks a little to the left of every New Yorker who takes the subway. The poster asks the New Yorkers to keep their distance from the kid but to call a cop immediately. This is not the time for citizen intervention, no matter how concerned a citizen might be. Besides, as the PR rep says, the police need a picture of the kid getting out of a cop car — *not* in handcuffs, the PR rep explains slowly — and being returned to his mother. This will be a victory for the NYPD.

The cops talk to more reporters; they've been told it's okay. Be more human, they're instructed. The mother reads the articles about her boy online. The city is with her; the city blesses her.

One paper runs an article with new findings about the school for the city's most vulnerable. The school is astonishingly negligent in many regards. The city demands justice from this school. The mother reads the article.

TIME OUT

Ginny feels a heavy responsibility for her sister. She wants to protect her. She always feels this, but it means she wants to muffle her sister. She wants her sister to be quieter, meeker, more compliant.

Her little sister refuses to speak. She folds her pudgy arms and won't get up off the rug. She insists that her older sister be pulled out of French and that they be alone.

When the adults won't leave the room, Ginny crouches down and puts her ear next to her sister's lips.

"They're after Mom."

And then there are two quiet Palm girls. Eventually they're both put back into class, although French is over. Ginny Palm's off to English, and Jane Palm is tearfully taken back for fractions, and allegations of head lice are made. Jane kicks a snotty boy in her class and is sent to the cloakroom again, this time for a time-out. Overwhelmed,

Jane's teacher finds Ginny again in English and asks her to come back to help with her sister. She's kicking the boys.

So Ginny goes to sit with Jane but does not advise less violent behavior. She's just glad her sister isn't crying about their mother anymore. "Kick all the boys you want," Ginny tells Jane. Jane is content: the Palm girls are united at last.

MARION HAS HER HAIR DONE

In a new neighborhood, Marion Palm buys herself some red hair.

On the beauty parlor wall there is a framed picture of a rouged model with a spiky short haircut. "I don't want that done to me," Marion says, pointing to the poster, and this upsets her hairdresser, a fleshy smocked woman with a haircut similar to the one in the picture. *Bad start,* Marion thinks. So she chats the woman up, coos at her to regain her trust. The woman is easily won back, and then they are that repulsive thing: girlfriends.

Marion has found this difficult in the past; she doesn't like giving up her feet, her hands, her head to another woman for superficial betterment. The exchange makes her uneasy. She is paying to be held hostage, all in the hope of becoming a slightly better woman at the end of it. She will have accomplished something that is both necessity

135

and luxury. She is treating herself; she is maintaining herself. Cuticles must be eliminated, roots retouched. Marion would like to scoff at these rituals but still believes there is something safe about a beauty parlor. Besides, this time it's different. She's not Marion Palm being dragged into a nail salon against her will by a cloying lunch date. She's a wife on the run.

She's been imagining what kind of person she will be on the run, and toying with battered wife. That would allow for her lack of identification, and she can admit to a lot. Her fake name becomes a fake name for a reason. Her new hair is a safety measure, and people won't pry or investigate.

She imagines being hit by her husband (not Nathan — she cannot imagine Nathan doing this. It is another husband, a taller one who perhaps she would have loved more and better than Nathan). Maybe she's had a few teeth loosened. She's hit her head against a sink. She's put concealer on black eyes. It was difficult because the skin was puffy and sore, but she needed to hide the marks or else. She's been disguising herself for years, and this is another round. Another do-or-die situation. Do-or-die dye job. Does the battered wife believe she'll get away with it? No, but this is her last chance to survive.

"Isn't there a movie where Julia Roberts literally swims away from an abusive husband?" she asks the hairdresser.

"Oh, I remember that one. I remember that perm too. You want to look like Julia Roberts?"

Marion shakes her head. She does not want a perm. But isn't it funny? The weirdest things can pop into your head. The hairdresser starts gossiping about a friend of hers whose piece-of-shit husband used to beat the shit out of her on a semiregular basis. She didn't understand why her friend wouldn't just leave him — he was bad news, they'd told her so before the wedding. But the friend was stubborn in her love.

"Well, it's complicated sometimes," Marion says. The hairdresser pauses to take in Marion's supposition with a big open mouth.

"Oh, honey," she says. "Don't tell me about complicated."

Marion's hair is washed, trimmed, dyed, and tinfoiled. She's given a magazine to kill the time, and she learns about new sexual positions that she should try if she wants to keep the mystery, aka keep the man. She listens in on conversations around her. This is not Carroll Gardens or Boerum Hill. The girls are not in yoga pants with swishy ponytails and enormous purses. The women who work in this establishment are from the same social class as the clientele, or at least this is the pretense. Coolness is not a commodity here. Rather, it's a contest of how much they can relate to one another. *I've been there. Don't tell me. I know you. I am you.*

Marion looks at herself not talking in the mirror. She isn't agreeing. Instead she's sitting in judgment of all these women she doesn't know. She has to become one of them again, and she hates them. She remembers when her mother stopped liking her. It happened one evening at dinner when Marion was sixteen; her mother passed her the potatoes and wished Marion would just go away. She said, *I don't care where to.* Marion thought there would come a time when she would look across the dinner table at one of her two daughters and vocalize a similar desire. At least she's avoided that, Marion thinks. At least either Ginny or Jane has been spared.

BOARD OF TRUSTEES

Good afternoon.

May I just interrupt? One teeny tiny second, I promise. I just want to give a big thank-you to everyone for the kind wishes about my recent health concerns. I'm happy to report that my doctors feel very confident: it's benign.

Thank you for sharing.

Congratulations.

Yes. Well. The audit. The audit is what we need to discuss here today. It seems that Daniel felt the need to reach out to the IRS to explain Marion's absence. He seemed to feel that this was necessary, and Deb — apparently — encouraged him to do so.

I thought we told him, no emails.

Can we fire him? Why can't we ever fire anyone?

I've talked to Daniel, and he's very sorry. He thought he was helping.

So now they know.

They know, and they would very much like

to meet with Marion, to discuss some peculiar transactions and the odd deduction. I've been in touch, and they were — to give credit where credit is due — understanding. However, they made it clear to me that sooner or later they will need to speak to her. Or there will be consequences. For the school.

What kind of consequences?

Financial. Financial consequences that we cannot, well, afford right now. So I just wanted to gather the board and ask once more, has anyone seen Marion Palm?

No. As you know, I've been in the hospital —

Anyone else?

Anyone? No? That is complicated.

The lawyers are still —

Concerned. Yes, I know.

How did the conversation with the daughters go?

Unfruitfully. They seemed to get the strange idea that we were *after* their mother.

After? How funny. Cute, almost.

Like the Mob? Like the CIA?

Something like that. So they refused to say anything.

Is that not, if I may, troubling?

How so?

The Palm girls believe their mother must be protected from us. From the school. What has

Marion Palm done that requires such protection?

I hadn't thought about that.

Perhaps it would be wise to find out.

DINNERTIME

Marion buys more black beans and rice from the taqueria. The woman behind the counter compliments her hair. It's time to move on from the Sunset Park sex motel.

The Palm family has dinner without Marion for the third time. Indian takeout. Ginny avoids cubes of cheese in her spinach. Jane eats all of her chicken masala to please her father. Nathan drinks a bottle of wine quickly.

A boy intrudes on a train of commuters. He rocks, and a space clears around him. The commuters look down at their phones, thumbs dart across screens, while the boy makes sounds of terror. He moans and rocks. A space clears where he is.

DEMANDS

In her room, Jane marries and divorces her dolls. The marriages are elaborate and shoeless, because she cannot keep those little shoes on her Barbies' frustrating feet, but other than that, they are whirling operas of chaos. Fights break out, outfits are changed, sex is had.

Jane is supposed to be in bed but felt like playing, so she's playing.

The divorces are simple, somber, and usually only one other doll is in attendance: the lawyer. Most of her classmates' parents are divorced, and she's seen some movies, so she has the basic principle down. As she understands it, two people sit on opposite sides of a table, with a lawyer in between. They fight and argue about money and children. Usually one person is hoping to marry a different person. But both the mother and the father are there at the table. Even if one person moves to a smaller apartment in Manhattan or to a house on the other side of the park while the other remains in the brownstone, they are both still around. Her mother's absolute absence throws off her logic. But dolls do disappear, it's true; it's like they walk away.

Jane expects to hear her mother's voice, and as it does not come, she cannot be stilled, and so she is always in motion. At first she imagines her mother in the room, but now this doesn't help. She knows too well that her mother is *not* in the house. She hasn't gotten a clear answer from anyone on when her mother is coming back.

Grown-ups look past her, and she wants to kick their shins to make them notice her. Everyone tells her what to do. You should be patient and not kick. No one listens to her. Her father listens to Ginny because he is frightened of her. Ginny has mutated from a child into something else.

Jane rages. She opens her mouth and howls.

Ginny's watching a television show about teenagers with dramatic lives and quirky syntaxes. All of Ginny's friends watch this show and text each other as they watch. One friend tried to text Ginny, but her mother told her to stop playing with her fucking phone. Ginny was relieved, because she didn't know what her friend wanted.

Nathan's watching too when Jane begins yelling. He doesn't hear the tantrum until Ginny points it out. "Oh, right," he says, and gets up. Nathan was in the process of passing out; otherwise he would not have consented to watch the television show.

Upstairs, a thud and Nathan's voice, words indistinguishable but the tone clear: *Goddamnit,* the tone says.

Ginny smiles, because she remembers how her father and Jane spoke to each other the first night. Simpering singsong voices about stories. They were pretending. Ginny was not pretending, so tonight she is not bellowing. She is apart from that.

A boy on the screen kisses a girl on the screen and gathers the back of her dress in his fist, and the girl has her hands starfished on the sides of the boy's face. Ginny makes a note of this. She is trying to learn how to kiss from a television show. When they break apart, the girl's face is glistening with fake tears. They weren't supposed to be kissing. The bellowing happens once more and a door slams. Nathan is back.

"Turn off that crap," he says to Ginny. "Go to bed."

Jane's demand: if she has to go to bed, so does her sister.

145

"No," Ginny says. "I want to finish."

"Bed," Nathan says.

"No," Ginny says.

"Please?"

Ginny turns down the volume.

"How's that?"

Jane is behind her father.

"She has to go to bed too. It's not fair."

"I'm older than you. I will always be older than you."

"It's not fair."

Jane pushes her father, who stumbles and submits.

"Fine. No one goes to bed. We all watch television."

Jane blinks a little but deposits herself in an armchair. Ginny curls up in hers. Nathan lies back down on the couch with a wineglass cloudy with fingerprints, and the whole family watches the inappropriate television show. They watch another. Nathan passes out. Jane falls asleep. Ginny eventually goes to bed, and leaves the television on.

MARION AT TWENTY-TWO

Marion at twenty-two feels no hope for her future. She works six shifts a week at the restaurant, and when she returns home, she must sit in a dark room and watch television. If it's a comedy, she won't laugh at the jokes. If it's a crime show, she won't be bothered by the murder. If it's about a relationship, Marion switches the channel. Marion at twenty-two will be either at the restaurant or watching television.

The café has several regulars, and they pride themselves on their regularity above all else. They know how the café works, and even more impressively, they remember the names of the waitstaff. They have tables they like and are offended when they are not available.

Marion tries to fit in. She mimics the enthusiasm of the other waiters and waitresses. She practices making her face smile when a regular walks in, as if it's spontaneous. She's not certain whether it's spontaneous for the others but knows it's not so difficult for them either.

When Marion makes a mistake with an order, she fails these regulars in an indelible way, and they must let her know. These regulars must be unhappy, Marion tells herself, but their pathetic maneuverings enrage her. She hates the way they tip. These regulars slide the bills over the bar to her as if they are both members of a secret but fun club. As if Marion's livelihood is a made-up construct of some game they are both playing. Where do these pitiful people make their money? Who would give these wretches a livable income, and why won't they give one to her? She and Nick are living off credit cards and leftover food from the restaurant. Nick's boyfriends seem to enjoy this young poverty. They are artists or musicians, or they have been to college or are in college, and plan on growing up eventually. Marion doesn't know how to say *This is me grown up. This is as good as it's going to get.*

When the owner storms into the restaurant during one slow Tuesday morning shift, the waitstaff freeze like frightened rabbits, and she screams that they should be working faster. It's comical in the abstract, but the reality is debilitating. The owner swipes her finger over a petal from the floral arrangement and cries out that it is dusty. Marion snaps to attention and begins to run a rag up the stems. The flowers are not dusty, so Marion is pretending to dust. The owner must notice, because she snatches the rag out of Marion's hands and says, "Are you stupid? Are you deficient? What specifically is wrong with you?" The head chef pours Marion a glass of Barolo when the owner leaves. She gulps it back and asks for another.

That night as she counts the drawer, she thinks about dusting and finds herself writing a fictitious receipt for window washing. She slips $20 from the drawer in with her tips. She puts the rest of the cash in an envelope, except for the $150 that remains in the drawer, and she puts the envelope in the safe along with the fake receipt, with a rubber band around it all. She puts her tips and the twenty in her purse and feels, fleetingly, vindicated.

Nathan's Insomnia

Nathan wakes up once more with the television on. His younger daughter sleeps in the chair beside him. Nathan carries her to her room and puts her to bed. His head hurts; his tongue is dry and rough. He gulps water, takes three Advils, and climbs into his own bed, but Nathan Palm can't sleep. It's like he's not allowed to. His thighs itch. *This is just guilt,* he thinks. *Go to sleep.*

He wasn't guilty when he called Denise. His wife wasn't there anymore, perhaps not even in the same state, and she wasn't calling him back. He needed to feel better, and calling Denise would help. He even reasoned that it would make him a better father, better able to present a calm front to his daughters if he accepted that he had been left.

But when he and Denise were fooling around in the kitchen, it did not feel like he had been left. It felt like he had a wife who

150

was visiting a friend in Tarrytown and would be back in a week or so. Denise made Nathan feel like an opportunist.

Three years ago, Marion went through a phase when she seemed frightened all the time, and Nathan couldn't understand what she was frightened of. He wanted her to get over it. It was scaring the girls. He watched as they squirmed away from their mother and she gripped their little bodies all the tighter. She had panic attacks in the early hours of the morning, and he would find her balled up at the foot of the bed. Nathan suggested she see a therapist.

"I'm from Sheepshead Bay — I'm not like you, I'm not like your family."

Marion's accusation had stung. He had seen a therapist. He'd been sent there by his mother.

Marion was working longer hours at the school, coming home later than her children, usually with more work to do, more phone calls to make and emails to write.

"This doesn't make any sense — this is a part-time job!" she'd wail. She often left the house with watery eyes, with two mascara-tinted teardrops under the lower lash line, like Pagliacci, not because she had been sad or angry but because she hadn't been able to find her keys. Nathan would help her search the house while she wept and opened and slammed shut drawers. He would eventually find the missing keys, and rather than praise him for this accomplishment, she'd shake her head, still inconsolable. Nathan told his wife that he lost his keys all the time and it never upset him much. And Marion said that that was very nice, but he didn't have any real responsibilities, now, did he?

Marion was at her most biting and mean after she had lost something.

That was the last time he had called Denise. He needed Denise then as he needs her now.

Nathan remembers that bad time in his marriage, which he thought was over and done with. Marion, without therapy, had righted herself, and Nathan did not ask how. A good memory floats up, and he hopes it will soothe him back to sleep. He closes his eyes and relaxes his body to prepare for it. A few weeks before Christmas. It's dark and he's coming home from seeing Denise. The streetlights are on, and snow lightly dusts the cars, the sidewalk, his shoulders.

His house glows yellow from the interior lights. Nathan sees his younger daughter at the window on the first floor. She must be standing on the sofa, something she's not supposed to do, but from the outside looking in, it's charming. She presses her hands against the glass. He waves to her, and she waves back, but she's looking beyond him at an old Volkswagen Beetle, painted pink with multi-colored polka dots, inching through the snow.

He lets himself in, and his house smells like dinner. It's clean. He exhales. Jane runs to him and allows herself to be picked up, but still looks behind him at the car.

"What do you see, Janey?"

"A car. A silly car."

"A silly car?"

"I want one."

He puts her down, and she returns to stand on the sofa by the window. Nathan finds Marion in the kitchen. He says, "Jane's got a car thing now?"

"I know. I bought her a Barbie sports car for Christmas," Marion says, and she seems proud and happy. She reaches for Nathan and keeps her arm around his waist as she stirs a simmering pot of gravy and tells him about the Christmas gifts she's purchased for her girls that day. Nathan never learns the reason for Marion's pride. He believes it is a kind of psychological breakthrough and does not question its mechanisms.

Instead he peers into the pot of gravy.

Nathan never knows that Marion is celebrating. It has been a four-month-long close call at the school, but she has won. Shelley, the suspicious head of the PTA, has been deactivated; instead of accusing Marion of embezzlement, she will be getting a messy divorce, and Marion is her new confidante. Marion is reveling in her moment of victory. She has once again kept her crime from this house. She can stay.

HEADLINES THAT MATTER

Headlines tell of a missing boy in the subway. The missing boy can't talk. The city is on the lookout for the missing boy.

It is a story about disability. It is a story about incompetence. It is a story about a story. It is a story about one family. It is a story about one school. It is a story about one borough, then five boroughs. The boy loves the subway and that changes everything.

Jane studies the photo of the boy in the newspaper open on the kitchen table. He looks like he could be her age, even though he is a teenager. His shirt is buttoned all the way up, and Jane imagines his mother buttoning it for him.

The Palms are late and the bus has to be sent away once more. Jane is going to school with her sister again on the subway because they are so late. Nathan drinks black coffee at the kitchen table. He gives them granola bars for breakfast. He couldn't sleep, he says, but it's fine.

"I'm going to look for the boy on the subway," Jane says, and her father and Ginny say okay and go back to their coffee and granola bar.

In the subway station, Ginny sees his face on a poster. *Have you seen this boy?* the poster inquires.

"Is this the kid you were talking about?" Ginny asks. "I thought you were making it up." She reads the fine print while the F train roars in.

On the train, Jane looks left and right for the missing boy.

"He's not here," she says, disappointed. "Should we put up posters like that for Mom?"

Jane says this loudly, and the passengers of the car look at her over their smart-phones, iPads, and folded newspapers.

Ginny shakes her head, not only at the idea but at Jane's decibel level.

"What?" Jane says.

Ginny tells Jane to shut up.

Jane lets go of the train pole, says, "Excuse me," and slips away from her sister into the morning rush-hour crowd. Ginny chases her. The two sisters change the tenor of the train, and Jane is apprehended trying to change cars.

"Have you lost your mind?" an older man asks Jane. He detains the little girl by gripping a strap of her backpack until her sister can reach her. Jane kicks him in the shins.

The man swears, and keeps Jane at arm's length so she can't kick him again but doesn't let go of her backpack. It is Jay Street, and Ginny takes her sister's arm and pulls her off the train, away from the angry man.

Jane reaches up and scratches her sister's face. Three red lines appear from her temple down to her cheek. Ginny grimaces but does not release her grip.

"I hate you," Jane says.

"I hate you too," Ginny replies.

THE BUSINESS CENTER
OF THE DAYS INN

Marion visits the Business Center of the Days Inn, which consists of an old PC and a black-and-white printer. It suits her fine. She has a computer again after days of not having a computer, and her fingers itch for the keys. She's sitting down, she's tapping away, she's looking at Ginny's Facebook page. Her online routes are familiar. She checks the news, reads the school's PTA blog, looks up her husband's ranking on Amazon, and it hasn't changed; she Googles his name to see if anyone has mentioned him. They haven't.

She types "women who embezzle" into the search bar, and a list of articles appears. Most she's read before. The topic has not been adequately explored, and the current research contains none of the nuances one might hope for. Recently a woman embezzled over $400,000 from a cement factory in Biloxi. The author of the article sneers at the car the woman chose to buy herself with the stolen money. It was a new car, but beige and practical. The article implies that it's funny and quaint how the woman chose to spend the embezzled money. Marion Palm bristles in the Biloxi woman's defense. It seems like a fine car. Very reliable.

The next article is about a study that says there need to be more studies about women who embezzle. Marion Palm wholeheartedly agrees, and checks the sources. They seem to stand up but could use more stats.

And so on. This is her expertise, and she's lost in her world. This is where she comes for tips, for clues, for balance, for nurturing, for love, for sorrow, for community.

Three pages down, she finds an article written in the first person. One woman who embezzles to another woman who embezzles. Charlene is in prison serving the second year of a five-year sentence and is innocent. She claims it was a case of identity fraud, overzealous and most likely criminal police, and a tragically incompetent female lawyer. The lawyer giggled before sentencing. Charlene is in her cell writing on lined paper with a cheap ballpoint pen and she's sent it to a feminist blog.

Charlene is full of shit. This is uncharacteristic of women who embezzle, Marion knows. Women who embezzle confess easily, honestly, and they involve their families. *I took a risk and made this sacrifice so my daughters and sons and sisters and husbands and brothers and mothers and fathers could live a better life. It's not about me.* That's what women who embezzle say, and Marion believes she will say something similar if and when she's caught. She feels it's true; her husband and daughters have lived better, happier lives because of her crimes.

This woman is different, a variable, an outlier in the data. She offers the excuse of nonguilt. She believes her own lies. Charlene is her own victim. An appealing perspective, Marion thinks.

She reads through the story once more and does a cursory background check. It leads her into the strange world of marathon blogs, and Marion thinks of her husband. He's always wanted to run a marathon, and every year he thinks about submitting his name for the New York City Marathon lottery. But he bemoans the amount of time training would take, which would be time away from his family and his writing. Still, he's got to run it once in his life, before his knees go. The issue is effortlessly forgotten until the day of the marathon. Then he's depressed on Fifth Avenue, watching the runners go by. *Next year,* he repeats with great sadness and determination. Marion refused to engage last time. *This is meaningless and boring,* she wanted to tell him. *How and why can you not see how meaningless this is? How boring you are?*

A thread of comments unfolds under an article Marion has found.

BE ON THE LOOKOUT FOR CHARLENE SHE CHEATS. Note to all marathon organizers and volunteers and runners: if you see this woman, beware.

A photo of Charlene has been removed. Marion feels disappointment but reads on.

This woman is a notorious marathon CHEAT. She joins in for the last three miles and finishes with a TOP TEN TIME. She's done this about 7 times THAT WE KNOW OF.

>She did this in Providence in '08. UNBELIEVABLE.

>>SERIOUSLY. What's the point?

>>>My cousin saw her in Jersey. Charlene finished and CRIED.

The writers seem personally victimized by this fraud. Marion guesses she understands. A marathon is meaningless and boring unless it is metaphorical. By trying to cheapen whatever that metaphor might be, Charlene has trampled on something specifically hazardous. Still, Marion can't intuit what this woman needs. It could be fame or a cheering crowd, but cheating at a marathon seems stupidly risky for such a small reward. Perhaps Charlene is not really a woman who embezzles after all; she's a cheater of marathons, a hog of the spotlight. She might even enjoy her own pursuit by the law.

Marion Palm clicks to the NYC Marathon website and enters her husband for the lottery. She remembers his credit card number, the code required, and the expiration date. She hums a little as she perpetrates this tiny fraud, clicks the button to say she understands the health risks and wants to proceed. Yes. She hacks into his email and reads the confirmation that he has entered the marathon lottery. It tries to sell her some running gear and a training guide, and she deletes the email. She hopes Nathan wins. She imagines Ginny and Jane cheering for their father on Fifth Avenue. Jane hands him a paper cup of Gatorade. Ginny makes fun of his clothes. He'll see them in three hours, he says boyishly. Ginny and Jane go home and watch the marathon on the news. Nathan crosses the finish line alone.

She moves on virtually to her real purpose. The Days Inn has lost its allure, and Marion Palm needs a room. While it was helpful and necessary to recuperate after her bout with homelessness, her stasis must end. She searches neighborhoods that her husband and his friends would never go to and certainly would never live in. She'd like to be by the water, she thinks. She starts to look around Coney Island and Brighton Beach. The summer is over; there may be rooms available.

She creates a new email account and writes emails to the Craigslist ads. "Hello. I'm a recent divorcée and I'm looking for a furnished room. I'm very clean and want to pay in cash in advance." Emails out, she waits for a response.

MISSING PERSONS

In the basement, Denise discovers a small pink armoire under a mouse-turd-encrusted tarp. The armoire reaches Denise's waist and is hand-painted, possibly handmade. There are two doors on top and three drawers underneath. The drawers are small, the hardware tiny and delicate. Denise guesses a grandfather built this for a granddaughter. She kneels and opens one of the small doors. She finds several naked Barbies sitting on the shelves, and a glass of water with an iPhone in it. She pulls open one of the drawers and finds a stack of credit cards. She shuffles through them, and it's not only credit cards. Here is Marion Palm's driver's license. Here is her Social Security card. Denise sweeps her hand to the back of the drawer and finds Marion's passport. The day before, she found $700 bundled with a rubber band in a shoebox on a shelf above the washer and dryer, next to the detergent.

She leaves her discovery and finds Nathan passed out in the living room. She shoves him awake. Nathan must call the police. The argument isn't difficult. He gives in because Denise is usually right about these things and it has been four days. Nathan still feels uneasy about calling the cops. He remembers the last time he did this. He called 911. The operator yelled at him for tying up the line, and then the detective scoffed at his story. Marion walked through the door three hours later.

Denise knows she must tell Nathan about her discovery but can't find the right moment or words.

Nathan Googles "missing persons BK." The number he needs is for the Missing Persons Squad, which feels like something a television show would make up. He tells his story to the officer who picks up, and the officer does not scoff at him. In fact, he sounds concerned. He says that a detective will be by shortly to investigate. Nathan gives his address, and the officer says, "Thank you, sir."

Denise wants to stay, but Nathan asks her to leave. He says, "They'll ask who you are." She says, "I'm an old friend of the family." Nathan says, "Yes, but my face will tell the cops what else you are." Denise gives in and gathers her belongings. Nathan washes their two coffee cups and leaves one out to dry; the other he puts away in the cabinet. Before she goes, Denise manages to tell Nathan about what she found. "Is that normal?" she asks. Nathan has no answer. She leaves, and Nathan examines the pink armoire in the basement, and it's as Denise described. The doorbell rings. He pulls the tarp back over the evidence and turns off the basement light. The money he leaves in the shoebox.

Nathan opens the front door. A man in a suit and a uniformed officer stand on the stoop. A camera on a strap hangs from the officer's neck.

He cannot tell them about the basement. What will the police think? What will the police do? Nathan reminds himself that Marion always comes home.

So he eagerly welcomes the police into his home. The man in the suit identifies himself as a detective, and Nathan offers them coffee, tea, water, anything. The detective says he'll have a glass of water. Nathan turns to the officer with an open face, but the young man shakes his head. "No?" Nathan says, and goes to the kitchen.

He returns with the water, and the detective asks Nathan if his family has cats.

Nathan says they don't, and the detective nods and seats himself in an armchair. The officer sits on a piano bench and takes out a notepad. The detective fidgets in his suit, which is not expensive, nor tailored. Nathan is happy in his jeans and T-shirt, as he always is when he talks to a man in a suit.

The detective sneezes into a tissue and asks, "So, what happened?" Nathan tells the detective the same story he told Denise, but with less swearing. The next questions are: *Why did you wait so long to report your wife as missing? Do you think your wife has left you? Where do you think she would go?*

Nathan replies that he does believe his wife has left him, but there has been no contact and no one knows where she is, and that's odd. He feels he has to be safe but also doesn't want to waste the police's time. He doesn't believe anything is really wrong, but as he says this, he thinks of the pink armoire. He's checked all the places she might go, and she's not there. Nathan answers questions about his wife's mental history, not that there is one beyond the occasional intense mood swing. Some depression runs in her family. The officer takes notes while the detective sits uncomfortably in the chair, his ankles almost daintily crossed and his belly spilling a little over his belt. Nathan might be tempted to dismiss the detective, but he looked at Nathan sharply when he thought about the armoire.

"What was your wife wearing the last time you saw her?" the detective asks.

"A nightgown. She'd have changed her clothes. My daughters would know."

"They were the last to see Mrs. Palm, correct? So I'll need to talk to them."

"Really? I don't want to worry them."

"They're not worried now?"

"I think they think Marion is visiting a friend," Nathan says slowly.

"You think," the detective repeats.

"We haven't really been talking about it."

"I'll be very tactful."

Nathan realizes he has no choice and so grants his permission. "Well, they'll be home soon. They're at school."

The detective asks if he and the officer can take a look around, and Nathan says of course. Instead of leading them to the basement, to the strange evidence, he takes them to the second floor, to his and Marion's bedroom. Nathan shows the detective the closet. "So she didn't take much with her," he says, hiding the fact that Marion took nothing with her with the word *much*. The detective says, "Huh." The officer takes pictures.

"Is there any reason your wife might have left you?"

Nathan's mouth goes dry. "Not that I can think of. But, well, she's done this before."

"When was that?" the detective asks, knowing all about it. There's a record of Nathan's previous call.

"Ginny was maybe seven, so six years ago? She disappeared for a couple of days. She just needs the time sometimes. I guess she needs the time away from me."

"Is that what you think is happening?"

"Yes. Yes, I do."

"So she'll come back."

"Won't she? Isn't that the pattern?" Nathan asks the detective, and what he's really asking is, *Don't wives occasionally do this?*

When the girls arrive home, the detective trundles down to the first floor, taking careful steps in his large black orthopedic shoes, and scares the hell out of both of them. He asks each girl separately about the last time she saw her mother. Neither mentions the check at the Greek diner. Jane doesn't like to think about it but isn't sure her mother did anything wrong. Ginny knows but won't tell.

Before he leaves, the detective has a quiet conversation alone with Nathan in the kitchen about the reality of missing persons.

He will post a picture of Marion online, along with a description of her physical attributes. He now has a description of her clothes from Ginny. He'll file a report and he'll look into her credit activity, but there is very little the police can do when foul play is not suspected.

"Is there anything you can tell me that would contradict that? Should we be concerned?"

Nathan should show them the basement, he knows, but he's seen too much television. He thinks he will be suspected of harming his wife. He decides to show them half of the evidence. He leads the detective to the washer and dryer, to a green shoebox that once held a new pair of sneakers for Ginny. Nathan opens the lid and shows the detective the cash.

"Why do you think this is here?" the detective asks.

"It's probably just for emergencies," Nathan says.

"But you didn't know about it?"

"My wife handles the finances."

The detective scratches his neck but thinks that this box of cash is not enough. He must take into consideration Marion's habit of taking time off from her marriage. This seems like a private matter. He'll still look, he says. But if the police do find Marion Palm, he can only report to Nathan that she is safe. He won't be able to tell him where she is. She's an adult, he says, and this is America.

"Can you give her a message if you find her?" Nathan asks.

"Sure," the detective says.

"Remind her that she has children ages thirteen and eight and they would like to see their mother."

The police leave the Palm brownstone, and the officer begins to talk. He's confident that this crazy Brooklyn woman has abandoned her family, as she does from time to time, and that's sad. But the husband's just covering his ass. It's funny, actually, this Brooklyn housewife taking off. She decides she wants something else, or someone else, and instead of hiring a divorce lawyer like a normal person, she takes off. "After a cheeseburger," he says and laughs. "God bless. God bless."

The officer is still on duty, but the detective's shift is finally over. They've all been looking for the missing boy. The officer drops the detective off at his house in Windsor Terrace and wishes him a restful night. The detective does not return the sentiment.

The detective unlocks the front door, opens it slightly, makes a clicking noise, and blocks the opening with the side of his foot. Nothing's on the other side. He slips in and shuts the door fast behind him. "Walter?" he calls out. "Walter!" No movement, but he knows where Walter is. He goes to his bedroom and eases himself down onto his knees and then his belly. He lifts up the sheet, and two small orbs glow from under the center of the bed. The detective reaches and grabs the cat by its scruff and pulls Walter out. The cat lets out a low growl of protest and hisses. The detective does not let go but sits on his carpet with the cat in his lap, holding its scruff with his left hand, and reaches for a bottle on his nightstand with his right. Walter's ears are flat, and the stink of urine rises up. "Jesus, Walter," the detective says, and he unscrews the bottle. He works the cat's mouth open and lets three drops of the medication land on the cat's tongue. He holds the cat's jaw shut, counts to ten, then releases Walter, who springs away to find an impossibly small space to hide in. The detective looks down at the damp spot on his suit and wonders once again why he doesn't remember to change before he goes through this sad ritual. He should shower, but instead he sits on his floor. It's been a long day, yet the detective wants to know more about that box of cash. The children were lying to him about something. He lifts himself up onto the bed, shrugs the urine-stained jacket from his shoulders, and loosens his tie. He kicks off his shoes. The missing boy is the priority, he reminds himself. For a while the privileged class of Brooklyn must fend for itself. The detective unbuttons his shirt. Abandonment happens. Missing people are common. And if Marion Palm wasn't rich, if she didn't own a brownstone with her husband in Carroll Gardens, he would not have interviewed Nathan in person. The officer would have gone alone. The detective visualizes the daughters looking up at him on the stairs. Nathan tells the girls not to look so scared, and the girls smile for their dad.

The detective hears Walter heaving in the carpeted hallway, and he rushes to move the ailing cat to the bathroom tiles.

BRIGHTON BEACH

In Sunset Park, Marion buys new clothes in dusty shops that sell everything. She could buy a mother-of-the-bride suit there. She could buy a brooch to put on the suit. She could also buy vacuum cleaner bags. She buys colorful tops and tight skirts and new underpants. With the red hair, she looks like a Carol Burnett character. She rips the tags off.

Marion takes the F to Coney Island to look at a room in an apartment on Mermaid Avenue. When she gets off the train, she feels the cold wind full of salt on her cheeks, and she shivers, then smiles.

This isn't like last time. The other time she used her credit cards. She turned off her phone but kept it in her pocket. The girls were young enough that they either wouldn't remember or would believe Nathan when he lied about where she was. She stayed with Nick, her former roommate, who assumed it was mere heartache or heartbreak and didn't ask questions. Nathan never called Nick, because he'd forgotten Nick existed, because Nathan has forgotten that Marion existed before they married. So she slept on Nick's couch and watched television. She couldn't go to Nick this time, she knew; she'd eventually be found. Nathan may not remember premarital Marion, but Nick's apartment is an official previous address, credit history would show, and soon the police would be at the door. The other time was practice. She didn't have a knapsack full of cash then.

She'd left when Nathan became arrogant and vain. When he was like that, she knew he wanted to brag to her about some infidelity. She could smell Denise (or whoever else) on him, and she wanted to destroy him for the cliché. He kept looking at her, silently begging for a reaction. She would not join Nathan in being trite, she'd vowed, but couldn't look at his face without wanting to hurt it. She left and waited for her rage to subside. When she returned, Nathan opened the door and his face had changed back and she could enter the house again. Her daughters ran to her, full of tales of what she'd missed while she was gone.

The knapsack doesn't go with her new

outfit, but she still slings it over her shoulder. She bought a small purse, and this crosses her chest. She reaches into the new purse and pulls out a small piece of paper with the address and directions. Living without a cell phone again is freeing. She looks up more.

The apartment building is a block away from the beach. The rent includes a single bed, a bureau, and a shared bathroom.

Marion finds the entrance for the large apartment building and selects the correct buzzer. After a blast of static, the door latch makes a mechanical grinding sound, and Marion is able to enter.

"Third floor," an accented voice calls out. There is an echo in the dingy lobby from the old marble on the floor and the walls.

"Okay! I'm coming!"

She hasn't survived a Brooklyn walk-up in a while, and soon she is sweating through her new synthetic fabrics. A woman in a robe waits for her in the doorway.

"Take your shoes off, please," she instructs, not kindly, but not unkindly either. She gives Marion a pair of slippers to wear.

The woman has a figure that Marion immediately envies. It is the figure of a French movie star in her forties, soft but thin and appropriately curved. The woman's face is

176

lined and her teeth are yellow, but she wears eye shadow and a dash of lipstick. Some blush. It's not a lot of makeup, but it's enough.

"I am Sveyta," she says.

"Sveyta," Marion repeats. "I am Marion."

"A pleasure to meet you," Sveyta says.

A short tour of the immaculate apartment comes next. The windows look out onto the street, and if they were open, Marion believes she could hear the ocean. However, Sveyta is adamant that the windows stay closed. She has a chill always.

Sveyta ends the tour at the available room for rent, which contains a twin bed with a white coverlet, a nightstand, and a white bureau. The walls are painted pink. There is no closet. Marion believes that Jane would love this room, and because Jane would love it, she will love it too. She will even tolerate the cross above the bed.

Marion leans forward to look out the window and sees that Sveyta has nailed the window shut. The window faces a brick wall.

"It is perfect," Marion says.

"There is no closet," Sveyta says.

They return to the kitchen for tea and a short interview.

"Where do you come from?" Sveyta asks, and lights a cigarette. The smoke from the cigarette mixes with the steam from the tea.

"I'd rather not say," Marion says. "I have cash."

"You've mentioned that. It makes me somewhat nervous."

"I can pay up front."

"Why don't you want to say where you come from? It's a simple question."

"I'm from Brooklyn."

"Then you have family here."

"Not anymore."

"Why not?"

"May I have a cigarette?"

"Of course."

Marion pulls the cigarette out of the pack on the table. She hasn't smoked since the first weeks she was pregnant with Ginny and didn't know.

"I'm hiding from my family. My husband. He was abusive. Physically abusive."

"You have not gotten very far. Why do you stay in Brooklyn?"

"I don't want to leave. Brooklyn is a large place and my home. It isn't fair. Besides, I'm not much of a driver."

"Will your husband find you?"

"No."

"Why not?"

"Because he wouldn't look here. I'm sure

178

of it. He can't even see beyond Prospect Park."

"I don't know. This makes me very nervous."

Marion reaches for Sveyta's left hand, which lies on the table next to her teacup.

"Please. If there is any trouble, I'll go. But I love the room. I need the room."

"Do you have children?" Sveyta says after a long pause.

"No," Marion says. She instructs herself to believe this. "I am childless."

Sveyta slips her hand out from under Marion's. "That will be three months up front."

"Thank you. Thank you."

Sveyta does not say that Marion is welcome, but Marion feels welcome anyway.

THE MISSING BOY

Now New York commuters wrestle daily with how easy it is for some to disappear.

They've read the fine print of the posters. They've made mental notes of the boy's features. They've imagined themselves finding the boy, rescuing the boy, and becoming brief New York heroes. The mayor would shake their hand. They look into the faces of all the young people on the train, temporarily aware. A quiet boy becomes a person of interest in New York, and all the quiet boys and young-looking men of the city are now responsible for speaking up and telling strangers that they are neither lost nor autistic. It's an unusual thing to declare about oneself.

The commuters peer into the faces of these adolescent boys and, after imaginings of heroism, have differing reactions. Some feel nothing besides faint curiosity; some feel pride — they remembered to look and therefore have committed an act of service; some think about their own quiet and lost adolescences; others think about their children or their brothers. Those with their own missing people remember them. The commuters become the mother of the boy. They all fail to protect. The commuters become the boy. They find themselves utterly missing. Then they reach their destination, and their days either begin or end.

Board of Trustees

Thank you. I'd first like to say how glad I am everyone could make it here on such short notice.

It's fine.

It's important to me that you understand my gratitude.

Can we for once begin and end on time, Eugene?

Duly noted. Well, as you may or may not have heard, the Marion issue has become more . . . well, urgent.

Good Lord.

It just hurts.

This is not a personal matter.

Then why does it hurt? We welcomed her into our community.

Yes, and you all did an *incredible* job of making her feel right at home, absolutely.

Was that sarcasm?

No.

Because it sounded like sarcasm.

It was unintentional.

Can we stay focused? Can we? Thank you. It took some digging, but it seems that before Marion left, she transferred the entire Wing Initiative fund into a personal account. That account has now been closed. The good news: it only held roughly four thousand dollars. Thank God the initiative hadn't begun in earnest.

Why did she do it? I don't know what more she wanted. She was invited to the cocktail hours, the barbecues, the block parties. We gave her a job when she asked for one.

The lawyers say that we must go to the police.

Well, I don't know. The Palm family was very generous after the fire.

That was a hundred years ago.

This is not up for debate. We have to initiate an official investigation.

Our ability to honor our past sets us apart — it's what makes us great. We have a history.

Please, listen to me. We have to act fast or we could be liable. I suggest we hire a forensic accountant on our own, although the NYPD may have someone they want us to use.

Excuse me?

We've reached the limit of our accounting capabilities. Marion appears to have been skillful at covering her tracks. We need a professional, a specialist.

Ahem.

But we don't want the NYPD to have full access, considering our donors.

May I interject? Is that necessary?

What do you mean?

This isn't the first time Marion has done this sort of thing.

She's the reason we are being audited.

The Palms owe us what they stole.

Yes, I'm not arguing that point. My only concern is that we are rushing to inform the police because we are scared and upset.

We need a course of action, urgently.

We need to get our money back.

From whom?

Well, from Nathan. Right?

Well.

Yes, the lawyers think that eventually we will need to prosecute. There's also a civil case to be made.

Let's put aside the lawyers, put aside the audit, let's breathe, and remember, we expect the Palms to make a considerable donation to the Wing Initiative.

So?

Perhaps we don't want to accuse a Palm of stealing a comparatively small amount when the family might pledge a much larger one.

Won't it come out eventually? That Marion's been embezzling?

Let's not use that word. I propose we find Marion on our own.

Why?

If we find Marion, we can say that she has been at the bedside of a sick relative or something. She can explain whatever the hell she was doing with our taxes to the auditors — and we all know that Marion is good at that sort of thing. Meanwhile, the Palms will fully fund the Wing Initiative, and no one needs to know that a part-time employee has been swindling us for possibly a decade.

It's risky.

I still think we should call the police.

I agree. Put the cunt behind bars.

Give me a few days. I'll explain to the lawyers. I'll put off the auditors. Trust me.

Any ideas on how to start? Where to look?

Some. Some. We've been monitoring her email account, but so far we haven't found anything that would pinpoint her location.

Has Nathan called the cops yet?

I don't know.

Well, that seems important, don't you think?

What about the children? The daughters know more than they say.

Perhaps if the Palms were more inclined to trust us. At least one of us. Perhaps in a dif-

185

ferent setting, a less official capacity . . .

Okay, not a horrible idea.

Leave it to me. For the time being.

For the record, I still say we should go to the police.

What record?

DINNER PARTY

Nathan Palm receives an email. *HOW ARE YOU DOING????* The subject says. It's written by the mother of a family that lives in the neighborhood and whose children also attend the school. She's one of those involved parents, Nathan thinks, as Marion has mentioned working with her on a few projects. She has a large smile, an excitable manner, and she wears fashionable knit hats. Her husband was an actor, a failing one, who started illustrating children's books about his dog. The children's books have become a huge success. The couple is famous for their generosity. The husband, Tom, seems genuinely baffled by the money he makes. He is unfailingly polite, and always defers to Nathan as *the real writer*. He asks Nathan how his writing is going and shakes his head with wonder at the process of writing poetry, telling Nathan that he couldn't do that in a million years, it is so beyond him. *I just like to draw and tell stupid stories,* Tom says, with kind eyes.

Nathan hates this couple, this family, with a wild passion usually reserved for social injustice and grocery stores on the weekends.

In the body of the email, Anna, the wife, invites him and the girls over to dinner with the caveat that if he's not "up for it," "no worries," and that she just wanted him to know that they are "there for him." The dinner invitation includes offers for both free babysitting ("!!!") and a glass of wine ("or THREE!!!").

Anna is being nice; Nathan should be more kind, and the truth is he has been feeling lonely in this house, overwhelmed by it. He needs to be with people again in order to reset. He can sink too deep into his thoughts, and this isn't good for him, and it isn't good for Jane. Ginny, he's not sure. Jane is also deeply in love with Anna and Tom's daughter, Beatrice, a seventeen-year-old, the babysitter whose services were offered. Jane loves Beatrice in a way that makes Nathan think Jane could be a Secret Service agent; she would happily take a bullet for Beatrice. The pair also have a precocious young son who can be funny, and he sometimes plays with Ginny. Nathan accepts the invitation.

On the night of the dinner, Nathan is wearing a clean shirt and jeans, and Jane has overbaked a batch of chocolate-chip cookies and transferred them into a Tupperware container. Nathan's got a bottle of wine by the neck in a brown paper bag. Ginny is in her room, listening to loud music, and so Nathan must climb the stairs to fetch her. He opens the door and finds her sitting in front of her computer with poor posture.

"Come on," he says over the music. "Let's go."

Ginny taps the touchpad of her laptop with her thumb impatiently and the bleating singer stops.

"I said let's go."

"I don't want to. I always end up stuck with Ben."

"You can stay with me. That won't happen."

Ginny shakes her head again and returns to the computer screen. Nathan sees she's reading some blog about celebrities.

"There's nothing to eat."

"I don't feel well."

"You feel fine. Let's go." Nathan suddenly believes his daughter knows about him and Denise. That communicated message is in her poor posture. He says, "Fine. Order a pizza. Feel better."

Jane and Nathan leave Ginny behind and embark into the night together. The wind is picking up, the eerie vigor of autumn in the air.

On the stoop of the Fishers', Jane rings the doorbell, and the damn family dog barks and barks and barks. The dog is the subject of Tom's famed children's books, a large gray bearded collie named Scooter. Tom takes great pride in this dog, as well as in shoveling snow and overtipping waiters. He's been there, he says of the waiters, with that half-smile, while wearing a $300 sweater.

Tom opens the door and beams at Nathan and Jane.

"Come in, come in. Anna, they're here."

Tom screws up Jane's hair — she laughs — and squeezes the upper part of Nathan's arm and then pats it twice. He takes the Tupperware container of cookies from Jane. He asks, "Where is Ginny?" And Nathan makes up a big test for her: "She's studying hard." "Good for her," Tom says. "Good for her."

Anna rushes out from the kitchen, rubbing her hands dry on a dishtowel. She swings it over her shoulder and leaves it there. The house smells like chicken. The woman: she is allowed to hug, whereas Tom is not. She hugs Nathan first, rocking him in an exaggerated fashion back and forth, lets him go, and does the same with Jane. She is the official tactile greeter of this family. She asks after Ginny, and Tom informs her of the test. Anna also finds this admirable behavior.

"You know," Anna says theatrically to Jane, "Bea's upstairs working on her homework, but I bet she would love to be distracted."

Jane runs up the stairs, almost tripping over her own feet to reach the teenager she adores.

With the child gone, the tone of the greeting drops like a weather event.

"Nathan," Anna says. "How are you?"

"Oh, you know."

"Yeah, okay, yeah. Wine?"

Nathan offers the wine in the bag. The couple coos over it for a while, and it's uncorked and poured. Bland but international music plays on the stereo and the three settle in the living room. Anna curls into a sofa, tucking her socked feet under her thighs, and pulls a wrap over her shoulders. Tom sits but moves, taps his feet, shifts at his end of the sofa. Nathan sits in an

191

armchair and takes too many sips of his red wine too quickly, and feels happy to be there. The living room is warm, and the house is complete. He can hear the children upstairs, and the bright light in the living room is cheerful. Anna has put out a plate of cheese and olives and crackers, and they talk about the block, and it is all subtle and calm. He doesn't like this couple, but he appreciates their lack of neuroses. Their unhappiness is competently expressed and dealt with. Their needs are usually met.

Anna is telling a story about the co-op, Tom interrupting in a funny manner — "They have us by the balls" — and they make each other laugh, so Nathan laughs too.

They tell a story about their son and the girl who has a crush on him. The son doesn't understand what's happening. They tell a story about the daughter, who has been waitlisted at Brown. They talk about their recent renovations and the difficulty and humor of choosing and buying a new toilet. Industrial flushing power is mentioned by Tom, and Anna shushes him comically.

This couple is performing, and Nathan watches. It's strange not to have his own partner. His stories are good too, but without Marion, he can become cerebral. He's on his third glass now, and aware that he's on his way to being drunk but doesn't care. It seems fine.

The chicken is ready, so the children are called down. Plates are carried out from the kitchen to the dining room. Anna has given her guests and her family members each a small piece of chicken, a spoonful of rice, and some vegetables. This family is thin because they don't eat very much, rather than purely because of genetics. Looking down at his plate, Nathan knows that he and Jane will need seconds, and if they aren't offered, he may order takeout when he gets home. If it isn't too chilly, he may even take Jane for ice cream.

Beatrice whines about not getting into Brown. She eats with her fingers (the chicken and the vegetables; she doesn't eat the rice) and rolls her eyes when her mother talks. Nathan finds himself staring at her throughout the meal. She still looks like a little girl; she is slim, and her skin is unblemished. He is not attracted to her, thank God, but he's curious if this is what will happen to Ginny. Beatrice says she doesn't want to go to college, and the family fights about it for a while. Beatrice talks about taking a year off, and Tom is worried that she'll never go, and Beatrice asks if that is so bad. Nathan won't say anything, but he agrees with Beatrice. *Let her wait tables,* Marion would say. *Let her enjoy the world without a degree and see how far she gets. She'll be begging to go to college in a year, maybe less.*

The fight escalates, but the family isn't embarrassed that this is happening in front of guests. The fight concludes when the boy starts talking about his favorite television shows — he favors half-hour comedies that feature wacky thirtysomething women — and the college topic is tabled for the time being.

Then the boy asks, abruptly, where Ginny and Marion are. Beatrice kicks him under the table, and he looks wounded and says "What?" Only younger siblings can feel these wounds in this particular way.

"Well, Ginny is home studying, and Marion is visiting her friend upstate," Nathan says, and he says it well. He says it on cue, and the boy goes back to talking about his favorite TV shows. Nathan puts his hand on Jane's shoulder and notices that her breathing is off. He looks at her, and she's crying again.

"Did you see *SNL* last night?" Nathan asks Ben.

Ben looks to his mother for permission to

re-create his favorite sketches. She gives it with a nod, and he gets up from the table and plays all the different characters and explains why it's funny, and the table laughs and is thankful.

MOTHERS WHO ABANDON THEIR FAMILIES

Ginny takes her laptop down to the kitchen because she is wildly hungry. Her father was correct — there isn't any food in the house save a bowl of raw cookie dough. Ginny takes it out of the fridge along with one of her father's beers and places both on the table next to her computer. She's been Googling.

She Googles her mother's name. Her mother's work profile appears, as well as the photo of an orthopedist from New Jersey who is particularly active on LinkedIn. She traces her mother's past, and looks into the orthopedist because why not? The orthopedist has long dark hair that falls lushly around her shoulders but doesn't distract enough from a beaked nose.

Next Ginny Googles mothers who abandon their families. It is a rarer occurrence than fathers who abandon their families. Not as rare as Ginny expected, however;

she is in good company. The side effects on the children are extensive. Experts say the absence of her mother will define Ginny's adulthood.

She opens the beer and takes a swallow. It tastes bitter and alive, and she immediately burps into the empty room. She eats a spoonful of cookie dough. She eats another. She can taste the butter, and this is nauseating, so she concentrates on the chocolate chips as they break between her teeth.

Ginny has a history exam on ancient Mesopotamia the next day. She has a chapter she should be reading, and notes she should be revisiting. She should be memorizing the geography of the region: two rivers, the Tigris and the other one.

She clicks on her mother's picture and it gets larger. Her mother's behavior has not been unforeseeable, but Ginny can't explain why. She loves her mother and also misses her, but there was something lacking in her mother's eyes, or maybe her forehead, when she looked at Ginny.

Ginny tries to hack into her mother's personal email. She tries her own name, her birthday, her nicknames as passwords. She tries Jane's name and birthday, but it is all unworkable. The spoon digs into the cookie dough repeatedly. A headache mounts behind Ginny's temples. The beer fizzes away.

Ginny's grandmother, Marion's mother, died last winter, and Marion went to the funeral alone. Nathan wanted to go, and Jane wanted to go. Ginny didn't want to go but would have for her mother. Marion shook her head to all of this, just spent the week in Sheepshead Bay. She slept at home, but every morning she took the train far away and didn't return until late. When she did, she looked in on Ginny and Jane before going to bed. Her hair seemed frizzier, and her outfits became strange. She wore long shapeless skirts with scuffed running shoes. One day Ginny noticed that her mother had forgotten a bra. When asked what she was doing in Sheepshead Bay, Marion answered that she was mostly throwing away food. When asked about her family in Sheepshead Bay, Marion said they looked like her but they didn't talk like her, and most everyone owned a boat. Boats were all they talked about, actually, she said. She said she wished her mother had died over the summer because then they would be out on their boats and they wouldn't be cooking so many casseroles. After a short pause, she retracted that statement. Then she would have to deal with the catch from Long

Island Sound, a suspect food group if ever there was one. January was better. Better to hear about the catch than to eat it.

She said this sitting on Ginny's bed, as if she were talking to someone else in the room, but it was just Ginny, so Ginny agreed. Her mother looked at her sharply. "Don't pretend."

DINNER PARTY

After dinner the adults move to the living room to drink more, but to drink differently. Nathan is handed a single malt of some kind that he won't properly appreciate. He wishes Marion were here to make an exclamation of gratitude over the something-something-aged-something years.

Jane is supposed to leave and play with the other children so the adults can talk about grim realities now that they are sufficiently liquored, but Jane doesn't want to go.

"I don't want to play," she says.

"Sure you do. I bet Bea could show you some new YouTube videos."

Beatrice is unexpectedly helpful. She reaches out for Jane's hand and says in an upbeat voice, "Come on. We'll have fun upstairs. It's boring here." This is the older sister of Jane's dreams.

"Go play with the girls," Tom says to his

son, who resists. He says he would rather stay with the adults, but he is eventually persuaded to the second floor. The adults then have one of those pauses that happen when they've gotten their way. But Nathan is confused about why he wanted Jane to leave. He felt like he should make her leave so that the sensitive questions could be asked, but he never wanted to answer those questions. Also, he misses her.

"So how are you doing?" This is Tom.

Nathan sucks his cheeks in and puts his glass on the coffee table. He leans forward and rests his elbows on his knees. He opens his hands, splays them, stretches the fingers, and brings them back together with a light clap. He raises his eyebrows.

"Oh, you know. You know, it's just hard."

Tom and Anna are serious now; they are concentrating on empathizing deeply with Nathan. They are saying that Nathan is not alone with their faces of concern.

"You had to have known this was coming, right?" Anna says.

"No, well, not really. I don't know what you mean."

Anna explains: "Partners don't just take off with no word. It's not normal. If, God forbid, God forbid, Tom left without any warning, I would be going crazy."

Anna keeps her gaze steady on Nathan, and Nathan understands that despite her warmth, he is being held responsible for his marriage's sudden ruin. He wonders if Anna knows about the woman in Dumbo. Or worse: Nathan tries to recall if he ever made a pass at Anna.

"I am going crazy," Nathan says.

"I'd have called the police," she says.

Nathan almost tells Anna that he has. He catches himself. They'd ask more questions, and he might answer. He shakes his head sadly, as if he knows the help of the police is not available to him, but he's thought about it. "No, Marion hasn't been snatched or something. A crime hasn't been committed."

"You don't think so?" Anna says.

"Of course not. I don't . . . I don't know why she left me. And why she didn't tell me why. Let Marion tell you when she comes back. She knows."

"Come on, come on." Tom's late but here to defend his wife.

"Maybe it's your fault," Nathan continues. "You guys could be such snobs to her."

"Come on," Tom says.

"Marion never went to college. She knew you all judged her for that."

"What you're saying is simply not true. I

202

am angry with her now, for leaving you and her daughters, but I always respected her."

"Fuck you."

After fourteen years with Marion, Nathan can only swear and throw things when he is angry. She laughed when he tried to express himself any other way. It is difficult, especially for a poet, that when Nathan feels angry or attacked, he is not more eloquent. But his rage now dismantles his vocabulary, and so he can only swear at the Fishers when they easily express themselves. Nathan thinks about what it will be like if Marion never comes back, and exhales all the oxygen from his lungs but can't sufficiently refill them, and sweat beads on his brow and lower back.

Anna and Tom shift in their seats, eager to accept this as a moment of catharsis from which they will be able to move on to dessert; Nathan refuses to be saved.

"Fuck you both. Jane! Jane, we're leaving."

"I think you should stay," Anna says. "Let's talk about this."

"I don't know why Marion left, and neither do you. It's fucking condescending that you would invite me and my daughter over to your house to figure it out."

"That was never my intention."

"Jane!"

"I think you have a lot of nerve to come in here and eat our food and lash out like this. I know this is a hard time for your family, but we haven't done anything except be your friends."

"Jane. Get down here right now."

"But if we're being honest, Nathan, and I feel that we are, I have to tell you something."

"I am going to count to three."

"We do have a vested interest in finding her, just like you. Nathan, sit down."

Nathan looks at Anna and can't read her. Gone is the Brooklyn earth mother in organic threads walking the dog at five in the morning. This is an entirely different sort of woman standing with her hands on her hips, peering at him through round tortoiseshell glasses. Tom still sits but looks at his wife with something like awe and fear.

"Marion has chosen a very poor time to disappear. Despite what you may think, I like your family and I like your daughters and I like you. I like Marion too, but I feel very angry with her right now. As you know, the school is being audited."

"Anna, what does this matter?"

"Marion's disappearance is upsetting to you and your family, but it could be disastrous to the school. Do you get that?"

Jane appears in the doorway of the living room. "Daddy, what?"

"We're going for ice cream," he says. "Get your coat."

"I'll do it," Tom says, and he scurries away. Jane follows.

Anna continues once Jane is gone. "We think Marion has been embezzling from the school. She emptied a few accounts before she left."

Nathan pictures the cash in the shoebox.

"You made a mistake. Or Marion . . ." Nathan can't finish the sentence. Tom returns with two coats and Jane.

"Any information about Marion's whereabouts would be helpful. That's all," Anna says quietly, so as not to be overheard by Jane. "And it seems like the least the Palms can do. Considering."

"Are you fucking with me?" Nathan asks. Anna smiles and shrugs.

Nathan and Jane abandon the Tupperware for the cookies in their escape from the Fisher brownstone. Nathan reaches for Jane's hand, and Jane skips a little to keep up. Anna watches the Palms from her stoop until they turn the corner.

Anna wishes that the scene with Nathan had gone a little differently but doesn't think it could have. She was angry that he was swearing at her, so perhaps she's showed her hand. At least she's now certain that Nathan doesn't know anything. She has a meeting in the morning with the other trustees. She promised she would follow up with them after the dinner.

Anna pities Nathan but also feels some glee that this is happening to him. She wants the money back, and she'll get it, but there is something deeply funny about what Marion has done. Marion, even with the embezzlement, was highly competent, more than her honest counterparts. She was a pleasure to organize with. Her clear head, her methodical manner. She had a kind of poetically rational mind. In a different world, Anna would want Marion to have the money. But it's this world, and Marion has gone too far. More of Marion's doings have been uncovered, and though they can't officially prove it, it seems she's embezzled more than $100,000 over the years. She needs to be punished. Nathan allowed too much, ignored too often. Anna aches to tell him precisely what his wife has been doing while he's been writing poetry, but she can't. The Palm family must not know the details until the timing is right and perfect. When told, the Wing Initiative will be fully

206

funded. Anna knows. But first Marion Palm needs to be found. A penitent wife will seal this deal.

She returns to her living room and smiles about Marion while Tom leashes the dog for his last walk of the day.

"Beatrice, would you come down here for a minute?" she yells into the air. Brownstones have their own intercom system: thin walls.

Minutes later, the teenager appears at the top of the stairs. "What?"

"How was Jane?"

"I don't know. Upset."

"About what?"

Beatrice rolls her eyes. "Her mom?"

"I mean, anything in particular. Did she say anything to you?"

"She talked a lot about Ginny. She says they're going to school together now on the train. She, like, bragged about it."

"Anything about Marion?"

"No. It was weird. She talked more about that missing kid."

"The autistic one?"

"Yeah. So. I have an essay, so —"

"Dishes first, honey."

"But I've got so much homework to do."

"Better do the dishes fast, then."

Beatrice slinks off to the kitchen. Anna

finishes her wine on the couch. Soon Beatrice is back.

"So, like, she said her mother ran away from a diner. The one on Montague, I think."

"Thank you, Bea, that's helpful. I'll finish up the dishes — go work on your essay. Goodnight, honey."

"Night."

Beatrice is a beautiful, sullen narcissist. She helps only when it is in her own best interests to do so. Often Anna must sit with her daughter in some public place while Beatrice cries and whines about a perceived injustice done to her. Anna listens, as she would for no one else, and tries to fix the injustice for her beautiful daughter. It's difficult to say no to a person who is stunning when they cry. But tonight Bea was helpful; Anna will return to this moment often because it will make her feel like a good parent. Anna is raising a helpful daughter.

MISSING PERSONS

The officer returned to the Fort Greene precinct after dropping off the detective and told everyone about the plug-ugly housewife who bolted after a diner cheeseburger. When the detective begins his next shift, he's asked for details on what is now the most popular running joke of the station. He's asked what Nathan looks like, what Marion looks like, but they know. They've seen the picture. They know how unattractive she is. Detectives and officers alike offer humorous suppositions about Marion's possible destinations. To find a bag to put over her head. A quest for more and better cheeseburgers. Fat camp.

The detective smiles at the jokes, admits that Marion is nothing much to look at, but says that there might be more going on. What about the two kids she left behind? Why didn't she take a suitcase? The humor dissipates, and the crowd of law enforcers becomes uncomfortable. The detective has a reputation for doing this, and one of the newly sulky group reminds him that Marion Palm is not a priority. The crowd nods solemnly. They can be more serious than the detective, they say with their chins, and they return to their own desks. They're all looking for the missing boy.

The detective's task for the day is to listen to recordings of phone calls made to the tip hotline. He's digging for a legitimate lead among the false identifications, but it's clear to him that the kid is, sadly, gone. But the missing person's case is now a city cause. It's uniting the city, and he supposes that is worthwhile, if hopeless. The police haven't told the press: not only does the boy have a fascination with the subway system, he's also mesmerized by the ocean. These are not encouraging qualities in a missing person.

The detective shifts in his seat and runs a check on Marion Palm. She ceased to exist electronically the day she left. Nathan Palm admitted she struggled with depression. The detective believes we all struggle with depression and it's just now been labeled as a problem. It's the truly afflicted who take off and are a danger to themselves and others. Those lost are found walking through

Prospect Park, muttering or bellowing, in a robe and slippers or their underwear or naked. They've soiled themselves. They're walking into traffic, off a bridge. They've left behind sick and starving cats.

Nathan Palm's bland phrases for his wife's illness were not urgent enough; he would not have used the words *admit* and *struggle.* Nathan Palm would have been on the phone with the police the first day, reading names off prescription bottles and explaining that Marion was no longer on those medications. He would have used the shorthand, *meds.* If Marion Palm has left, the detective deduces, it is for a rational reason or she is dead.

A voice says the missing boy climbed into the back of a van off Flatbush. The detective marks the call for follow-up but doesn't believe in it. The voice is too pleased to be helping.

The detective thinks of Nathan Palm and his helpful answers. Nathan Palm called the police but wanted them to leave as soon as they entered the house.

Another voice claims the missing boy is the son of God. Sometimes the boy is Elijah. Other times the boy is a warrior for Satan. It's the end of the world.

Marion Palm has a history of leaving her

husband and returning. She is not a vulnerable adult; if she were, she would not have become this figure of derision and mockery in the precinct. There is a boy who is missing, vulnerable, and a likely victim of a crime. The boy should come first. The detective squints into his computer screen. He tries to focus on the correct missing person.

Marion at Twenty-Three

Marion has worked at the café for over three years when she meets Nathan. She is now the night manager, and an integral part of the operation. She does the front-of-house schedule as well as preliminary training of new waitstaff. More important, she's in charge of ordering for the bar, which means developing relationships with suppliers. She rotates a few personalities to get the best deal: brassy New Yorker, good-time girl/alcoholic, and idiot.

She and the head chef drink regularly together in the basement as Marion pays bills and he works out the specials for the upcoming week. At first it was a glass of wine or two, and now they are sipping tequila out of small plastic cups meant for sauce-on-the-side takeout orders. The head chef is dour and yells to communicate but is essentially a pushover. They gossip about the owner, narrating to each other the latest crazy thing Gabrielle did or said. There is always something new. However, Gabrielle now trusts Marion unconditionally. She still screams at her in a mix of Portuguese and English, but more often than not ends by collapsing into Marion's arms. *I'm so unhappy,* the owner says.

Marion earns a little more than minimum wage for managing the restaurant. She transitions from petty theft to full embezzlement when Gabrielle, overwhelmed, hands her the books. Marion promises to do the best she can and teaches herself to forge Gabrielle's signature. She gives herself a raise.

Nathan comes into the café after work. Nathan at thirty-three wears his hair short and his glasses large. He smiles often. He works part-time at an anarchist bookstore near Marion's café. Nathan is not an anarchist, not even that political, but he is good at sounding political. Still, it's exhausting to feign indignation, so when he's finished for the day, he likes to get a little drunk at the café where Marion works.

He chooses Marion's café because it's nearby and because of the large windows. It is the kind of room that looks pleasant in all weather. He doesn't like bars because he doesn't like televisions; he can't not watch them. This café is quiet around four and five, and so Nathan comes in to drink wine. Between four and five is when Marion likes to check inventory and write fictitious receipts.

At thirty-three, Nathan is not great with women. He'll be better when he's in his forties. Marion will be part of the reason that he's better.

The first conversations happen about wine. Nathan knows nothing except that he likes it, and Marion knows a lot but doesn't judge. He tries new wines with her, and they talk. Marion lets her hair be big, and has wide hips but a slender waist, which is accentuated by the apron. Her breasts are large, and if Marion's mother taught her anything, it was how to purchase and maintain a bra.

Marion manages the conversation, because Nathan is first a customer and then a regular. She knows how to deal with regulars at this point, has developed her own style of familiarity, which is warm but cautious. She harbors no animosity toward the customers, she says with her voice. Nathan responds to her persona by tipping well.

At first he sits at a table by the window, and the conversations happen with Marion standing and cradling an open bottle of wine. This is awkward for Nathan, so he sits at the bar, even though it is away from the window. Marion notices the move and begins to shift the persona slightly. She doesn't do this often, preferring the distance, but there is something about Nathan that is trustworthy. It may be the age difference; Nathan has mentioned that he is in his thirties. But she also thinks he might see her as a person. If they saw each other on the street, Nathan would greet her easily, Marion believes.

Nathan keeps a notebook open as if he is going to write, but it is a prop. He is aware, though, that he wants to write in front of her. He wants to impress her, and the only thing he finds impressive about himself is his ability to focus. He sometimes claims he isn't even that smart but he is able to concentrate in a way that other people aren't.

He will say this later to Marion, after they are married, and he will say it often when he is feeling expansive. It is only after Jane is born that Marion will admit how patronizing she finds this statement, but her anger comes later. At the café, the notebook works, and when he eventually summons up the courage to ask her out, Marion accepts. Nathan seems interesting. Also rich.

Marion looks at the label of his jacket when he's in the bathroom. It's not that she's looking for a wealthy boyfriend. There is another waitress at the café, and she is absolutely out to marry a rich man. Marion looks at the label because there is something unrecognizable in Nathan that he is trying to hide, but he's also impossibly familiar. She's not surprised by anything he may do or say.

She can't lie: on the subway home after he asks her out, she envisions her life with him and how money would make things much easier. A possible future clicks smoothly into place.

NATHAN IN BED WITH DENISE

Every day since the police came and went, Denise arrives at the Palm brownstone around ten, searches the basement, and then joins Nathan in his bed. The first time, Nathan had to remove her clothes for her, even her shoes. Now, days later, she undresses herself but is still distracted.

Denise says, "Explain to me, where do you think that money came from? Why do you think she left it there?"

Anna Fisher stands in her foyer and tells Nathan that Marion has been stealing. "To be honest," Nathan says to Denise, "I haven't really thought about it."

"Incredible," Denise says, and leaves unspoken: *It is incredible what you, Nathan Palm, don't think about.*

How can he explain that his wife's secrets are strange, severe, vast, and undiscoverable? He's more troubled by the phone, because it could mean that Marion isn't coming back this time. He can't say this sort of thing to Denise. He's sure of that, at least.

She stands to put on her clothes.

"Please don't go yet," he says.

"Why not?" Denise says.

Nathan is ashamed of his answer, so he doesn't say it.

"Incredible," she says.

BRIGHTON BEACH

The first days with Sveyta are like soft dreams, because Marion is proud that she is safe. She becomes familiar with her new room and the alley outside. Even though the window is nailed shut, she can hear voices from the other apartments and has a vague sense of where they are coming from. She believes she hears the voices from five other apartments. She hears a lot of sex, like at the Days Inn. It seems she won't be able to avoid the sound of intimacy in her escape. The sex is a little different, because it's between partners rather than people having affairs and people paying for sex. It's less ecstatic, but the participants are also in less of a hurry. She is analytical of the breathy or guttural moanings and exclamations, which all sound somewhat similar, no matter the duration of the lovemaking; what she decides is that we have all been conditioned to sound the same way during sex.

She wonders what sex sounded like before film stars, TV stars, and porn stars started showing us how it was done. Or we are all the same. That is what we all sound like.

She hears parties, televisions, long phone calls. She hears belching and furniture rearrangement. She's heard long, keening sobs from a young girl who lives in the apartment directly above Sveyta. Or so she imagines. She doesn't know if the girl is young or not. Across the alley, a couple has loud drunken arguments about their cat. What Marion has learned about drunks when they argue: they repeat themselves without awareness. "Why don't you just go die?" the woman says on a loop. Marion is unsure whether she's talking to her boyfriend or to the cat. Sometimes she finishes with "Why don't I just go die?" but not always.

Sometimes she hears Sveyta speaking Russian down the hallway, and that is a luxurious sound. Sveyta makes her phone calls in the morning to various family members and friends in Moscow. She chats casually but is also businesslike on the phone. Sometimes she laughs. Marion doesn't know if she's telling jokes. It's a possibility. Sometimes the phone calls have a deathly kind of seriousness. One call in particular made

Marion worry. She gathered herself out of bed (where she has been spending most of her time since moving in) and poked her head into the kitchen. Sveyta saw her, smiled, and gestured with a cigarette between her fingers to a teapot of steeping tea. Marion poured herself a cup and added sugar, and the smile never manifested in Sveyta's voice; the seriousness was throughout.

Sveyta is the caretaker for New York City apartments owned by fantastically wealthy Muscovites, who use the apartments two weekends out of the year to go shopping. These beautiful light-filled apartments furnished with gorgeous things accumulate dust. She tours the empty apartments once a week and manages a large team of cleaning ladies. Marion says that sounds like a good gig, but Sveyta corrects her. No, she says, it is difficult and thankless work.

Marion can't understand why Sveyta doesn't occupy the apartments when the Muscovites are gone. She could live rent-free in penthouses all year round and wouldn't need to rent rooms to women who embezzle. No one would know. She would ask Sveyta this, but she's concerned it's a wrong idea, possibly amoral.

She's read that the criminal mind is victim

to poor impulse control. Her brain will look different from her husband's. After fourteen years of marriage, Marion knows this to be true. Marion's guilt has never really existed like other people's. She's heard a lot about guilt from her so-called friends. (Marion believes that the friends are friends with her husband and not with her. She is the limp side salad of the marriage.) Her husband's guilt is somewhere. She could feel it at night when they slept in a house that he bought with money he never earned. When he wasn't feeling proud that now women often wanted to fuck him, he was guilty about that too. Jane feels guilt like a disease; it wrecks her. Ginny's guilt: maybe Marion and Ginny have more in common there.

But Marion is childless, so they have nothing in common. Ginny is Nathan's daughter, she reminds herself.

Marion's lack of normal guilt has given her some control in their marriage, and yet Nathan can surprise her with his reactions, and therefore she has always felt that he is in charge. She attributed it at first to the age difference, and perhaps that's still all it is. But Nathan's guilt matters too.

Marion Palm is not guilty, because the money was unwatched and therefore hers. All that is unwatched or unguarded belongs to Marion or should belong to Marion. She watches, therefore she owns. She sets her own perimeters. If others don't, it's not her fault for trespassing.

She's not sure what this makes her. She's never felt free or unburdened. She's never gotten ahead, like hedge-fund managers or politicians. Maybe she is not very smart. The other possibility is that lack of guilt in men is socially more acceptable and admired. Or perhaps if Marion had no guilt and was very attractive, she might have made her way in the world. But since she is saddled with a wide dimpled ass, thick thighs, and a lacking chin, her diminished capacity for empathy sits unused because it is almost unusable. Even at her most attractive, she was voluptuous, not glamorous or mysterious. Her body made her intentions and thoughts more knowable, more familiar. Besides, she was young. She didn't even know what she had, and couldn't use it to her advantage. The guiltless have body-image problems too, she wants to write somewhere.

Sveyta leaves the apartment after her phone calls. She wears three outfits in rotation and they are stunning. When she returns, she takes the outfit off in her bedroom and puts on her robe to press the outfit and hang it up again in the small closet off the hallway. The outfits are composed of classic pieces by well-known designers. Marion inspects them when Sveyta's out; each piece has been mended several times.

Marion is ashamed of her fabrics and cuts, and she wants to ask Sveyta how she maintains her beautiful wardrobe with such frugality. But if Sveyta told her, would Marion even be able to adopt such a skill? It could be beyond her. So she must wear the clothes she has, and she cannot explain them to Sveyta. Marion would like to tell Sveyta what she does well, what she excels at, but that, of course, cannot be mentioned.

Marion is woken from a midafternoon nap when Sveyta knocks on her bedroom door. Marion, still groggy with sleep, finds her landlady/roommate in the hallway. Sveyta's blond hair is swept up from her forehead and pinned in the back in a delicate yet unmoving French twist. She wears a dark red wool pencil skirt and an off-white blouse with a gold necklace. She's still in her slippers; she will put on her heels when she is on the doormat by the front door.

She looks into Marion's eyes. "Marion. I would like to offer you a job."

The cleaning lady who works Tuesdays at a midtown apartment has been unexpectedly deported. The owners of the apartment are returning on Wednesday for an extended stay, and Sveyta is consequently in something of a bind. She would do it herself, but she's already booked uptown.

"Marion," she says. "You must be honest with me. Can you clean?"

"Sure," Marion says.

"No. I mean, I don't mean 'I put the book back on the bookshelf where it's supposed to be' or 'I remember to wipe down counters.' I mean, can you clean?"

"Yes. I can clean. Before I married, I managed a café. We had to meet the city health codes or we would be fined. I can clean."

Sveyta looks behind Marion to her room. She sweeps her eyes over the floor, the windowsill, the mirror. She looks at the unmade bed, and Marion tells her she was just sleeping in it. It will be made soon.

"All right. You will begin tomorrow at nine. I will give you a ride. I have supplies for you. You will be compensated."

Why does Marion want to clean an apartment? Why has she said yes to this menial labor? She will now despise Sveyta because Sveyta has offered her this pitiful opportunity. Why must she always say yes? And yes, she knows she'll go, she'll spend hours scrubbing floors and toilets and the apartment will be spotless, and Sveyta will be pleased. Marion will fume with both satisfaction and malice, thankfulness and resentment, hope and despair. And this will all be absurd because the pay will be — maybe — $100.

"I'll be ready," Marion says.

The knapsack is under the bed. The knapsack is under the bed.

How will she be smart this time? How will Marion be good?

GINNY'S DETENTIONS

Ginny and her Bible-sock-wearing homeroom teacher are in a standoff. Since Marion left, Ginny has been accumulating detentions. Each afternoon she chooses not to go to her mandated detention. The following morning the homeroom teacher asks if Ginny went to detention. Ginny says she did. The homeroom teacher smiles and corrects: *Ginny, you did not.* Ginny's number of required detentions is rising exponentially, but the school hasn't figured out a way to make her go to them. Eventually the homeroom teacher meets Ginny after her last class of the day and personally escorts her to detention. She watches Ginny settle in for her hour of forced repentance and leaves. When the detention proctor goes to the window to investigate the sound of a possible car collision (squealing brakes, multiple car alarms, low-toned swearing), Ginny walks out again. She's getting pretty good at this.

When she ignores her detentions, she doesn't go home. Sometimes she goes to the Greek diner to see her friend, who gives her Cokes. Sometimes she hangs out with the smokers of the middle school on the steps of the courthouse. The smokers are a strange clique. They are welcoming but hard to read. For a reason unknown to Ginny, they've begun to invite her to join them. So far, she's declined the cigarette but sometimes follows them to the courthouse. Other times, when she doesn't feel like company, she walks to the promenade. She doesn't look at the skyline but at the highway below. The cars look like they are traveling faster than they are. She convinces herself to be back home by dinner, knowing that her father will worry. She's having a hard time looking at him, but she doesn't want him to worry more. Her father's worry is visible and upsetting.

There comes a morning when the teachers of the school will not stand. They've connected Ginny's disobedience to her mother's. A theory develops that the Palms, as a family, are willful. While the teachers don't know what Marion did, they feel that she has broken some rule. They are used to minding children and scanning for misbehavior; the Palm family glows under this gaze. This must be corrected, and they will start with Ginny. It's unfortunate timing, but she must learn that rules are meant to be followed. If she does not learn this now, when will she? Is this not a watershed moment for Ginny Palm?

Ginny's homeroom teacher is triumphant when the middle-school dean schedules a meeting to discuss the seventh grader's multiple infractions. Ginny sits next to her father, and the dean sits behind his desk. He wears a brightly patterned shirt with a textured tie and jeans and insists that Nathan call him George. No need for formalities here, he says. The homeroom teacher stands in the corner, smiling.

"We understand there have been some issues at home," the dean begins politely.

"No," Ginny says.

"Your sister has been pretty vocal about the issues."

"Jane exaggerates sometimes," Nathan says.

"No," Ginny says again.

"Settle down," Nathan says.

"No, everything's fine. May I go?"

"You may not, young lady." This is the homeroom teacher.

"Hey, watch it," Nathan says. "What did

she do again?"

"She has missed all nine of her assigned detentions."

"But the detentions were for missing detentions. What was her original, I don't know, crime?"

Nathan meant to be sarcastic but thinks of his wife and reddens at his word choice.

George kindly interrupts the silence to explain. "Ginny has been consistently tardy for homeroom."

"Can someone explain to me the point of homeroom? Because it doesn't seem like it has a point," Ginny says.

"Quiet. How tardy?"

"She was three to seven minutes late."

"Three minutes? And now she is being suspended?"

"We did not want to escalate, but Ginny has forced our hand."

"When? Ginny has been taking her sister to school."

"We should have been informed."

"Listen, George, my wife is, my wife is . . ."

"Outta town."

"Quiet, Ginny. She is out of town, and Ginny has been helping."

"Again, this would not be an issue a) if we had known about the excused tardies or b)

231

if she had attended a single detention. We really have no choice in the matter but to suspend Ginny for three days."

"Well, you do have a choice. Everyone has a choice."

"If we make this exception —"

"Riots in the hallways? Anarchy and mayhem?"

"*Quiet,* Ginny. Just wait outside."

"Fine."

Ginny leaves the office and stands in the center of the small waiting room. There are doors to other offices, an empty desk, and four chairs with upholstered seats. The walls are the pale pink of her mother's office. That color of paint must be cheap.

Inside, Nathan tries to negotiate the terms of Ginny's punishment. He does not want his daughter to be punished, and also does not want her around the house during the day. He needs Denise and the hours without children. The dean is unmoved by Nathan's pleas for leniency. Nathan thinks of Anna Fisher's accusation in her foyer and concedes.

The suspension begins today, and he's to take Ginny home. The dean ends the meeting, and Nathan leaves without shaking hands. Unfortunately, Ginny has disappeared. Nathan rushes out of the waiting room and into the hallway to find his daughter. It's a sea of short people fighting to get to their lockers, and he cannot find his own short person. Realizing that he has lost another member of his family, Nathan places his hand over his heart and tells himself to steady.

MISSING PERSONS

The detective takes some time off from the calls to speak to Walter's veterinarian. The vet is invested in Walter's survival and the functioning of his kidneys. The detective finds it difficult to dissuade the vet from taking these extraordinary measures. The detective believes that if Walter was his cat, he would be able to tell the vet to put Walter down, but Walter's all that's left.

The detective knows that missing people do not leave a void for long, because detritus rushes in to fill the empty space, and as mundane as that detritus usually is, it must be acknowledged. Some may point to the detritus as a saving grace, something to take one's mind off a missing person. The detective knows this is false. The detritus has no meaning. It's just there, and the missing person is not. Still, the detective will regret killing the cat. However, he will not pay for feline dialysis.

As a distraction from Walter and the missing boy, the detective investigates Marion Palm in a cursory manner. He reads her work profile on the school's website. It lists her current projects, and it seems that there are a lot of them. Marion smiles grimly in her headshot. She looks like she has better things she could be doing.

He clicks on Marion's latest project, which leads him to a gallery of architectural renderings. He recognizes the exterior of the building, but the inside looks like a spaceship. Realistic cartoons of students with backpacks slung over their shoulders traverse the corridors in friendly pairs and trios. He clicks the bottom link: *DONATE NOW*. Instead of taking the detective to a user-friendly fundraising site, the link apologizes to him for any inconvenience, tells him that the Wing Initiative is taking a brief hiatus, and instructs him to call a phone number with any questions. The detective gets off the phone with the vet by confirming Walter's next appointment. He calls the number. Daniel picks up.

Forty-five minutes later, the detective is able to work himself out of this conversation, but he has a list of odd and seemingly random things Daniel has told him. Marion Palm is with a sick relative. Nathan Palm is an alumnus of the school. The school is being audited. Ginny Palm has been suspended. The Wing Initiative has been shelved. Daniel may be developing a slight drinking problem (it's not that Daniel is drinking in the morning; it's just that he's starting to want to). Everyone knows that Marion Palm married up.

It's against protocol, but the detective dials Nathan's cell. Nathan accepts the call after one ring, even though he doesn't recognize the number. He says, "Where are you?"

The detective identifies himself and asks if Nathan would mind coming into the precinct to answer a few more questions. "When?" Nathan Palm asks. "How about right now," the detective replies. Nathan says, "Now is not a great time." The detective asks why. Nathan can't say why and tells himself that it will be easy to find his missing daughter. "Right, sure, got it," he says into the phone. "I'll be there as soon as I can."

The detective hangs up. A conversation should solve this, he thinks. That's all I need.

GINNY'S SUSPENSION

Ginny sits on the cold concrete rim of a fountain and holds her arms. The smokers are above her, on the raised north facade of Brooklyn Borough Hall, behind the Greek Revival columns. The doors of the north facade are all boarded up; the basement entrance on Court Street is used instead. At night, homeless people sleep on the north facade. During the lunch hour and after school, the smokers take over the space. It's well hidden from view because of the columns, and if a teacher from the school does catch sight of them, the smokers can easily stub out their cigarettes and escape. It also feels good to be twenty feet above everyone else.

Ginny was on her way to join the smokers when she saw the fountain without water and decided this would be a more suitable destination. She doesn't want to be responsible for finding her own caretaker. She wants someone to ask if she's okay. She'd say *Fine,* but the person would persist, and she'd reveal hesitantly how broken she feels.

"Ginny! Ginny." Nathan runs at her from across the square. Pigeons take flight, and the smokers look down to see Ginny being found by her father. In her mortification, Ginny can say nothing as Nathan puts his arm over her shoulders and steers her to the Borough Hall train station. The smokers watch from the portico.

Once underground, Ginny asks, "Where are we going?" as Nathan fails to understand a MetroCard vending machine.

"The police station," Nathan says. "Do you have your pass?" Ginny waves her green MetroCard as evidence of how ignorant Nathan really is.

On the subway platform, Nathan taps his toes and looks down the tunnel the wrong way for the train. Ginny corrects him, because it seems he cannot embarrass her enough today. Nathan says "Oh" and turns around but does not apologize for his stupidity.

Posters for the missing boy are taped to each column. "Is that the boy your sister is always talking about?" Nathan asks. Ginny won't answer. Nathan reads the description on the poster and memorizes the details in case he sees the boy. The poster has clearly been up for a while, so the boy is gone, but Nathan memorizes anyway.

The train arrives, and Nathan puts his arm over Ginny's shoulders again to guide her onto the train. Ginny sits; Nathan stands, grips the safety bar, and squints at the subway map behind her head.

"So you are suspended for three days."

"Why are we going to the police station?" Ginny asks.

"A detective wants to ask me some more questions about your mother."

"Questions about what?"

"I don't know."

"Maybe they found her."

"I don't think so, honey — they would have told me." Nathan looks back up to the map, as if it has answers for him. Ginny concentrates on looking like an orphan.

A few stops and Nathan and Ginny find the Fort Greene precinct. Cop cars and minivans are parked diagonally around the gray fortress of a building. Both Palms feel like they have broken the law. When they walk into the station, Nathan realizes that he should not have brought his daughter to this place, because it is not appropriate for a child. However, it's a nonissue because they're already there, and also he can't let

239

Ginny out of his sight.

Nathan gives his name at the front desk, and the policewoman tells him it will be a minute and gestures to a bench. Nathan and Ginny sit. There are a few homeless women on the bench across from them, or at least that's what Nathan assumes. He is uncomfortable, and he looks at Ginny; her eyes slide over the homeless women. She either doesn't know that the women are homeless or has already learned how not to see homeless people. Is this because his daughter takes the subway to school every day? Nathan walked.

The detective is in front of them and shaking hands. He's kind to Ginny and makes space for her beside his desk. He takes Nathan into a room with a table and a few chairs and a lot of filing cabinets. Alone, Nathan says, "My daughter, she was suspended because she keeps running away. I'm afraid that she's going to do it again if I don't watch her."

"My colleagues will keep an eye. Your daughter isn't going anywhere."

Nathan doesn't stop talking for the next thirty minutes, and when it's over, he can't recall what he said. He can't remember the questions the detective asked either. He can't remember why he agreed to let the

240

detective talk to Ginny again, on her own, without him. He has no memory.

Nathan waits for his daughter back on the bench. He holds his coat folded over his arm and scrolls through his phone. He texts Denise that he is at the police station and looks at the screen, expecting her reply. None comes. He reads articles. The articles are about lifestyles, social constructs, deconstructing social constructs, politics, motherhood, decorating. He consumes. A few sound-bites of his interview resurface. Was his wife unhappy? How was she unhappy? Was it work? Was it the kids? Was it him? All three, Nathan told the detective. Both Nathan and the school undervalued her. Both expected her to respond to emotion robotically, expected her to calm others' anxieties, whims, and manias, and this meant she could never have any of her own. Of course, that's what's so funny about Marion, Nathan told the detective. She sees herself as a calm person, and she's not. Although she is rational.

"How was she unhappy with her children?" the detective asked.

"Ginny's a teenager, and Jane's a little weird. But it's not that she was unhappy with them. Is unhappy. She's unhappy with who she becomes when she's around them.

She deals with a lot of parents in her position, in her job, and many of the parents seem unsatisfactory to her. She said it was as if they were performing an idea of parenthood."

"Did Marion parent or perform?"

"She parented. She couldn't let herself perform. She's very hard on herself."

"But she didn't like how she parented."

"No. She didn't like being a parent."

The detective's questions seem odd to Nathan now, on the bench, but at the time it felt like he was with a doctor or a priest. Nathan had to answer for his health or his soul. He reads articles. He tells himself, *I didn't say anything about the woman in Dumbo. I didn't mention the phone Marion drowned. I did what I was supposed to do.*

Meanwhile, the detective questions Ginny in a benign manner. He asks questions to make her feel more comfortable, and then he asks why she keeps running away from school. She doesn't tell him that she feels like she's being watched. She doesn't tell him about her strong belief that she shouldn't be there anymore. The way the teachers peer at her — it's not that they are concerned. They want her somewhere else.

Then the detective asks the same questions about her mother that he asked in their first interview. Ginny gives answers as if they are different, but they are the same answers as before. The detective never asks her where she thinks her mother has gone, and she appreciates that. He does ask her about her father, how he is doing. She shrugs her shoulders to say fine. The detective waits for her to elaborate, to fill in the quiet with chatter, as her father has done, but Ginny likes the quiet. It doesn't make her feel like she's done something wrong. The detective sighs and releases Ginny back to her father. He shakes the father's hand and he shakes Ginny's hand. Nathan Palm repeats that he is grateful for the detective's time and attention. The detective says, "This is my job."

Ginny wants to walk home from the police station, and Nathan agrees. A long walk, but he could use the exercise. He offers to carry Ginny's backpack, and she lets him. He makes a noise when he shifts it onto his back, and she remembers her mother with her backpack. She looks at Nathan and thinks about telling him about the check at the diner, but he's preoccupied with her backpack because it's hurting his shoulders. They're nearing the Gowanus Canal when he tells her to hang on. "This is unacceptable," he says. "You are a child."

Nathan opens the backpack, violates a boundary, and pulls out a health textbook. "What is this? You don't need this." He walks to the fetid canal, smelling of chemicals, shit, smog, and oil, and throws *The Mystery of the Human Body* into the water. It makes a splash in the crud. "What do they want from you? What do they want from us? Are we supposed to carry whatever weight they give us? Are we at their mercy?"

Her father is gripping the railing and swearing loudly and repeatedly. Ginny looks up and down Union Street to see if anyone has noticed. Nathan swears a final time, leans back from the railing, and hangs his head down.

"I have homework to do," Ginny says.

This gets her father going again, and he reaches into the backpack once more. He pitches into the canal a copy of *Frankenstein* and a folder of Xeroxes. "This is unacceptable."

"This is not a book burning," Ginny says.

"This is a book sinking," Nathan says.

"A book disintegration."

"A book melting." As father and daughter name this strange event, Nathan launches the entire contents of the backpack into the dark water. Ginny counts the gloopy splashes.

244

"Doesn't this canal catch fire sometimes?"

Nathan laughs and resumes his journey back to the brownstone with the limp backpack on his shoulder. Ginny trails behind. The walk from Gowanus to the house is charmed for Nathan after the release at the canal.

When he unlocks the front door of his house, Nathan finds himself regretting his behavior. Should a writer throw books into a Superfund site? The dog-eared copy of *Frankenstein* is particularly troubling. How would this be received by the literary community? How will his daughter remember it? Still, he felt gleeful and empty afterward. Now he recognizes the emptiness as hunger. He should make lunch. He looks at his daughter.

At this time of day, they aren't usually around each other. She seems to realize this as well, and looks up at him as if he's a species other than human. Nathan asks if she is hungry, and she guesses she is.

Nathan will heat up tomato soup and make grilled cheese sandwiches. He asks Ginny to start constructing the sandwiches and she agrees easily, so he is allowed to be human again. Fuck the literary community. Fuck Mary Shelley. Fuck the school. He's furious on behalf of his daughter, who is being punished because or instead of her mother. He pictures the shoebox of cash in the basement but replaces this image with the new memory of slinging the textbooks into the canal. He has unburdened his daughter. She should feel free from the school and its rigidity. And so Nathan is congratulating himself on his accidentally good antiestablishment-dad move when he notices that Ginny's hands are shaking as she holds the knife. He should say, "Let me," but instead he says, "What's wrong?"

"All my books are in the Gowanus."

"So?"

"So I have homework I need to do. I'm not allowed to fall behind."

"That fucking school. I'll buy you new books."

"They had notes in them."

Nathan is hurt. "I'm sorry," he says. "I thought it was funny."

Ginny looks like she is considering storming off to her room, but instead she chooses to smile.

"It was funny, Dad."

Nathan takes over the sandwiches. The soup is beginning to heat, so he puts a few slabs of butter on the griddle and lets them melt.

"Where do you think Mom is?"

"She's probably with her cousins. You know, the ones in Utica."

He places sandwiches on the griddle as he lies. He called the distant cousins days ago and had an uncomfortable conversation, as they of course hadn't seen Marion.

"Yeah, but they don't like her," Ginny says. "No one really does. She doesn't have any friends."

"People like your mom."

"No. She makes people feel weird about themselves. They need her. That's different."

"Need her for what?"

"I don't know. Whatever it is they don't feel like doing. Dad, the soup."

The soup has formed into one large bubble and risen to the brim of the pot. Nathan turns off the heat.

"I mean, did you like her when you first met her?" Ginny asks, eating a piece of cheese from the cutting board.

"Of course I did," he says, but he doesn't remember.

He ladles soup into two bowls and slices two sandwiches into triangles. They carry the meal to the den and turn on the television. As they watch an episode, Nathan texts Denise warnings: *Don't come over, my daughter's home.*

After lunch and television watching, Ginny and Nathan clean the kitchen. In the course of this rote activity, Nathan thinks it over and becomes sure once again that Marion would never embezzle. He shouldn't have let Anna scare him. The money in the shoebox is a kind of Sheepshead Bay practice that Nathan doesn't know about. But the abandoned phone and the credit cards: what does that mean? He returns to his disbelief.

Ginny interrupts his inner monologue by saying that she will attempt to do her homework. Many of the texts are online, she admits, but she needs to purchase them. Nathan gives her a credit card from his wallet, and she runs the plastic rectangle along her fingers quietly.

Nathan watches her and is grateful that Jane doesn't understand what's happening. A few tantrums, a few meltdowns, but other than that, she's going about her days. Ginny, on the other hand, taps a mysterious Morse code with the credit card on the kitchen table and then, after a low hum, leaves. He hears her climb the stairs, and, so quickly he doesn't investigate the feeling, he believes it could be Marion.

When Nathan wrote, he would often go looking for Marion when he was stuck, or when he was pleased. He could read lines to her, tell her his latest word count, his latest email from his publisher. It's been a while since he's had one of those emails, but it's undeniable in the kitchen that Nathan has something to say.

He closes his eyes and deliberately pretends it is Marion going up the stairs. Her heavy gait. Her exhalation at the top of the stairs. Nathan opens his eyes and calls up, "I'm going to work too. Let's work together." His office is next to his daughter's bedroom. Her door is open, and she's sitting in front of her laptop. Nathan can barely stand how industrious he feels.

In his office, he turns on his computer. He usually works off a legal pad, but today it's just going to happen. This isn't a poem; this is something large, this is something to send to his old publisher: *My wife left me, and it opened all these doors, it just flowed — here is my pain!*

Blank document up, Nathan taps away. It's coming easily; he's writing for Marion in absentia. An hour passes this way.

"I'm at nine hundred and eighty-seven words!" he yells to Marion.

"What?" Ginny responds.

BOARD OF TRUSTEES

How did this happen? Who let this happen?

Good afternoon to you, too, Anna. Pleasure to see you, as always.

Who let the Palm girl be suspended?

No one let her. It was that history teacher. The one who wears the socks with the, you know, Bible verse.

She was insistent, and then George felt like it was an issue of consistency and fairness —

It was a coup.

How could it be a coup? The teachers don't know anything.

Oh, they know. They know.

They're just trying to make themselves feel important. Involved. Necessary.

Aren't they?

Whatever.

It's only for three days.

We can offer to expunge it from her record.

The Palms will never forget. We protect the Palms. Doesn't George know that? Wasn't

250

that made clear to him?

I think this Marion business has the faculty questioning their priorities. And to be fair, Ginny has become harder to handle now that her mother is gone.

Nathan's never going to forgive us.

He will if he has to, if we threaten to send his criminal wife to prison where she belongs.

Isn't that . . . What is that called? Extortion?

Well. We wouldn't necessarily have to be formal about it.

STRATEGY

During recess, Jane explains certain things about the courtyard to the missing boy. She tells him who plays where: the popular girls stay on the monkey bars, the fourth-grade boys by the tetherball court, the nerdy kids by the ginkgo trees. That's where Jane should belong, by the ginkgoes, but she never has. The nerds find her playing style too romantic.

The missing boy and Jane sit on a pair of swings and swing high. She would like to see over the cast iron fence separating the courtyard from the street, because her mother might be out there. Would it be okay if they looked?

Jane knows the missing boy is nonverbal, so she just assumes he approves of her idea, because he starts pumping his legs stronger and higher. Jane does the same, and they shoot up. Jane leans forward and back, forward and back, and yet she cannot see over the fence. They oscillate back down. Time for Plan B.

In order to get to the fence, she says, you have to climb into no-man's-land, the flower beds. The flower beds are sectioned off by a low railing, but the teachers are vigilant in their patrol. They need a diversion. A gift: the ill-located zip-line. The zip-line is for middle schoolers, and only with adult supervision. Concussions have been common since it was installed. Jane encourages a solitary first grader to give it a go when the teacher isn't looking. The tiny girl launches herself into a large maple tree, and the teachers come running. Jane and the missing boy make their move.

They squeeze through the bare Brooklyn bushes and reach the severe cast iron bars that surround the school. Jane and the missing boy wrap their hands around the bars and look out. Parked cars, more trees, a row of brownstones, but no people.

Don't worry, the missing boy says. *We'll find her.*

The missing boy's words settle Jane in a way that her father's words can't. The boy's words remind her of her mother's words, even though he sounds different.

However, Jane is still preoccupied by injustice. She believes it unfair that other kids have their mothers while hers is lost.

Her father and her sister have dismissed all her ideas to get her mother back. She recommended fliers first, even volunteered to post them. Her suggestion was met with clipped sarcasm from her sister and a shake of the head from her father. They weren't listening to her because she was eight and the youngest. If she had been the oldest, they might have done it.

Next she thought it would be good to go on television. They did it for the missing boy. There were segments on the news, and they made his family seem close and real. This could also be a useful strategy. Jane asked over dinner how difficult it was to get on television. Her father's response: *Very.*

Jane at thirty will look back and think, actually, those weren't bad ideas. It still astounds her that as a family they collectively did nothing. It must have been hard to do so little. It had to be. Jane at thirty has a face that people tell things to. She's heard about abortions by the water cooler, addictions to online gambling on airport shuttles, cancer from the checkout girl at the mall. It's her face that invites these tales of misery, she tells herself, but maybe not. Maybe humans are naturally inclined to share their pain. And maybe, because of her mother, Jane is not allowed to judge.

Why didn't her family want to talk? Maybe her father knew. Maybe her sister suspected. This would mean she was the only one in the family who had a missing family member. Her sister and her father had someone to protect, and Marion was safer for everyone as a missing person.

Jane the adult sympathizes with Jane the child. And that's good, she supposes, but it's hard to think about Jane the child asking at the dinner table what's so wrong with her ideas. Do they have better ones? Someone should do something.

Jane the child places the missing boy next to her at the table, and she looks at him for support, and he winks, meaning, *Those are good ideas. How smart you are,* he says.

MISSING PERSONS

Walter's in the backseat throwing up while the detective navigates downtown Brooklyn traffic. The only opening the vet and Walter shared was during peak rush hour. The detective looks at the caged Walter in the rearview mirror. He sometimes thinks the cat is saying "Kill me." Other times the cat is saying "Never let me die."

The detective had hoped that a follow-up interview with Nathan would subdue his curiosity, and for a while it looked like it would. Nathan spoke about his wife in a more conventional way, and the detective was able to draw a picture of a woman who never wanted to be a mother and who hated her job. If Marion was a man, the detective found himself thinking, I doubt I would be interested.

The detective imagines that the Palm marriage was a peculiar one from the beginning. He thinks about the picture of Marion that Nathan gave him. There weren't many to choose from, Nathan admitted, but this was the most recent. Marion Palm wears what looks like a maternity dress, but she is not pregnant. She's smiling, but the smile could be taken for a grimace. She's at a backyard barbecue and holds a glass of wine in her left hand, and that hand is the only part of her that seems relaxed. Her shoulders are nearly touching her ears. Nathan Palm, next to her, is midlaugh, arms crossed, bending slightly forward toward the camera with locked knees. The couple is not touching; in fact, they seem to be in different photos, or even different backyards. The detective looks more closely at Marion and thinks that she could have been attractive once.

The Marion Palm disappearance was on its way to seeming sad but expected, and then the detective spoke to Ginny. Ginny Palm wanted her mother back but didn't seem at all sure that her mother *should* come back. She admitted that she felt responsible. The detective reassured her that it wasn't her fault, and she scoffed. She said, "I don't mean me, I mean all of us. My father, my sister, and me. If someone runs away from a group of people, most likely that group of people was the reason. It's not like my mother had anything to run toward."

The detective feels that most of the time people do run *toward* something — a person, a place, a feeling, an idea — unless they are desperate. He believes it takes desperation to get a person running. Was Marion's marriage that bad? And what about her children? What would make her leave them? What kind of mother does that?

Walter howls, then gags. The detective sits and watches the light go from red to green to red again. He considers putting Walter out on the curb and opening his cage door. He believes that Walter would be fine, would thrive, would live forever.

Marion Palm is not a vulnerable adult, and the detective cannot prove she was the victim of a crime. We don't hunt people down in America unless they owe us something, and Marion Palm paid her bills before she left. If she were pretty and blond, it might be a different matter, but Marion Palm is not, to put it lightly, photogenic. But her coworker Daniel seemed more interested in finding Marion than her husband did. The detective briefly considers an affair between Daniel and Marion, but that feels wrong. Daniel is overwhelmed, not by grief but by a new workload.

The detective calls Daniel on his cell. He needs a few more details about Marion, if Daniel doesn't mind. Daniel stammers, says something about a meeting, but the detective urges him on. He cajoles; he won't let Daniel go without an explanation. Daniel confesses. "I'm not supposed to be talking to you," he says, and hangs up.

The detective makes it to the vet, and Walter is given another week of precious domesticated life.

WOMEN WHO CHEAT

A new woman has cheated at marathon racing in St. Louis. Marion reads about it in a free newspaper she took from a man wearing a red smock. The cheater appeared from nowhere, members of the crowd say, to fly across the finish line and earn herself a record time. She'd pinned her bib to her shorts and had to lift her shirt for someone to see it. She said she had removed the time tracker. She seemed embarrassed at the finish line and not very sweaty. She stood behind a large banner declaring her the winner and looked to the left of the photographer.

Marion enjoys the woman's face and the article. The medal is given to the actual winner and the cheating woman is banned from all future races. Marion is curious about how it will be for this cheating woman at work on Monday. She imagines her driving a Hyundai to an office outside St. Louis, hair neatly pulled back into a ponytail, her tight young body shrouded in a J. Crew cardigan and skirt. She wears sensible shoes. She hates her life. The only reason to cheat so publicly, to take that risk, is to hate. Without the hate and also the entitlement, it wouldn't be worth it.

On the way to the midtown apartment, Marion asks Sveyta what she thinks of this strange cheat. She shows her the picture from the article, which she has clipped out and put in her purse. They are in Sveyta's car, driving into the city.

"Was there a cash prize?" Sveyta asks.

"Fifteen hundred dollars," Marion says.

"That is something, but not enough. There are other ways to make that money."

"Not for everyone."

"But she's running a marathon, or at least pretending to. She could ask her family for the money."

"What if she couldn't?"

"She could. Look at her clothes. Expensive activewear. It wasn't about money."

Marion looks at Sveyta, who is looking at her blind spot to change lanes. Sveyta should be telling Marion that she's glad she's here, or glad that she was available on such short notice to clean the apartment. An American woman would tell Marion all

261

these things, and Marion would have to re-
assure the American woman how well it
works for her, this opportunity, that it is
actually perfect to be wearing a housecoat
and driving into Manhattan with a bucket
of chemicals. But Sveyta says nothing, only
concentrates on her driving, which is timid.
Sveyta is aware that she is timid and tries to
be bold.

"When does the family arrive?"

"Day after tomorrow, around eight."

"What are they like?"

"Russian, wealthy, young. The mother,
that is. She has two daughters who are also
young. The husband is older. They are all
very beautiful."

Marion wonders for the umpteenth time
what it might be like to be beautiful. What
doors would that open? What could she
concentrate on if she weren't concentrating
on her blocked pores, her asymmetrical
face, her eyebrows all askew?

"How long will they stay in New York?"

"Seven weeks. The daughters are both
dancers and will be training at the Joffrey."

"I love the ballet."

"Really?" Sveyta says. "We should go
sometime."

Marion's heart leaps; she would love to go
to the ballet with Sveyta. She pictures them

262

sitting in a box together, in beautiful outfits. They are beautiful together.

"I would love that. Only I have nothing to wear."

Sveyta makes no suggestion that Marion's clothes are good enough. She says, "You should go shopping."

Marion thinks of the knapsack of cash, already dwindling, but yes, she should go shopping, she should impress Sveyta. Cleaning lady by day, patron of the arts by night.

They pull up to a glassy high-rise off Central Park near Columbus Circle. Sveyta peers out the window and allows herself a few wrinkles as she looks at the building with disdain.

"Ridiculous," she says. She reaches into her purse, pulls out a set of keys, and gives them to Marion. "Apartment 2626. You may call if you have any questions. I can't take you up, unfortunately — there is nowhere to park — but the doormen know that you are expected. Give them your name. Yes?"

"Yes," Marion says, and wonders if she and Sveyta will ever go to the ballet together. She will buy the clothes anyway.

Marion at Twenty-Three

For their first date, Nathan takes Marion to a bar near his apartment in Cobble Hill. It has dark paneling on the walls, a jukebox, and a small garden in the back with picnic tables. Marion orders a glass of white wine, but the bartender doesn't ask any follow-up questions, so she changes her order to an IPA. Nathan watches the interaction and approves. Of what, Marion isn't sure.

Nathan suggests the backyard and Marion says great, although she would prefer cool air. She sweats when she drinks, but Nathan seems to want her to be someone who enjoys picnic tables. He recommends that she put some music on the jukebox, but she wants to drink her beer first. She needs to figure out what music he likes. She doesn't really listen to music all that much.

Without the bar of the café between them, they are figuring out how to be. It was lucky when they found out they both lived in

Brooklyn, but the BQE intersects their two apartments. It was an ugly twenty-five-minute walk for Marion to meet Nathan. Nathan doesn't seem to understand that.

Nathan Palm is nervous, and so he talks a lot, which Marion likes. She doesn't date often, because she doesn't like being responsible for ending small silences. Also, not many ask for dates. He tells her a funny story, and when she laughs, he runs his fingers through his hair. He's wearing a large watch with a thick leather strap, and it looks like it belongs to someone older.

He's drinking whiskey, and Marion thinks it affects him quickly. He's softly slurring his words, and he becomes more casual, more confident. His accidental drunkenness is endearing. She thinks it proves that he doesn't drink that much, and this is true. He made a mistake. She takes her time with her beer and then goes to the jukebox. She hasn't figured out what he likes, so she puts on the Velvet Underground for the next six songs and returns with another beer for her, a beer for him, and two glasses of water on a tray. He approves of everything she does: the music, the water, the choice of beer for him. He is glowing with positivity and acceptance. He tells another funny story, this one about sailing, and Marion waits for him to finish before she tells him about her experiences with sailing. They are different experiences. One is Nantucket, the other the Long Island Sound. The coolers have different contents (gin and limes in one, light beers in the other). They've stumbled on their one commonality, their one shared experience, but it takes a long time to admit to each other that they hate sailing. They admit that they've connected sailing with unhappy times from childhood. They order another round.

Marion's music choices continue, and Nico slow-moans odd vowels, and Nathan's eyes get wide.

"This is college," he says.

"Me too," Marion says, not elaborating. She doesn't say that by college she means one semester, and even then, Velvet Underground came up in a conversation she overheard between classmates. She never listened to the album they were discussing but stored away the information. She thought it might be useful.

Marion thinks they stumbled out of the bar with stomachs full of beer and the glow of finding someone who likes their company, and Nathan offered to walk her home. He made the offer, but she believes it might have been her idea; she wanted Nathan to see where and how she lived. At some point they got very close to each other. Marion thinks she let him up to her apartment with the promise of tea.

Nathan has difficulty performing because they've had so much to drink. She doesn't mind; she's tired, and isn't so sure she wants to have sex anyway. But she lets him lie on top of her, and she gently coaxes him back to life. In a rush he enters her, and it's the first time she's had sex without a condom, and the feeling breaks her apart. Nathan's selfishness courses through her, but she feels entirely required.

NARRATIVE STRUCTURE

During the three days of Ginny's suspension, Nathan works in his office next to Ginny's bedroom. He writes but often stops, and then he's in her doorway. Sometimes he even sits on her bed. He says he wants to talk out problems with her. He says he's writing a story. He's drawn to narrative in a way that he's never been before, but he's rusty. He hasn't built a character in years. Ginny pretends that she understands Nathan's anxieties. She just needs to nod, and then Nathan talks his way into some kind of resolution. He thanks Ginny brightly. Confused, she replies, "No problem."

On the third day he rushes into her room with an idea. "We should work on this together," he says. "It should be a collaborative project."

"About what?" Ginny says, and Nathan says, "About missing. About absence."

When Ginny's quiet, Nathan adds, "Think it over," and he's back in his room, tapping away.

Her father is violent with the keys, and the typing happens in noisy waves. When the typing fades into a silence, Ginny counts to ten, and Nathan's either calling out or in her room again.

He thinks she's working on her homework, but for the past day and a half she's been researching her mother's past. She copied down Nathan's credit card number, expiration date, and the three-digit security code on an index card and put it in her desk drawer before returning the credit card to her father. With the numbers she buys a membership to a site that promises to sort through public records on the customer's behalf. The intended customer is a small business, the site publicizes, but all it needs is $99 for the first year and an address. *You can reconnect with childhood friends!* the site boasts.

Ginny knows her father doesn't look at his credit card statements. Nathan drops bills on Marion's desk in the den without opening them. He's still doing it even though Marion's gone. The envelopes are piling up.

The first report is in Ginny's inbox, and

she's about to open it when her father is in the doorway. "Lunch?" he says. Ginny's relieved by the interruption. She isn't ready for her mother to reappear that way.

"Is it okay if I meet Becca after school? She says she has notes for me."

This is a lie. No one has contacted Ginny from school since she was suspended. They heard that her mother has abandoned her. They don't know what to say about that.

"Sure. Where?"

"Gino's, on Ninth."

"Do you need some money?"

Nathan takes out his wallet and hands Ginny a twenty. She takes it and notices that her father looks upset. He doesn't want her to leave, but she has to.

After lunch she downloads and opens the report. There is an address.

Marion Cleans
an Apartment

The apartment hums with emptiness. There is no clutter. There are vases on all the tables, and when the Russians arrive, Marion assumes, Sveyta will fill them with flowers. A large sectional sofa is in the middle of the living room facing a large television. The furniture is either black leather or glass. Marion believes this is a show apartment. No one could live here.

She settles into a rhythm quickly. She dusts. She sweeps. She scrubs. Her mother taught her how to clean, and how to be livid that Marion's father wouldn't help. "You are better at it than me," he would say with a smile, gesturing to a sink full of dishes. Her father's laziness was masterful and spectacular. Marion now believes he was correct in his ignorance, so she hasn't taught her daughters to clean. She demands that they do it but will not instruct them how. A little experiment. She wants to see if they teach themselves or if they convince someone else to do it. She's hoping it's the latter. When she read to them, she read *Tom Sawyer,* hoping to get her message across.

I'll never find out if it worked, Marion reminds herself, *because I am childless.* She's been dreaming of her daughters. They are all of their ages. Sometimes Jane is older than Ginny. Ginny is an infant again and Jane is tying her shoelaces. Sometimes they are the same age. Sometimes they are old, but not Jane and Ginny, just blurry women with their names. She never dreams of one without the other, and one is always touching her, grabbing at her clothes. Nathan is sometimes there. Her mother is sometimes there. Sometimes no one is there but she feels Jane's skull under her palm. When she looks down at Jane, it is another child grinning up at her, ugly, small, and mean. Then the child splits like a cell and becomes Jane and Ginny again and they are hungry, so hungry they don't recognize hunger; instead they feel pain and sadness. They are astounded by their hunger because they've never been hungry before, not once, and Marion searches her purse for a baggie of fresh carrot sticks.

Floor-to-ceiling windows look out onto the park. Marion needs a step stool to Windex properly, and when she's up there, she thinks of Jimmy Stewart fainting into Barbara Bel Geddes's arms. Marion doesn't have vertigo. She's not claustrophobic; she has no fear of snakes or spiders. Sometimes as a child she made up phobias when she felt left out, wanting an unexplainable anxiety of her own. Marion tries to open the window but is allowed only eight inches. She lets her left arm and shoulder rest on the ledge. The arm waves in the breeze, as if she's in a car on an empty highway. Twenty-six stories up, she can see hawks circling over the park, undisturbed by the city below.

SIGN LANGUAGE

In class, on the bus, at the dinner table, Jane's hands make letter shapes. The missing boy wraps his hand around her hand and in this way they communicate when there are people around, spelling out words in a slow but thoroughly satisfying exercise. Jane can't decide who in this scenario is Helen Keller and who is Annie. It goes back and forth. The letters are half American sign language — Jane learned the ASL alphabet last year at summer camp — and half joyful shapes. Her fingers twist and contort; she creates new symbols, and the missing boy learns each one, then teaches Jane a few of his own. She can feel his hand in her hand, pressing two fingers against her palm.

Jane is caught talking to the missing boy with her hand by a classmate during math. "What are you doing?" the girl asks loudly. "Fractions," Jane says. "No. What are you doing with your hand?" "Fractions," Jane says. Ginny would be proud of Jane's attempt to fit in, but it's not working, the girl won't accept, and at recess boys and girls mimic Jane's frenetic hand gestures and mutterings, because Jane didn't know that as she was signing, she was also mouthing the letters. Sometimes even a sound came out.

After recess, during her vocabulary quiz, Jane raises her hand and asks, "May I go to the bathroom?" Her teacher says, "You may." In the hallway, she smiles at her small lie. She didn't need to use the bathroom; she just wanted to be alone in the corridor. She listens to other lessons being taught, and it's amazing to her that the rooms are filled with people, all having their own thoughts, while she is in the corridor, apart. She walks down the corridor, she doesn't run, but she's on her way. In her mouth a tooth wiggles, one that should not move, then comes an ache, a thump, rolling waves of nausea. Jane believes her hair is falling out too.

Her mother worked in the basement. Sometimes Jane would ask to go to the bathroom but would go to her mother's office instead. She would have to be brought back for a time-out in the cloakroom, but it was worth it. She liked to see her mother behind her desk.

She's looking into other rooms for her mother. She puts her hand into her jean jacket pocket, the jean jacket with the rhinestones on the collar, and she holds the missing boy's hand.

Ask her what the boy's doing and Jane could fill you in. But first you have to learn that he exists, and Jane's dying to tell you but can't. That's the agreement. Jane is on the fifth floor. She's found the dark art room with the ceiling fans. She discovers a table of crude clay figurines, painted wrong, waiting for the kiln. Jane and the missing boy dismember the figurines and return them to their original clumps of clay.

DENISE AND JANE

Nathan hears the front door shut. He's in the kitchen, drinking flavored seltzer from a can, and Ginny has left. Jane will be home soon. Just another forty-five minutes. Before Marion left, he would have appreciated this time alone, but now he can't find anything to occupy himself. Besides, it was a good day of work. He wants to celebrate. He texts Denise. *Come over,* he says. *I've got the house to myself.*

She doesn't text back, so he calls her. In the middle of the second ring he's sent to Denise's outgoing voicemail message. It's brusque, low, and uncharming, yet he is charmed by it. He tells Denise's voicemail that he has the house for the next forty-five, no, forty minutes. He'd like to see her.

Nathan spends thirty-five minutes checking all his screens, all modes of communication, one after another, waiting for a reply. None comes, but at least Jane will be home soon. In the kitchen he plates a snack for his daughter. Celery sticks with peanut butter and two home-baked chocolate chip cookies. He even pours her a glass of milk. He takes a picture of the meal in the slanting autumn sunlight of the afternoon. The doorbell goes at 3:40 and he thinks that she is a little early, so he opens the door happily and it is Denise, not Jane. She doesn't take her sunglasses off. Nathan sees the small yellow school bus inching down the street.

"It's too late. You can't be here right now," he says.

"I don't appreciate your messages. They don't make me feel good about myself," she says.

"So why did you come?"

"To prove a point."

Denise walks into the house and settles herself on the couch in the living room. It's the darkest room of the house, but the sunglasses stay on. Black jeans, worn T-shirt hanging from her shoulder blades. Her hair swept forward onto her face. Nathan thinks of her angular hips digging into his pelvic bone. Bone to bone. They are not matched. At first Nathan can't place what is different, and then he registers the shoes. She's wearing motorcycle boots. She's usually in the same beat-up pair of blue Sauconys that she's been wearing since high school. Denise is in costume, and Nathan believes it's to scare him, or scare his daughter. He still can't understand her point.

The doorbell rings again, and Nathan leaves Denise in the living room. His daughter on the stoop looks down the street with a faraway look on her face. She enters with a small "Hello, Daddy." He waves to the bus driver, whom he seems to have been winning back to his side, and takes his daughter's backpack from her, and her lunchbox. "I made you a snack — it's in the kitchen." She heads to the back of the house and doesn't look into the living room, doesn't see the frightening woman on the Pottery Barn couch. Nathan trails after her, and they eat the snack together. When Nathan returns to the living room alone, Denise is gone. She must have let herself out.

Nathan will compose an email to Denise and fix what just happened. He tells her what she means to him and what she's been to him since Marion left. *Come back, and let's talk. I could be a better boyfriend (ha ha ha).* He almost deletes the part about being a boyfriend and doesn't, because he wants to be honest.

He sends the email. His heart pounds at

having opened himself up to Denise's antipathy, scorn, and laughter. He checks his email on his phone. Nothing's new, nothing's new. Another email. He watches his phone as it uploads. It's a newsletter from the co-op. He deletes it. Another. The subject line is *Hey, asshole.*

You owe us money, the email says. *You and your cunt wife.* Nathan deletes the email. He's certain it's a joke.

SHEEPSHEAD BAY

Ginny has found the Q. She's never taken this train before, and she tries to make her face a blank so it won't betray her discomfort. When the train rises aboveground, she believes she's lost. She checks her phone again and again to confirm her location, that she's on the same island and not as far from home as she feels.

Leaning forward with her brow furrowed, Ginny Palm bolts off the train at her mother's old stop. She checks her phone to make sure this is the right direction. She passes Laundromats, fruit stands, a Hallmark store, shops with strange lettering. She believes that people stare at her as she passes, and she might be right. She looks lost, even if she knows exactly where she's going.

A bridal shop. A ninety-nine-cent store. An optometrist. Another fruit stand. She turns off this thoroughfare to a residential block. The houses are red brick with small stoops, and each house has a driveway. Some have gardens in front, others pavement. The front door is on the right, and three or four windows are on the left. The houses have three floors, but the window on the top is small, so the space behind it might be an attic and not a room. Still, Ginny Palm imagines this is her mother's childhood bedroom.

She finds her mother's old house, and it looks like all the rest. It has a small lawn in the front, no flowers, only grass, and it's bordered by a low white cast iron fence. A car is parked in the driveway. Unlike the avenue, this street is empty of people and very quiet.

Ginny Palm wants to wait, because she feels that her mom might come walking up the street with a bag of groceries and her keys out, ready to unlock her front door. She crosses the street and sits on one of the small stoops to stake out her mother's childhood home.

She was never allowed to come here. She asked her mother about her grandparents, and her mother always said, "Don't worry about it." Her grandmother died, and she knows that her grandfather retired and moved upstate, so Ginny doesn't know who's living in this house. She guesses it's been sold. She tries to imagine her mother playing in this front yard, but it would look strange to play on this sterile square of grass. Also, Ginny's not good at pretending things like this. Her sister would be better. She's about to stand, pat the dust off the seat of her jeans, give up, and go home when she hears a voice.

"You're not supposed to be sitting here." It's a boy, around her age, maybe a little younger. He's shorter than Ginny, has a scooter, and wears a bike helmet. "If my mom catches you, she'll yell at you."

"My dad says the stoops belong to the city. To the neighborhood."

"My mom says you're loitering."

"Whatever. I'm leaving anyway."

Ginny stands and crosses the street back to the house. She looks at the attic window again.

"What are you doing?" the boy asks. He's behind her, and he's left his scooter on the stoop, but he's still wearing his helmet.

"None of your business."

"My mom says Sandy is a drunk."

"Who's Sandy?"

"The woman who lives here."

"Oh. Yeah, how does she know?"

"Sandy hangs out at a bar all day. She

doesn't work either. My mom says she gets disability checks because she's crazy but that she's crazy because she's a drunk. If you don't know Sandy, why are you staring at her house?"

"I was looking for someone else."

"Who?"

"No one."

"Come on, tell."

Ginny Palm looks at the short boy and thinks, why not tell? It might feel good.

"My mom left us."

"So? My dad lives in Queens with his girlfriend."

"No, I mean, like, she's gone."

"My dad's gone too."

"No, like missing."

The boy, in the end, admits that Ginny's situation is worse. He looks at the house with Ginny for a while and then he says: "Sandy once came outside in only her underwear and yelled about income tax for an hour. My mom called the cops."

Ginny laughs, and the boy laughs too. He mimics Sandy, waving his arms around, practically crowing, and pacing the sidewalk. It's spectacular. Then the front door opens and the boy yells, "Run!" Ginny turns, catches a glimpse of a woman a decade older than her mother, with frizzier hair, holding a bag of garbage. Ginny and the boy run until they are panting joyfully two blocks away. The boy raises himself on his tiptoes and kisses her on the lips. His helmet knocks her forehead. He runs away.

A confused Ginny returns to the train station and swipes her MetroCard again. The platform is now a different kind of busy. It's all high schoolers in groups having uninhibited conversations, eating candy bars, and taking large swigs from plastic soda bottles. There are smaller groups of girls and larger ones with boys and girls. Some of the girls wear jackets that are too large for them, and let them drop below their shoulder blades. Some of the boys wear tight pants and hold skateboards and have chains swinging from their belts. Some have cigarettes behind their ears. Even the ostensibly nerdy kids loom large over Ginny, because they speak easily with one another. They have energetic conversations and laugh hard, with their whole bodies.

The train arrives, and Ginny tries to find a place to be. A seat opens up, and she takes it. She digs through her backpack for her headphones to listen to music. She sits with her backpack on her lap; her ear cartilage cups the earbuds, music pipes in, but voices invade anyway. To mute them she turns her music up, but there is a girl in front of her, snapping fingers in her face. Ginny pulls one earbud out, and the music is half replaced by a whisper of girlish profanities. This young girl, this stranger, pretends that she is a boy looking forward to devirginizing Ginny. She invites Ginny to suck her cock. The train is crowded; this girl's words aren't heard by anyone else, or if they are, they are not acknowledged. The girl is murmuring, gesturing at her own crotch and Ginny's breasts, and Ginny is now too frightened to put the earbud back in her ear. She's transfixed by this anonymous bully. The girl asks Ginny a question, and repeats it until Ginny must respond: "Yes, I have a boyfriend." Ginny calculates this is the safer response. The girl laughs, leans closer so Ginny can smell her spearmint breath. "No, you don't, bitch. Why do you lie?" Ginny rises and moves to the doors. She turns and the girl has taken her seat. She's snapping open a makeup compact.

This sort of thing would never happen to her mother, even when she was Ginny's age. Her mother would still have her seat, and the frightening girl would have to stand to apply her makeup.

SMILING

After her first day as a cleaning lady, Marion takes the train home and despises her body. Her fingers smell of disinfectant. Her scalp sweats and causes a curly halo of thin hair to appear around her head. Her housecoat is balled up in a plastic bag she found in one of the kitchen cabinets. She was lucky to find it, as most of the cabinets in the kitchen were empty, save for a few cheap and flimsy skillets and one spatula. She imagines all meals are delivered to the Russians, including coffee in the morning. Including the milk in the coffee. Marion looks at all the other women in wrinkled slacks on the train at 5 p.m. After Park Slope, a seat opens for her, and she's with the remaining women, and they are strong, beefy women with smile lines, though they clearly don't smile often.

Marion's in bed with achy joints when Sveyta knocks on her door. Marion rises up and lets her in. Sveyta still wears her outfit, but with slippers. Her good heels swing from two fingers on her left hand. An envelope is in her right. Sveyta's arms are crossed, and Marion is worried she oversold her cleaning skills. An American woman will never be as good at cleaning as an Eastern European, after all.

"I went by the apartment," Sveyta says. "You did a good job."

Marion exhales. "I'm glad you think so."

"A good job, yes. I think the family will be pleased. If they are, this could be a permanent position. If you are interested."

No, Marion thinks. *I am not interested. I am better than this.* "Sure, yes, that would be great."

"Good." Sveyta hands Marion the envelope. "For today. I'll let you know about the position. They will expect you there five days a week from eight to twelve. And you will need to purchase a uniform."

Marion is howling internally. This isn't what she wanted. She wanted to go to the ballet with Sveyta. Will Sveyta ever go to the ballet with a cleaning woman?

"Just let me know if the family is satisfied," Marion says, and Sveyta moves to her closet, where she puts away her shoes in the correct shoebox. Marion waits to be invited for tea and a cigarette. Then they can discuss the apartment, the family, the type of people she will be working for, these rich who are different from you and me. Let's discuss how different.

But Sveyta makes no suggestion, and so Marion closes her door. A brief impasse, she tells herself. She looks at the envelope in her hand. It's sealed. Sveyta didn't want her to look inside when they were together. She sits on the bed and works open the flap.

There are two twenties in there. Forty dollars. Marion upends the envelope and lets the offensive pay waft to the floor. Her back hurts.

NATHAN AT THIRTY-FOUR

Nathan at thirty-four hasn't had many relationships. It's not that they have been disasters, but they have had a tendency to deflate. Many of Nathan's friends and relatives are marrying and having children. Nathan tries to point to his poetry as proof that he's been doing something too as an adult, but his friends and relatives say, *Oh yes,* and turn back to their respective spouses and children.

After the first night with Marion, Nathan is tempted to let it all go. They are so different, he and Marion, and he's not sure if she likes him or not. She's interesting-looking, but not necessarily his type. Then he remembers that he is thirty-four and that this is not a common occurrence for him and calls the number she left.

Marion comes over to his apartment and essentially never leaves.

What happens next for Nathan: a period

of high productivity. Marion works nights, drinks with the head chef, and then takes the F back to Carroll Gardens to fuck him. He writes in the morning while Marion slips in and out of ill-defined hungover sleep. She's thinking about whether her stomach can handle eggs, and he's thinking about work. But they find they easily live together in the same space. They sleep well and they eat well. They both know that this natural cadence they have with one another is rare.

Nathan's book comes out, gets some good reviews, and wins an award. Marion takes off a few weeks from the restaurant to go on tour with him. She handles the directions, the rental cars, the flights. Nathan pays for everything, but it's Marion who coordinates. Nathan says, *Thank you, thank you.* She says, *I like your poetry.*

It comes quickly in the night after the book tour is over: Nathan wants kids. It's a genetic ache. Nathan asks Marion to marry him. She takes the ring and says, *But no wedding.* She's watched brides, and she can't do what they do. She can't smile for that many pictures. Also, there's a chance that Nathan hasn't realized that he is more attractive than she is. Photographic evidence of her plainness might hurt her cause. Last, her family is better left to itself in Sheepshead Bay.

She waits for Nathan to throw a tantrum, but he smiles. *Just so long as I get to marry you.* Marion hides her revulsion at this greeting-card sentiment.

Nathan and Marion go to City Hall on her next day off. She wears a dress, and Nathan hands her a bouquet that he bought at a floral shop near his apartment. He wears a new suit that fits him well and a flower through his lapel that matches the bouquet, and has had a haircut and a shave. Two friends of his are the witnesses, and Marion notices that they are frosty with her. One is his publisher; the other is Denise. They don't trust her. This must mean that there is more money than she thinks. She looks at Nathan's shoes. He says, *I even got a shoeshine.*

After, they all go to a bar. Nathan insists they order champagne. He hasn't told his family he's getting married. Marion told her mother, and her mother seemed happy. *Mom,* Marion said, *Mom, he's well-off.* Her mother said, *Good for you, honey.* Then she said, *Better make sure this sticks.*

She's not marrying him only because of money, Marion knows that she's not, but she's sick of being poor. She doesn't know how to do anything that will make her money. The only thing she can do well is steal, and she knows she shouldn't be doing that, even from the bipolar Brazilian woman who's asking for it.

Denise doesn't like Marion, can't understand why Nathan wants to marry this uneducated waitress who never smiles, this young woman who does not look young. Marion looks Denise up and down as if she is appraising the cost of her outfit, her makeup, her bag, her haircut. When Denise speaks, she swears she sees a slight curl to Marion's lip. However, Denise forces herself to acknowledge that Nathan seems happy with her. He rushes around the bar, telling strangers that he must return to his wife, have they met his wife, and he is proud. He tells everyone that he didn't believe this would happen for him. He believed that marriage was for other people.

Marion doesn't agree. She thinks Nathan was made for marriage. It will suit him. She wonders why it didn't happen earlier.

A RUSSIAN FAMILY
ARRIVES IN NEW YORK

It was a long flight, even in first class, and the teenagers moan in the back of the town car that they need sleep. They need their beds. Their mother sits in the passenger seat, next to her husband, the girls' step-father, who taps the wheel with his hand at stoplights.

"Soon, my darlings, soon."

It's been a difficult year, but in escaping Moscow just before the sun disappears, the mother feels she has done her duty. They've arrived in New York for the cool fall air, and she tells the girls that the sun remains in New York even in the winter. It is cold, but the sun shines.

The girls don't care; they know New York. They will be in ballet class every morning and part of the afternoon. Late afternoon, they will Skype with Russian tutors. Their mother will make them practice English by talking to waiters, salesgirls, and doormen.

They will not speak English in their ballet class, because it's not about language there, it is about movement. It is about grace, and the mother does not find anything graceful or elegant in English. There is no economy, and where there is no economy, there is no sophistication.

They arrive at the apartment building as the Central Park streetlamps flicker on. The mother points them out to her daughters, but they whimper and say they are tired. "Too tired to notice something lovely?" their mother asks. She tells her husband, "Look at the lights." He grunts and parks the car in front of the building. A valet is on her side, opening the car door for her, protecting her from the traffic. Her husband hands the keys to the valet and gives him instructions for the car in broken English.

The family rides an elevator up twenty-six flights in silence. The girls lean against the elevator walls, hips popped out, noses in their phones. On another day their mother would pinch the backs of their necks and tell them to stand up straight. But they've had a long plane ride. Let them slouch a little.

The doors open onto a gray hallway that smells like new carpet, and Sveyta is waiting for them. "This way," she purrs, "this way." Sveyta and the mother walk side by side, the daughters and the husband trail after them. Sveyta tells the mother about the arrangements she's made for their stay, and the mother approves them or offers small adjustments. Sveyta takes note.

They reach the apartment, Sveyta swings the door open, and the mother can see only the magnificent windows looking over Central Park with the glowing lights. Her daughters and husband rush in behind her to recharge their phones, to put down their luggage, to use the bathroom. They don't notice the lights, nor the lush flower arrangements. The mother, pulling her gaze away from the view, bends slightly to brush her fingertips over a petal, to lean in and smell.

"Lovely," she says to Sveyta.

"I'm so pleased," Sveyta replies. "I've hired a new cleaning lady for you. She cleaned the apartment for your arrival."

The apartment looks immaculate, but it's difficult to judge when an apartment has been sitting empty. The mother walks to a bookshelf and finds a small glass statue of a cat. She picks it up and runs her finger where the cat used to sit. It comes up clean.

"Have her come Monday to do the linens," the mother says.

"Good," Sveyta says.

Sveyta and the matriarch tell each other good evening.

Marion Shops at Saks

Rather than purchase a uniform to be a cleaning lady, Marion will shop for an outfit for the ballet. It will be worn only to the ballet, and it will be appropriate. She pulls ten $100 bills from the knapsack and puts those bills in her cross-body bag. She leaves behind the two twenties that Sveyta gave her, a pointless amount of money in New York. Marion has decided not to acknowledge the negligible pay until she understands why she is a cleaning lady. This was her epiphany: to wait, see why she's doing what she's doing, and the answer will come. In the meantime she'll buy an outfit at Saks.

On the train, aboveground, Marion contemplates her newfound contentment and congratulates herself. It is a clear marker that she is maturing and maturing well. Not everything needs meaning right away.

When the train dips belowground, Marion faces forward. She thinks about passing underneath Nathan's Brooklyn again. At his stop, she looks out the window for him, and for their daughters. This is a risk, but she needs the outfit. Besides, she has red hair, she's wearing different clothes, she's even lost some weight. Nathan will not see her. Her daughters might. Marion picks a discarded metro section from under her feet and ignores the expression of disgust from the woman sitting next to her. She flips open the paper and hides her face. She reads an article about a celebrity who threw a party a week ago.

In the middle of Manhattan, Marion climbs up from underground. She enters Saks with confidence, ignoring the perfume girls, the makeup girls, the hat girls, and the scarf girls, even the designer handbag girls. She knows what floor she needs and which floors to ignore. She will, for instance, pass the floor with the plus-size clothes. Marion needs a floor she's never been to, the designer floor. Marion arrives here with her contentment, steps off the escalator, and lets herself browse. Rhinestones abound; pantsuits flourish. She brushes her fingers over fabrics and shoulders of jackets. She's also in a box at Lincoln Center with Sveyta, watching *Giselle.*

In the distance, she sees a black skirt,

voluminous yet chic. It poofs out from the hanger, and there is a subtle sparkle in the layering. Perhaps it is all the tulle, allowing glimpses of light and space between each layer. It is beautiful. It is Grace Kelly.

Marion shouldn't even try on the skirt, that is how little it suits her, but she goes for the largest size anyway. She's rushing to a dressing room but thinks no, why try when she can own? She's at the cash register instead; bills are laid down to keep the skirt. The checkout girl maybe gives her a look, but Marion ignores it. The skirt is folded in tissue paper, and it's hers.

The train back to Brighton Beach is a happy blur. Before she left the department store, Marion also purchased large oval sunglasses, and she doesn't take them off. She catches sight of herself in the reflection and approves. Now she does not need the newspaper from the floor. Now she is perfect for the ballet.

THE RED HOOK
FISHMONGERS' COLLECTIVE

Get up, Nathan thinks. *Get up. Take a shower. Get out. Put on your shoes. Do something.* His daughters will be home soon. He looks at his last email to Denise and winces. *Come back, but just to talk — let's talk about this.* The desperation he thought he managed to hide is dazzling. *Go outside.* The farthest he can get is the backyard, but he can't make it off the patio. Maybe he'll grill for the girls, but he remembers there's nothing to grill. He researches how to get fresh fish delivered to a Carroll Gardens door in the next three hours. There is a service, of course; it's expensive, but Nathan's tapping in a credit card number. Three fresh tuna steaks are on their way. He can't go outside now. He has to wait for his fish. His daughters will be home soon. Maybe he'll vacuum.

The house needs the presence of two people. He never should have written that email. He should have gone quiet. He wants a warm body in the house but knows that want isn't particularly flattering to the warm bodies. An email confirms that the tuna is on its way. Also, he is now a bona fide member of the Red Hook Fishmongers' Collective. Here is his username. Another email appears above it: *Where did Marion go? Did you do something to her? You owe us.* Nathan archives it, puts it with the rest of these anonymous emails. He will rise from the couch to make a salad to go with the tuna. But first he must do more research.

The doorbell rings, and Nathan may have been saved. This cannot be his fish; this must be Denise. However, it is neither. The detective and the officer stand on his stoop.

"Sorry to bother you," the detective says. "I just wanted to check a few things."

"I wish you'd called. Now is not a good time."

"A few minutes, Mr. Palm."

Nathan yields. The first floor of the brownstone is a mess, and he does not apologize. The detective looks around and suggests to the officer that he start with the girls' rooms on the top floor and work his way down.

"Hey," Nathan says. "What about my daughters' privacy?"

"You're welcome to join him," the detective says. "I'll be in the basement."

Nathan bites the inside of his cheek. "No, it's okay. I mean, just don't touch anything."

The officer shrugs and climbs the stairs. The detective walks back to the kitchen. Nathan counts to five and attempts to follow casually. He finds the detective in the basement, peering into the green shoebox of cash again.

The detective nods, smiles, and sets the green lid back on the box. He then walks into the darkness of the basement, and a light goes on. Nathan follows and tries to take normal breaths. He hasn't been down here since Denise made her discovery. He realizes that Denise returned the basement to a state of order as she searched. The detective paces and makes a clicking sound with his tongue.

"And you never had cats?"

"No, I'm allergic."

Nathan could tell the detective about the unlocked basement door, at least, but doesn't know what that would prove. He thinks, *I'll say it if he gets close to the tarp.*

But why is he hiding it at all? Nathan tries to believe that he's protecting his daughters. The detective takes a step toward the tarp and bends at the waist as if he's about to lift it, and Nathan knows that he is protecting Marion, and by protecting Marion he is protecting himself.

He's about to tell about the unlocked door when the officer calls down into the basement. "Sir? It's the station."

"What now?" the detective asks as he leaves. Nathan coaxes his heartbeat back to a normal rhythm and turns off the basement light.

In the kitchen, the officer talks jargon into his cell and the detective looks out the window. "It must be nice to have a house like this in the city. Do the girls play out there?"

"Mostly Jane," Nathan says. "But yes. It is nice."

"It's a nice house. From what I've seen. All right, Nathan. May I call you Nathan? Nathan, we should get going. Sorry to have bothered you."

"It's fine, it's fine."

"Before I go, are you sure there isn't anything else you can tell me?" the detective asks, but Nathan's shaking his head before the detective can finish asking the question. "All right. Well, we're still looking. We haven't given up."

Nathan's eyes open wider. "Terrific," he says.

Back on the stoop, the officer says, "We

haven't given up? With all due respect, why the fuck not?"

The detective chooses not to tell the officer his motivation: that he wanted to see how Nathan Palm would react when given the chance to hope.

BROOKLYN BEACHES

Now that her sister is a delinquent, Jane has been forced back into her old routine of morning and afternoon school bus riding. It's better now that the missing boy sits next to her and holds her hand. But she misses seeing the missing boy's picture on the subway. The picture is what drew her to him, what fascinated her. And the missing boy sitting next to her is not exactly the missing boy of the posters. She wants to see another poster, but her sister won't be allowed to take her to school on the train anymore. Meanwhile, her father is no longer an outside dad. He's become an inside dad. She explains this to herself, to make sense of why he won't take her out to the school bus like he used to but instead prefers to wave from the front door.

She's been asking him to take her on the train to the water. She remembers that some trains lift out of the ground, and when they do, those trains usually take you to the beach. Jane takes subway beach trips with her mother and sister every summer, and they are delineated by the two long train rides. The first is exciting, anticipatory, then long. The second is sweaty, sandy, dirty, longer than the first train ride, but it always puts her to sleep. Jane is woken up by her mother a stop before Bergen Street, and she's been confused by the sleep because it was dead and heavy.

She wants to go on one of those trips again, even though it's colder. She believes this is where the missing boy wants to go or where he wants her to go.

A Description

The Grace Kelly skirt hangs above Marion's bed where Sveyta's cross used to rest. She would have kept the cross up if Sveyta had paid her like a person. Since she was paid next to nothing, Marion wants to shock Sveyta, leave her openmouthed. She wants Sveyta to be ashamed of paying her so little and prove that she is worth more than what Sveyta valued her at.

Marion lies on the bed in the opposite direction, her head at the foot, her feet on her pillow, and gazes at the skirt. She still has not tried it on, but she ripped the tags right off. The garment belongs to her, and she will not have the depressing walk back to the counter, the skirt folded up again, incorrectly, to be resteamed and rehung by a size 2 salesgirl. So what if it never fits her? She wants to own it. This is the closest to Grace Kelly she will ever feel.

The phone rings, and Marion listens to

Sveyta answering. She doesn't expect Sveyta to call out, "Marion. It's for you."

Sveyta must see terror in her eyes when Marion enters the kitchen to take her phone call, because she adds gently that it is Marion's new boss calling to sort out the details of the position. The subtext: *No one has found you.*

The Russian matriarch is all soft-spoken business. She tells Marion when she expects her at the apartment and details a list of new responsibilities alongside cleaning. Marion says, "Yes, sure." When she says *sure,* the matriarch admits that she's never hired an American cleaning lady before. Marion says, "Well, there's a first time for everything." The matriarch doesn't respond, because she doesn't believe the axiom means anything.

"So we will see you tomorrow at eight-thirty, yes?" the soft voice says.

"Yes, tomorrow, yes."

"Good. À bientôt."

Sveyta sits at the kitchen table smoking. She's poured two cups of tea, and she gestures for Marion to join her.

"I apologize for frightening you," Sveyta says. "It wasn't my intention."

"It's all right."

"You thought it was your husband on the

309

phone, the one who beat you?"

"Yes, he's the only one I have." Marion says this as a joke, but Sveyta doesn't smile.

"I had a boyfriend who beat me. A Ukrainian. A long time ago."

"It's unpleasant."

Marion wants to move on from this conversation, back to the ballet, for which she has bought the clothes. She wants to say, *I'll buy the tickets.*

"I have friends in this neighborhood. A few friends. If you give me a description of the husband, they will let me know if they see him around the building. Or the street."

"What kind of friends?"

"Old friends."

"I don't know about that."

"I'm afraid I will have to insist. One must protect oneself."

Marion bites her lower lip but gives Sveyta a detailed description of Nathan. She pictures him in the kitchen, reading the paper, drinking coffee, while her world caught fire. His height, hair color, build. Even the two moles on his left cheek, near his mouth. The graying spots at his temples. Sveyta takes notes in Cyrillic.

"And his name," she asks in a fill-in-the-blank kind of way.

"Nathan. His name is Nathan."

PANCAKES

Nathan shops online for groceries and simultaneously searches for recipes that will please his daughters. He hates the blogs he's found but admits they have a point. Playful colors in food entice children. One father recommends food dye in pancakes, but it seems this father puts food dye in everything, and that's not parenting, that's entertaining. *You're feeding toxins to your children, you stupid son of a bitch. You deserve to have your kids taken away by CPS,* the comments say. *We're calling them right now.* Nathan clicks on a packet of food dye anyway, and it's now in his basket. He's going to make chicken nuggets and pizza bites and ravioli, all from scratch, and when a recipe calls for beef, he will use turkey instead. He orders supplies to woo his children, because they no longer like him, and it's not because he's a single parent. They have begun to look at him like he's full of shit. The more he tries, the more full of shit they think he is. It's in their eyes, the knowledge that Nathan doesn't know what he's doing, that they have been stuck with the less capable parent.

The anonymous emails are occurring more often, and they have become more specific. *Be a man. Find your wife. You are responsible.* Nathan blames Marion in his head and gathers information from the Internet on perfect parenting in the millennium. He does know that perfection should not be his goal. He simply needs to learn how to get his children to trust him. Or at least to look like they trust him. Yes. That would be fine.

BOARD OF TRUSTEES

We've hired a private investigator. He's very good.

Where did you find him?

He was recommended by Elise from the parents' association.

So Elise finally caught on about Greg's late nights at the office. Good for her.

And you believe that he will be successful?

He's worked these types of cases before.

Doesn't Nathan need to be informed now?

He has been, in a manner.

But once we find her, then it will be different.

Then we'll need to discuss with Nathan what course of action he'd like to take.

Give us our money or we send your bitch wife to prison.

Do you have to say everything that comes into your head?

And if we never find her?

We will.

But if we never do?

313

This pessimism of yours is getting old.

It's a good question. The lawyers want to know. The longer we put off prosecution, the harder it will be to make a case in court. They'll want to know why we waited.

Okay, worst-case scenario, Marion Palm is a leaf in the wind, an untethered balloon, a needle in the proverbial haystack. Then we will ask the Palms to make reparations or we'll reconsider the girls' enrollment. Maybe the teachers had the right idea. The sins of the mother and all that.

Isn't that kind of spiteful?

Should we split the check?

I didn't have an appetizer.

But we are educators.

We are expected to continue to educate the spawn of criminals? No, that doesn't work.

I agree, cut the girls loose.

Not yet.

Not ever, probably. Most likely the Palm girls will graduate with their respective classes, and this distasteful episode will be entirely forgotten by all. We will find Marion Palm.

Who had the salmon?

GINNY'S INVITED TO A PARTY

Ginny has forfeited her right to go outside during her breaks, her homeroom teacher informs her; does Ginny understand? Ginny has no choice, so she says she does, but at lunch she sneaks by the hall master when a class trip returns from Greenwood Cemetery. It's the entire second grade wearing matching T-shirts under their coats, holding etchings of gravestones. They are showing them to the hall master, who is loudly appreciating them as masterpieces, when Ginny slips out the front door.

Ginny's friends didn't want her to sit with them at lunch. They've even found a replacement, an English transfer student. She has a plummy accent, freckles, and talks about stones and euros and a boyfriend she left behind. How can Ginny compete? She's returning to the smokers, who don't trust her much but at least let her sit down.

There were other addresses in the report.

One in Red Hook. There was also a work history; her mother worked at a Brazilian place in Manhattan. It's closed now. Ginny thought she would investigate, but Sandy haunts her imagination and she doesn't want to look at the report anymore. There's nothing to find anyway.

She returns to the steps at the courthouse. She walks up them, two at a time, and reaches the portico quickly and flushed. The smokers greet Ginny, and someone offers her a cigarette, as they always do. This time, she accepts. It's lit for her, and the smokers together teach her what to do. They tell her not to inhale this time, like they do; that takes practice. Three of the most seasoned smokers push smoke out their nostrils like angry bulls and smile. *Soon, Ginny, soon,* they say.

Ginny doesn't inhale, barely brings the cigarette to her lips, but she adores the weight of it between her two fingers. At last she feels like she belongs somewhere. She practices tapping off the ash at the end.

When the first cigarette is extinguished, Ginny has passed some initiation rite, because an older girl, Chloe, invites her to a party. *Come to my house first and we'll get ready. I'll text my address.* She's fourteen, wears eye shadow, and has several piercings

up her ears. Ginny asks for another cigarette.

LONG BATHS

Marion is conflicted by her satisfaction in cleaning the midtown apartment. She's good at cleaning, even likes cleaning, and when the Russian family praises her to Sveyta, Marion is gratified. They commend Marion's skill at displaying and organizing their beauty products. The bathrooms are now the bathrooms of magazines, the matriarch tells Sveyta. Sveyta tells Marion, and Marion is humble, bows her head, tilts her chin to her left shoulder; it's like a muscle spasm.

The Russian matriarch will never suspect that Marion's gift for the bathrooms is informed by the long baths she takes. She waits until the family is away at their activities (shopping, ballet, and the murky business of the stepfather). She cleans the breakfast dishes, makes the beds, and waves goodbye as they leave, one by one.

She's removing her clothes as soon as she

hears the door shut for the last time, and she's sitting on the edge of the bath, testing for the perfect temperature. Settled in, she massages their shampoos and conditioners into her scalp. She takes advantage of the Russians' multitude of masks, which peel, tighten, unclog, moisturize, or diminish the appearance of pores. When a product dips noticeably low, Marion adds water or cheaper versions of that product. Soon the Russians will be lathering themselves with Jergens. At the end of her bath, she dabs their scents from glass bottles on her wrists and the hollows of her neck.

After her bath, she blow-dries her hair and returns to work. She puts the polyester uniform back on, a blue-and-white tunic that she must wear with shapeless gray pants. She must press both garments at home each day. She does it while looking at the Grace Kelly skirt.

VERTICAL GARDENS

Nathan's online again. He can't help himself. Packages arrive in a constant stream. They are all things he needs, but he's building individual relationships with both the UPS guy and the FedEx guy. He's even begun to explain why he's at home so much. *I'm a writer, I'm a single dad.* They don't really care, but they need his signature. He elaborates: *It's a book I'm writing. I'm writing a book.*

He is not writing a book. He is buying shirts online. But he could be doing research. He must allow for this time, for his idea to germinate, percolate, do something. It should be growing. He wants to look back at the eight thousand words he wrote when Ginny was in the next room, but instead he plans dinners. He buys toilet paper for the year. He reads articles about urban gardening.

He's got a plan to build a vertical garden,

but first he must understand his sunlight. Is it full? Is it partial? Where's the wind coming from? How much rain will it get? He finds himself reading the weather report and learns that hurricane season is here. This delights him, because he has a new thing to shop for. He needs to prepare. The book must wait.

Nathan tries to set up a filter for the anonymous emails, but the sender uses a new email address each time. The messages are getting more specific about the amounts. *Your wife owes us $120,000. Find her, or the money, or else.* He writes back once: *Email me again and I'll tell the police.* The reply: *Go ahead. Do that. Be our guest.* Nathan has considered calling the Palm financial manager but doesn't know what he'd say.

He clicks on more items to put in his shopping bag; he right-clicks, left-clicks, right-clicks. In between looking for storm candles and flashlights, he drags his book to the trash-can icon and leaves it there. An hour later he empties the trash. The computer asks if he is sure that he wants to permanently erase the contents. It cannot be undone. He is sure and repeats the right-click. The office is filled with the computer-generated sound of paper crumpling.

An Introduction

Ginny's at her first party and it's not what she expected. The music is loud, so when she says something she must bellow it into an ear and turn her ear to the mouth in order to hear the response. She's holding a red cup with something sweet in it, and she is thirsty and nervous. She makes an excuse to the ear and the owner of the ear nods.

She weaves her way to the front of the house, or what feels like the front, and this is it, this is the front door. But Chloe catches her: "Hey, I was looking for you." She is pulled into a room where boys and girls of her class play spin the bottle. Ginny's a little surprised. "We actually do this?" she says. Chloe shrugs, says, "Why not?" Ginny looks around the room, and there's a girl in the corner without a shirt on, and a boy has latched himself to one of her small breasts with his mouth.

Ginny seats herself in the circle, and the

crowd looks at her, and it's decided that it's her turn. She spins the bottle and it lands on Chloe, and Ginny is relieved. When Chloe puts her tongue into Ginny's mouth, she shrieks a little, and the crowd laughs. When it's done, Ginny wipes her mouth with the back of her hand. "What, you never kissed a girl before?" Chloe asks, suddenly haughty, suddenly older. Ginny almost says that she'd never kissed anyone before a few days ago, but Chloe's already angry with her, and Ginny doesn't know why.

Since Chloe won't look at her now, Ginny figures she's allowed to go home. She's looking for her coat in a mountain of coats piled on the floor by the door when someone tugs at her elbow. It's a boy who sometimes stares at Ginny in French class. It's not that Ginny is special. He stares at all the girls. Now he's teetering back on his heels. He's gripping her shirt, and he's nuzzling Ginny's neck like a horse. Then she can feel his wet braces scrape the skin below her ear, and she could push him off, but she lets him do whatever it is that he is doing, and then he releases.

"There," he says.

"Okay," Ginny says. "There what?"

"I got you," the boy says.

He pivots back to the spin-the-bottle

room, and Ginny escapes. On the street she realizes she left her coat behind, but she isn't going back, so she hasn't forgotten her coat, she's lost her coat.

Her father allowed her to go out because he thought it was a sleepover with Chloe. He was happy that his daughter was making new friends. She was going to spend the night with Chloe to make the story credible, but now she's homeless for a few hours, so she makes alternative plans for her evening. She's been adventuring by herself a lot these days, and now she'll do it at night. She'll go home when she feels like it, she decides, and explain that Chloe's father dropped her off. It sounds kind of true. Ginny pauses her adventure to call her mother's cell, and the call goes to voicemail, which is full. She looks at her mother's Facebook page. She calls her mother again.

Ginny goes home around two. She unlocks the front door, ready with a story for her father, but the house is dark. She climbs to the second floor, and there is a bar of light under his bedroom door, but the door remains shut as she creeps by. Her mother would have caught her. Ginny takes note: this is her new existence, her new adolescence. She feels invisible but powerful.

In the morning Ginny finds an orange-

and-red mark on her neck under her ear. It is ugly like a bruise, but more speckled. She knows enough to hide it, to wear her hair down in front of her ears, but other than that, she's confused. It takes some time for her to associate it with the boy from the party and what he did to her when she was looking for her coat.

She's scared of Chloe, too. She wanted a new friend but ruined it. She's also a little in love with the boy from the party because he seemed to choose her.

She makes the mistake of tucking her hair behind her ear when she's getting her books from her locker. Her old best friend sees the mark, points at it, and asks what happened. Ginny doesn't know why she admits the truth, but she does, and her old best friend laughs into her open hand and then tells everyone. Ginny later sees the boy from the party walking proudly down the hallway. He is very thin — his T-shirts hang from his bony shoulders — and he never wears deodorant, but Ginny walks proudly too. She feels noticed. Everyone is talking about her. She puts her hair up. Let the school know. She exists.

MARION AT TWENTY-FOUR

Marion Palm quits the café two weeks after marrying Nathan. She tries to stay but has married a rich man, and so she can't handle customers anymore. Her reason to be nice has dissolved. She finds herself copying customer credit card numbers onto napkins and memorizing those numbers when the café is slow. It's not difficult, so she knows she's heading in a bad direction. She quits the restaurant, and the Brazilian owner does not cry or yell. It seems that Marion was on her way to being fired and hadn't noticed. The owner hasn't found out about the fictitious vendors. Marion is not being run out of town as a thief. The café simply no longer wants her there. Marion hopes it is because her financial need has diminished. She hopes this is progress. The chef, feeling that Marion is persona non grata with the owner, ignores her goodbyes to the kitchen. She leaves without ceremony and doesn't return for her last paycheck. Those three figures are insignificant to her now.

She finds a house to buy. She visits house after house with an upbeat real estate agent, driving through Brooklyn neighborhoods in the realtor's dinged and dented tan Saab. She chooses a brownstone in Carroll Gardens, and it needs work, but the Palms are young and they have money. It shouldn't be a problem, the realtor says. There shouldn't be any problems. They make an offer after Nathan approves. She and Nathan talk about possible renovations over dinner that night. Their offer is accepted. Marion gets pregnant. An accident but also Nathan's idea. He wants a family. He doesn't want to be an old man with young kids. For once, Marion has heeded her mother's advice: better make it stick. They pay extra for the current owners to vacate the premises as soon as possible.

They move. They don't have enough things for this house, so they buy more things. Their schedules are both very open. Marion and Nathan visit antique-furniture stores together. Marion is astonished by her new husband's ease in these expensive stores, but also sees the salespeople see Nathan coming. She must step in to redirect their focus. She must tell them and Nathan that actually, she makes the final decision. Nathan happily gives up the responsibility; the salespeople are annoyed. But she's pregnant, and she's found that this has made her into a person of authority. In Brooklyn, a rich white pregnant lady in leather sandals is sovereign.

Wanting a better understanding of her new power, she asks for financial records, specifically those concerning the Palm fortune. She wants to know precisely how much money they have. Nathan changes the subject. She asks again, and he makes an excuse, tells her it's complicated and she shouldn't worry so much. He treats her like a paranoid pregnant lady. It seems that as Marion gets bigger, she becomes more absurd, and so her sovereignty is fading with every pound gained. Alone one morning (Nathan's meeting a friend for coffee), she receives a bank statement in the mail, and she tears into it. She reads it like a novel in the kitchen. They don't have as much money as she thought. This house means they have no savings, and by *they,* she means she. She has no savings. Marion does a quick inflation projection for the next decade and knows that they aren't going to have enough. They should not have bought this house. She did not marry a rich man.

He's out of the house till midafternoon, so she calls the Palm family financial manager, after finding the number in Nathan's Rolodex. The financial manager is surprised to hear from her, tells her essentially to calm down and enjoy being the wife of a Palm, but Marion insists on seeing him. *I happen to be free right now,* she says. The financial manager grudgingly admits that he is too.

She takes the train to the financial district, and her belly is an anathema. It makes everyone wildly uncomfortable on the elevator. Here she is not a person who knows something special about the universe. It's also August, and the only thing she fits into is a short A-line dress, and her legs are on display. In the humidity of the subway this was fine, but in the chilly atmosphere of the skyscraper, she's freezing. The hair on her legs stands straight up. Her sweat is evaporating into the air of the elevator.

In the office, she tries to get the financial manager to take her seriously. It is impossible because she can't cross her legs and every minute or so must stuff her dress down between her thighs in order to not flash the man a shot of her underpants. With one fist keeping the dress down, she leans forward and rests her other hand on his desk. She pleads. She tells the financial manager that she knows the money they are getting will not be enough for a family in Brooklyn. She's run the numbers. Taxes will increase. Education will become more expensive. The mortgage payments could and probably will go up. The house needs work — not a new paint job, but a new boiler. They even found uncapped gas jets in the basement. Marion points to the sky to illustrate what is about to happen with living expenses.

The financial manager makes some noises, repeats that at least their child's college tuition is covered, Marion and Nathan don't need to worry about that. He says things that don't mean anything but ultimately admits that there isn't as much money left as everyone thinks. Great-Grandfather Henry Palm's fortune is not everything.

But he can make a few phone calls. Great-Grandfather Henry Palm is still owed a few favors. For instance, he helped rebuild a girls' school in Brooklyn Heights after a fire. The same school also graduated the young Nathan Palm. The Palm family has been good to the school, and the school knows this.

Marion Palm gets the job offer that afternoon. She accepts but knows it still won't be enough. A part-time job in development is not what she needs, and she knows she is being condescended to. But there are few options for pregnant college dropouts. The financial manager and Nathan feel that she is overreacting. She's a victim of pregnancy hormones. Nathan also implies that she's unaccustomed to her new financial status. This is a common reaction among the newly affluent. Marion knows otherwise; she is, and always will be, on the edge of poverty. She's suffering now because she forgot this fact. She still has the credit card numbers somewhere.

Jane Defends
the Missing Boy

At recess Jane observes her classmates playing a game she doesn't understand. They take turns looking slack-jawed and stupid; they make guttural noises and keep their arms crooked, the hands dangling, thwapping themselves on the chest, heads hanging to the side. They sway in place. The other children laugh at the rotating display of retardation. It's not until Jane gets closer that she realizes they are making a show of her friend, the missing boy. They've seen the posters too and have been, like Jane, inspired.

Jane steps into the middle of the game, and she's going to slap the boy who is currently mimicking her friend, but her open palm tightens into a fist, and she swings her arm back, keeps her feet planted, and throws her weight into the impact, and when the fist and face connect, it is an explosion of pain in her hand. Both the boy and Jane drop to the ground; Jane holds her fist, the boy his nose.

Teachers fly into the center of the courtyard where the children staged their game. Jane and the boy are separated from one another. The boy has conceded — he's hiding his nose, which is bleeding — but Jane isn't finished yet. Jane still wants to fight.

RUBLES

A computer in the couch. There's a computer in the couch. Slipped in between two seat cushions, a razor-thin laptop. The family has just left for a weekend stay on an island, and one of the leggy daughters has forgotten her computer in the couch.

Marion opens the laptop, brushes her fingertips over the silver edges and the soft black keys, and it whirs to life. She kneels in front of the couch to peer into the laptop for answers. Un-password-protected, this is a gift.

The daughter and two similar-looking friends (perhaps relatives) pout in the background, limbs twisted. A window of the girl's email pops up, and Marian is quickly searching for numbers: addresses, credit cards, bank accounts. She sinks to the floor, her bucket of cleaning supplies beside her, forgotten. She is both herself and the teenage Russian. She admires the Cyrillic. She spies on her husband.

She reads the news. A Queens city councilman's mother has been embezzling for years and funded her son's first campaign with her ill-gotten gains. She sheltered him, fed him, allowed him his pursuit of happiness. Meanwhile she embezzled over $1 million from the nonprofit she managed. The politician is expressing a kind of contrition to the press, but his mother looks unapologetic in the photos. She wears a pink suit and her hair is done.

Marion is mortified by the sum the politician's mother took. The woman simply wrote checks to herself, and no one noticed. The theft would have gone undetected if the councilman hadn't started talking about campaign finance reform. Marion is envious and insecure. Why didn't she take more from her daughters' school? She was hesitant, thoroughly female in her timidity and limited ambitions.

She stands regally and moves to the head of the dining room table, which has service for twelve. She places the laptop at the head of the table. She thinks she's hungry, but when she enters the kitchen, she realizes she is thirsty instead. She chooses a bottle from the wine refrigerator and opens it without resting it on the counter. The cork pops, and with one hand behind her back, Marion pours the wine into a thin-stemmed glass. She removes her tunic.

Sitting at the table in her bra and polyester pants, she easily gains access to the Russian girl's bank account; the girl keeps all her passwords in a file named, in Russian, *Passwords.* With a swift click, Marion translates the page and sees that the girl has over 50,000 rubles in her checking account. Marion tastes the wine. Another click, a currency conversion, reveals this to be $10,000. It's hers. It's hers.

MISSING PERSONS

The detective is going to initiate an official investigation into the disappearance of Marion Palm, after talking with Daniel into the night, both on their personal landlines. Daniel can't take a full breath; he's been using his inhaler too often. The school dismisses him and his worry, but Daniel persists. "I can't do this alone," he tells the detective. "Everything is going wrong. Everyone yells at me." Daniel whispers that he thinks Marion Palm could be dead. Or he thinks she's done something very wrong. Or Nathan has done something to Marion.

The detective asks, "Are you sure about this?"

Daniel asks, "Why is this happening to me?"

It was another day of hopelessness for the missing boy. The detective is returning from the mother's apartment, having sat with her and repeated the same bad news about her son. He's on the Q heading back to the precinct. He was offered a lift, but the detective made an excuse. He needs to be anonymous for a while. The mother didn't say one word. Not hello. Not goodbye.

Daniel's whispered allegations of foul play are enough for an investigation. It's enough for a search warrant of the Palm residence, where something secret lurks, the detective knows. This is a far-reaching conspiracy, Daniel concluded. Daniel knows nothing about the embezzlement, but he's hurt by the lack of faith in him the school has shown. His imagination responds to the hurt and to the faithless school and he spends his commutes fantasizing about what might have happened to Marion Palm. These fantasies are gruesome and violent and what he communicates to the detective in the night. The detective doesn't believe anything Daniel says but can use his hysteria to open the case officially.

The detective stands before the sliding doors as the train pulls into the station. He looks at his reflection and readjusts his belt as he waits for the train to stop and for the doors to open. Another train is arriving from the opposite direction. The train doors both open at once, and the detective looks into the other car. There sits Marion Palm, in strange sunglasses, with red hair.

"Marion?" the detective shouts, crossing the platform. "Marion Palm!"

The doors close, and both trains leave the station. The detective is left alone on the platform. He can't be sure, but he believes: when he shouted *Marion,* the woman looked at him. He swears she even smiled.

How can he be sure? He's been spending too much time with her photo. The detective may have conjured up Marion because he's looking for her. And perhaps the woman smiled because his behavior was odd, his movements uncoordinated.

He cannot open an investigation, because Marion Palm may not be dead. Unless Marion Palm is the victim of a crime, his hands are tied. No one can give him a good reason to look for Marion Palm.

But he also can't, in good faith, let the Palm family know that Marion Palm is safe, because that might not have been Marion Palm. He returns to the precinct and initiates nothing.

NATHAN STARTS A BLOG

Even though his book is gone, Nathan still feels like he has something to say, only it's about parenting. He feels like he's getting better at it. And his house: he understands it more with Marion gone. He's taking time to make it into a true and good home. He's conceptualizing a platform that will bridge these two topics as well as generate projects. He's going to start a blog.

He orders supplies while he sets up the site. A well-researched and well-reviewed camera will come in the mail soon, and he will take pictures of his meals and his rooms. He will start with his kitchen and retile the banquet. It's incredible what can be delivered to one's door.

The site is not an intuitive thing, but he's getting the hang of it. He makes aesthetic decisions. He organizes and categorizes. He buys the domain, and he's proud. The name of the site is classy, funny, apropos. He's even emailed an old friend who also has a blog, who also lives in Brooklyn. The friend will tweet about Nathan's new blog. Nathan will tweet too. He won't talk about Marion, because this is separate from her. He'll talk about his daughters, but only in a charming, anonymous, yet specific way. He's also going to repaint the downstairs bathroom and update the lighting fixtures. He's read articles about how to do it, and he's a careful person.

He turns off his phone so he can concentrate on this new project, so he doesn't get the calls about his younger daughter and the trouble she's in now that she's broken her classmate's nose. Later, when he does find out, he'll ask the school to send him emails in the future. He'll respond sooner. He checks his email religiously in order to catch the anonymous ones. *We're going to sue you,* the emails say. *Prepare yourself.*

Jane Talks to
the Missing Boy About
Her Defense of Him

In the nurse's office, with an ice pack on her knuckles, Jane is told by the missing boy that it wasn't necessary to punch the boy in the face. *He didn't hurt my feelings,* the missing boy says. *And they weren't making fun of you for once — you weren't the subject of their cruelty. Why didn't you leave them alone? Although I am touched that you care for me so deeply, I abhor violence.*

Jane can hear the grown-ups discussing her fate in the hallway. They can't get Nathan on the phone. Her teacher is defending her. The teacher says the kids were being offensive, and if she'd seen it she would have stopped it. Jane handled it poorly, but she was reacting to something real. "We'll tell her parents" — she means the father — "of course, but I wouldn't escalate this."

Jane can see that her teacher is talking to the principal again, pleading with him.

342

There's a pause in the conversation. Eventually the principal consents, for the time being. The teacher thinks she's won something.

No one gets to make fun of you, not ever, Jane says to the missing boy.

No one does because I don't hear it — I can't hear it.

Can you hear me?

I always hear you.

Why?

The missing boy shrugs. *I can't explain.*

The boy Jane punched is taken home by his mother. She hears the boy lie to his mother, and her teacher confirm the lie. They both say he fell on his face when he was running. The boy lies because he doesn't want to have been beaten up by a girl. The teacher lies because she feels that Jane needs to be in school. The missing boy puts his arm over Jane's shoulders and says, *See, they're all protecting you. Isn't that nice?*

CYRILLIC

The Russians return from the island, but Marion does not return the laptop. It stays in Brighton Beach. She researches into the dark hours of the night. When she turns the computer off in the morning, she slips it into her knapsack with the cash.

The Russian teenager, the owner of the laptop, has been struggling to ask Marion if she's seen it. Articles run amok, the subject and the objects are not clear, past, present, and future tenses collide, and Marion makes the girl speak correct English sentences before she'll answer at all. When the girl, her chest and neck red from frustration, forms the sentence "Have you seen my laptop?" and finally masters the present perfect, Marion replies like an English teacher. "No, I have not seen your laptop. Do you remember where you last saw it?" The girl needs time and a dictionary to construct her reply. Marion is enjoying herself.

The matriarch also asks her if she's seen the laptop, but with the weary air of a mother who assumes her daughter has been careless and stupid. Marion almost commiserates with her as a mother of daughters but remembers that she told Sveyta she didn't have any.

The stepfather stays above the issue. He's rarely there anyway, and Marion feels like he is always looking for his keys. She's started to hand them to him when he starts swearing in Russian and patting his pockets. At least, she believes he's swearing. It sounds like swearing.

She likes the family. She appreciates their directness. She loves their money. They have beautiful things, and as always, Marion wants their beautiful things to be hers. She has her Grace Kelly skirt, and she has her knapsack full of cash, but she's still living in a bedroom in Brighton Beach. It's not fulfilling her like it did in the beginning.

The man who yelled her name. His clothes didn't fit. His haircut was cheap. He could have been a friend of her parents from the neighborhood, but then why did he use her married name? She shouldn't have smiled, but he seemed so comical, and it felt wonderful to be recognized.

Marion's using the laptop to get to know

the girl and her spending habits. It's difficult because she does not understand the writing, so she teaches herself the Cyrillic alphabet. She can recognize English words spelled phonetically in Cyrillic and then can translate much of the girl's Facebook feed. The girl is, Marion parses, a very typical teenager.

To steal from her is easy. She begins to siphon small amounts from the Russian bank to an online account she set up for herself ages ago. It's an international account, and it will be difficult for Marion to withdraw the money, but that's not important right now. First it's the thrill of possessing the money; the Russian girl's loss is also good.

Marion comes into work one morning and the teenager is throwing a tantrum. She's stomping her flip-flopped feet and swinging her hair. Her laptop has been stolen, she yells, and Marion did it. It's all in Russian, but Marion hears her own name and sees the girl swing an accusatory finger in her direction. She puts on a blank face of confusion, and then a hurt one. She scurries out of the room as if she is embarrassed but not guilty at all. She hears the parents shout at the teenager. A door slams. An hour later, when Marion is unclogging a drain of hair, the teenager stands in the bathroom door. "I sorry," she says. "I *am* sorry," Marion corrects. "And what are you sorry for, precisely?" The Russian girl wails and storms back to her room to search for her Russian-English dictionary and textbook.

BOARD OF TRUSTEES

I'm glad you could meet on such short notice.

You said on the phone it was important.

Indeed.

Has the PI found Marion?

Not exactly. He's going to need a larger retainer.

Why?

Marion has done a good job of covering her tracks. The PI needs more manpower. And we're asking him to do this without informing the family. It's slightly unethical.

I don't see why we have to pay more for lack of results.

Perhaps this is a sign — perhaps we should let it go.

Our money? Impossible. The Wing Initiative would collapse.

We would seem vulnerable.

But if no one ever knows. If we keep quiet.

I'm afraid that's out of the question. Marion's departure was too suspicious. Too enticing to the gossips. That man she worked with — the pathetic one . . .

Daniel?

He's been telling everyone she's gone. The truth, or something like it, will come out.

I suppose. Well, how much more does the PI want? I can try to make some room in the budget.

Actually, that's not quite the issue. We've been talking —

Discussing —

And we feel that the board of trustees is no longer a good fit for you, Eugene. I'm sorry.

What do you mean?

We've appreciated all your hard work, with the holiday events and landscaping suggestions, but it's become clear that the time has come for you to go your own way.

But . . . my family.

Oh, for fuck's sake, Eugene. Just accept the facts. Don't make this worse.

Worse? My family has been on the board of trustees for decades.

And we've appreciated your service. But now it's over.

We appreciate you.

We appreciate you.

We do appreciate you.

But —

I said we appreciate you.

WEST VILLAGE ONE-BEDROOM

A week goes by and Ginny is not spoken to. She avoids the smokers because of Chloe. She keeps her head down. The boy from French class has been telling everyone how close he got to Ginny, but can no longer look her in the eye. She does not catch him staring at her anymore in French class. He stares at the girls on either side of her, and it seems deliberate, so Ginny stares at him. She remembers what it felt like to have his mouth on her neck. At the time it didn't make her feel anything, but now she becomes flushed thinking about the proximity of another person.

Ginny has adapted somewhat to this new reality when Chloe appears, waiting for Ginny at her locker. She says, "Come to my apartment after school. I'm with my dad this week."

Ginny says, "Oh, okay, yeah, totally." When the words come out, they are croaks, because she's been talking so little.

It turns out that Chloe's dad lives in the city, so they take the train in an unusual direction for Ginny. She rarely stands on this subway platform. Chloe leads Ginny into the West Village, to an apartment building on a cobblestone street. She skillfully enters the building with an electronic key, and six floors up, down a long corridor, the girls hang out in a white-walled one-bedroom with a view of the Hudson.

The bedroom of the one-bedroom is Chloe's. A mattress on the floor in the living room belongs to her father and stepmother. The art in the apartment is large and colorful. Everything else is black or white.

Chloe tells Ginny that she's forgiven her for the party. It took some time to get over it, but she now understands that Ginny was embarrassed. "I mean, you totally embarrassed me, but I don't think you meant to." Ginny agrees: she acted without motivation but was still thoughtless. Chloe nods with pursed lips, raised eyebrows, and large eyes. Then: "I have a Skype date with my boyfriend. Do you mind?" Chloe pushes Ginny back into the living room. "I haven't talked to him in, like, forever. I miss him like crazy, you know." The bedroom door closes.

Ginny sits on a black leather couch looking at the art while Chloe laughs loudly in the bedroom and then whispers. Ginny drinks a diet soda and wonders if this is what it's like to have friends who are older than you.

The door opens, and Chloe says, "Rafi wants to meet you. I told him about you."

Ginny's seated in front of the computer. The boy on the screen has curly dark hair, wears glasses, and looks maybe a little older than Chloe. Chloe says they fell in love at camp as CITs and now Skype every night.

Rafi says that Ginny is pretty cute. Chloe flicks her hair back over her shoulder, turns Ginny's face to her, and this time Ginny does not pull away when Chloe kisses her. Rafi wildly approves from the screen.

Nightmares About Nathan

One late afternoon Marion returns from midtown and Sveyta's waiting for her in the kitchen. She's on the phone but gestures to the teapot. Marion's tired; she was up late the night before, dissecting the Russian girl's account. Then the matriarch insisted that Marion clean the oven, even though it has never been used. Marion's head is pounding with noxious fumes and Cyrillic. Sveyta finishes her phone call and sits at the table.

"I've been having bad dreams," she says.

"I'm sorry," Marion says.

"They are about your husband. I feel like he's going to find us here."

Marion assures her that he won't.

"Ivan hunted me down. He could not rest until he had found me and made me his own again."

"Nathan doesn't care that much about

me. No one has ever cared that much about me."

"Still, I want his surname."

"To give to your friends?"

"Yes."

"I can't do that. An impossible thing to ask."

"I must insist."

Marion wants to cry. Nathan would never hunt her down like Ivan hunted Sveyta down.

"Can we please go to the ballet soon?" Marion says. "I'll buy the tickets."

"Maybe, but I would feel too ill at ease to enjoy the choreography. You must understand, the dreams are nightmares."

"I said I'm sorry."

"You do not have nightmares about Nathan?"

Marion says no, but doesn't explain that she's too busy dreaming of her daughters to dream about Nathan.

"If you don't give me his surname, I will have to ask you to leave. And I will need to find another cleaning lady."

"May I think about it? I just need a day to think."

Sveyta pauses.

"All right. One more nightmare. But if you give me his name, your problems will be over."

"Yes, you're right, but it's a major step. I want to think about it."

"Fine."

"And then we'll go to the ballet?"

NATHAN'S BLOG

The blog is blowing up. Nathan checks his analytics. New readers find his site, and they stay. Previous readers return. Nathan has found his voice. His blog persona is a lumberjack domestic god with a satirical, self-aware edge. If he had a beard, it would be a full one and casually groomed. He is so comfortable with himself that he writes about buying maxi pads for his older daughter. The voice comes easily, not like with a poem or a book. He simply tap-tap-taps and there it is, so it must be true.

A neighborhood acquaintance links to his blog from her blog on urban green spaces, and the readers slip over. They want more bright pictures. He takes selfies as he works. He's started to include the delicate hands and feet of Jane. Ginny would not give permission; she hasn't allowed her picture to be taken since she was eleven. She said something about her soul.

As the blog develops, so does the house. He's wallpapered the downstairs bathroom. He's fastened new mismatching knobs on all the kitchen cabinets. He's in the process of designing his new office. He's moving into a small, previously ill-used room on the first floor. He's talking about taking out a wall. He's talking to himself.

The readers comment on his posts: *Yes! More light!* They offer suggestions for wainscoting.

Nathan writes a post to the writers of his comments sections about how much he values their input and their ideas. *Without you, this blog would not be possible. I would be nothing without you,* he types.

Jane Is Sent to a Shrink

Jane is now an untouchable of the third grade. She's no longer bullied; she is avoided because she has somehow eluded punishment for her crime.

Jane's teacher, on the other hand, has been following her around. Ever since Jane punched the boy in the courtyard, the teacher can't look at her without a crease forming between her eyebrows, her head tilting to one side, and her arms crossing. She speaks in a different way now, and asks slow questions of Jane all the time. When Jane answers, she nods meaningfully, as if she understands what Jane is really trying to say. Jane knows she doesn't.

Jane gets some time to herself by claiming that she wants to print out something, a story she wrote. The teacher is busy with geography and Jane knows her state capitals, so the teacher lets her go to the computer lab by herself. Once there, Jane talks to the missing boy out loud and with pleasure. The missing boy says it's good to talk to her again. They make plans.

The missing boy whispers in Jane's ear. *There's going to be a storm. It's the culmination of hurricane season. Low-pressure systems are forming tropical cyclones in the Atlantic, building, building, and they are about to move inland. I feel it,* the missing boy says.

The missing boy and Jane watch clips of hurricanes or the aftermath of hurricanes with the sound off. Palm trees blown vertical, cars submerged in muddy water, people on top of their houses waving to rowboats. They find pictures of the Superdome. The missing boy predicts that a hurricane will cause widespread flooding of the New York City subway system and his two favorite things will collide.

Neither kid hears the teacher enter the room. The teacher listens to a good portion of the conversation before making her presence known, and the forehead crease is deeper than ever. Jane is escorted directly to the school therapist, the woman with the big breasts and thick wrists. The teacher says she will be back in an hour.

Jane and the missing boy sit across the desk from the school therapist.

"You miss your mommy, huh?"

Jane immediately begins to cry, not because she misses her mommy (although she does) but because she is frustrated. She doesn't call her mom Mommy anymore.

"Leave me alone," she wails.

"Oh, honey, I just want to make sure you're okay," the therapist says. "So, have you heard from your mommy at all — has she tried to contact you?"

Jane wants to leave this room. She offers a meek yes.

The therapist's face lights up, and she leans forward, exposing more of the line that separates her breasts. Her hands are on the table.

"When? When did you hear from your mommy?"

Jane says, "Last night. She talked to me last night. She said she was living by the ocean and that she was fine. She says she misses me and she loves me, but the ocean is where she needs to be. It's a long train ride away," Jane tells the therapist. "The train is underground at first, and then goes up."

Jane is set free from the office early and allowed to walk back to her classroom alone. The missing boy holds her hand and says, *Good, good.*

Jane says, *I said everything you told me to say.*

The missing boy says, *Yes, you were perfect. You said everything in a perfect way. She believed you.*

Jane says, *And they will leave me alone now?*

The missing boy says, *Yes, now they will leave us alone.*

MARION AT THIRTY

Marion at thirty is a mother. A young mother, by Brooklyn standards. In Sheepshead Bay she would be considered completely normal. In Carroll Gardens she has more in common with the babysitters than with the other mothers. To be thirty and have a six-year-old and a baby — the other mothers raise their eyebrows. They say, *At thirty I was still out at the bar. I was planning a wedding. I was starting to make a six-figure salary.* They laugh and say, *You must have so much energy. To be forty-five with two kids, all I want to do is nap.*

Marion does not have energy. Every muscle in her body is tired. Or, worse, asleep. The second pregnancy was harder than the first. It swelled her from the inside out. Jane took over her body, and she was nauseated the whole time. The other mothers talk about how they jogged or did prenatal yoga. Marion says, *I managed not to barf for nine months.* She wanted to barf, but her body wouldn't let her, so she peered into the toilet bowl while Ginny begged for her attention. Nathan stood in the bathroom door frame. He said, *I wish I was the one who felt sick. I wish I could share this with you.* Marion said, *Shut the door.*

So far, the money she's embezzled has all gone into the house, and now it's a lovely house. Nathan gives tours to his friends when they come over and talks about plans for more loveliness in the future. He carries Jane around, allows her one sip of his beer while he gestures to the patio. Ginny silently follows the crowd, in thrall to her daddy's voice. Marion stays put. She says, *I've taken the tour before.* She does not want to watch the women orbit her husband. She does not want to watch the gentle hands lightly swat her husband's shoulder. She's seen it too many times, so Marion Palm drinks her beer alone at her desk.

She wishes the attention from these women only inspired her husband to have extramarital affairs. She even understands; she and Nathan haven't had sex since she was pregnant with Jane. But Nathan seems to believe he needs to renovate the house in order to maintain his new sexual capital. This is more difficult to navigate.

When Nathan talks about a new project, a new extension, Marion thinks, *How will I find the money for this one? What will I have to do?* Because she can't say no to Nathan. She's tried, and it fails. He looks at her and says, *Why?* Not, *Why not?* But *Why?* And there is a universe she must explain to him; it is an answer that demands an infinity, as opposed to the answer to *Why not?* which asks for only one reason. *Why?* demands all the answers at once, or the perfect answer. Nathan gets what he wants.

Ginny falls back from the tour to find her mother. She wants to sit on Marion's lap, which is now soft and large. Marion at thirty looks into her older daughter's face and thinks about being somewhere else. While Ginny rests her small head on Marion's chest, Marion opens an online savings account for herself. She transfers her money (and it is her money; the effort she puts into stealing it means it belongs to her) from the joint checking account into the new account. She kisses her daughter on the forehead and sends her outside again. *Go tell Daddy that he should stop talking forever.*

Over the next year, Marion transfers small sums into the account, and they are designed to be unnoticeable. She then realizes that she wants the cash in her hands, so she adds small withdrawals to her routine. When Ginny's at school and Nathan's in his office, she takes Jane down to the basement. She settles Jane into an old playpen of Ginny's and hides her money. She makes it into a game, and Jane helps her decide where the money belongs by clapping her hands. They work together. When they've found the perfect place, sometimes they sit in the basement together for a while, even though it smells like cat piss, and Marion tells Jane stories about the ocean.

Board of Trustees

There's been, as they say, a development.

Finally.

Clarissa was able to get something out of the younger child. It took some coaxing, but the girl eventually opened up. She said something about the ocean. She said her mother had gone to the ocean.

Oh, yes, very helpful.

I'm not finished. She said Marion had taken a train that was underground and then went aboveground.

Oh, for fuck's sake. This is nothing. Why are we here?

Well, I told the PI and he was quite heartened by the news. So it's not nothing.

He asked for more money, didn't he? He's a con artist.

I think Marion Palm is still in Brooklyn, that's all.

Wild conjecture.

The PI agreed. And he has an idea. We can

366

place missing-person ads in some neighbor-hood newspapers. Very subtle. Very "Have you seen this woman? Her family is concerned." We'll offer a slight reward —

With what money? Everything is sunk to pay off our back taxes. I'll kill Marion if I ever see her again.

I'll handle the money. I'll handle the ads.

This is hopeless.

I miss Eugene.

Shut up, Barbara.

MARION EMBEZZLES
FROM THE RUSSIANS

It's been small amounts she's taken. The amounts are what a teenage girl would spend in an exciting, expensive new city. She's even managed to make the transactions look like they involve real New York businesses. There's nothing here that would raise any red flags, or a Russian bank manager's eyebrow.

She still doesn't know how to get it from the international account. She's only embezzled domestically before, and needs to educate herself in order to gain access to her money. She needs to move quickly when the time comes. This, however, is not that time. *Patience, patience,* she whispers to herself, but she also considers her history of timidity. Lately it's been difficult to trust her instincts.

She has avoided checking to see if anyone is looking for her, but now she should. Her instincts tell her that, and she'll trust them on this. She Googles her name, and all she finds is a brief police report with an unflattering photograph of herself from her fattest days. Of course Nathan would choose that one. There is nothing from the school. There is nothing about her daughters. There is only the man in the suit from the train. *Marion!* he called out. *Marion Palm!*

Then she Googles her husband and finds his blog. Nathan is growing a beard. He's renovating their house, still, still. Jane's hand reaches out in one of the falsely beautiful and bright photos. Nathan and Jane are cooking together. She scrolls down and types a comment. *What a very precious whole family.* She writes that, and clicks Publish. She would write more, perhaps to enlighten Nathan to the hypocrisy of a lifestyle blog when his lifestyle is funded by embezzlement, but she doesn't have the right. She also doesn't have the time.

She Googles, once more, "women who embezzle." She looks at all the small crimes, the same small sad mad women. She will become one of them unless she does something drastic. *Don't become one of the little people,* Marion says to herself. *You are better than them. You are smarter than them.*

She prepares to drain the girl's account entirely. This theft will be noticed. She must be able to disappear immediately after she acts. She looks up at the Grace Kelly skirt and prays.

NATHAN TELLS
THE COMMENTS THE TRUTH

Nathan's blog gets a rave review from an online Brooklyn magazine. The reviewer says it's charming, informative, and handsome. Nathan has a light touch but a compelling one. She asks, "May we have permission to use a photo of Nathan with Jane and a homemade margherita pizza with fresh basil?" and Nathan says absolutely. He is giddy with the popularity. He reads his comments late into the night. However, the absence of Marion is conspicuous. The comments are asking questions.

Dude, where's your wife?

>So are you a single dad or what?

>>Did she die?

>Are you lonely?

>So SWEET you're taking care of them on your own #heartbreaking

>>SO SWEET that he's just doing his job.

>Guys, guys, guys, we don't even know if his wife is gone — he just hasn't mentioned her.

>>Dude, his wife is totally not there.

Nathan feels that keeping something this significant from the comments is akin to being dishonest, and he wants to be transparent, because transparency is essential to the blog's tone.

Hi folks — some of you have been asking questions about my current marital status, and the truth is, my wife is out of the picture. Just me and the girls! We're doing fine, thanks for your concern. It means so much to me.

And it does. The faceless mass who read his work care about his and his daughters' well-being and happiness. Nathan publishes.

>Dude — she left you. What a whore.

Nathan laughs out loud. It's been decided:

he has a valid grievance. Then:

>He probably cheated on her.

It cuts, the truth of it, but he resists responding. He'll let this play out.

>>Why? Maybe she cheated on him.

>>>She obvs wouldn't leave the kids behind then.

>>>>Who says that's what happened?

Out of the picture, the fuck you think that means? We're not talking alternate weekend. Bitch is gone.

>How unfair. Those poor girls.

>>The poor man.

Nathan watches all this happen and finds himself holding his neck, craning toward the screen, hitting Refresh, Refresh, Refresh. The comments eventually taper off, having discussed and exhausted all reasons why Marion might have left. Nathan's possible infidelity fades as a motivation, and the blame comes to rest squarely on Marion's shoulders. Nathan wants to tell them more.

He writes a post on quick ways to ecologically and ruggedly clean a bathroom. He's discussing the ratio of vinegar to water to lemon juice when he slips in that not only has his wife left, he's not even sure where she is. She's not coming back. But back to the toilet. Don't forget to clean the handle.

We need more, the comments say. *We don't understand.* As Nathan plans his next post, he appreciates how good honesty made him feel. He opens the last anonymous email. He writes to MyMoney-Now11215@aol.com that he's sorry about what his wife did. He really is.

POETRY

Chloe's boyfriend, Rafi, admires Ginny. That's what Chloe tells Ginny. He's coming into the city soon from Westchester, and he wants to meet Ginny in real life. Ginny smiles shyly. Can't wait. Ginny adores the way Chloe and Rafi sometimes look at her, the moments when they appraise her and find her more than adequate. It doesn't happen often. Mostly Chloe looks at Rafi, and Rafi looks at them both but rarely at Ginny alone. Chloe and Rafi Skype privately and then Ginny's allowed in.

Ginny's never had friends like these before. They don't want to talk about television. Chloe sometimes talks about poetry. A moment of approval happens when she learns that Ginny's dad is a poet. She tries to buy his book, but it's out of print and Ginny doesn't offer her one of the hundred copies from a box in the basement. She regrets this, because Chloe finds Nathan

Palm's blog. As she scrolls down, her brief respect for Ginny evaporates. She sends the link to Rafi and the two of them begin to analyze the blog on Gchat as if it were a book of poetry, except it's about eclectic doorknobs and feng shui. They laugh at a video of Ginny's father lovingly polishing a candlestick with a rag. Chloe says, "It's like your dad thinks he's hot. It's so funny when guys think they're hot."

Then they try to find Ginny in the blog. They ask about an elbow. A bare foot on black-and-white bathroom tile. Fingers and knuckles wrapped around a fork. *Is that you? Is that you?* They want to catch Ginny, but Ginny says, *No, no, that's not me,* until she finds the back of her head in a post about spackle holes.

"But I didn't give my permission," Ginny says.

Chloe and Rafi are about to attack Ginny for her complicity in her father's lameness, but Chloe senses a shift in the group dynamic and signals Rafi to stand down. Ginny takes a breath and instructs Chloe and Rafi to write comments; Ginny will dictate. They each open a dialogue window and wait with fingers poised to attack. As anonymous Internet beings, Chloe and Rafi ask insensitive questions about Marion.

Nathan happens to be updating his blog, and so when they publish, they are able to watch him try to respond in real time. He believes these new comments have stumbled accidentally onto the truth. He tries to be charming to evade answering. Ginny's eyes narrow. She stands behind Chloe with her weight equally distributed on both feet and watches her father lie. "This will hurt," Ginny says.

ELECTRICITY

A storm is going to visit the borough. Brown packages fill the foyer until Nathan finally rips into each one with a butter knife and pulls the contents from the packing peanuts. Bottled water, canned goods, duct tape, batteries, candles, even walkie-talkies. Jane and the missing boy watch from the landing, communicating and laughing. They both feel the storm but want to see what it's made of.

Jane's father wants to burrow deep into the earth. Jane should explain to him what the missing boy has explained to her: that resisting the force of the storm makes the damage worse. Better to let the storm water in. Expect disaster to your infrastructure. All the deliveries in the world will not protect this family from wind and rising water.

When the hurricane comes, the missing boy says, *the sky will go impossibly dark and light at the same time. There is electricity up there. The birds will go mad. Dogs will bark. Cats will hide. It's very compelling, and it's powered by the ocean. You can feel it, the ocean above.*

But Jane can tell that Nathan no longer looks up. She asks her father, "Can we go to the beach someday? Can we take the train to the beach?" Nathan looks at Jane with confusion. He doesn't understand going to the beach anymore. Daddy is an inside dad. Daddy is no longer an outside dad. The missing boy goes to the front door and opens it for Nathan, and Nathan doesn't see. He's breaking down cardboard boxes to make room for other cardboard boxes. He'll ask Ginny to take them out to the curb.

THE MISSING BOY

The boy's body is found on Coney Island Beach. It washes ashore in pieces, which isn't normal for drowning victims. "What exactly disjoined the boy may never be understood," the detective says to the mother. "The ocean did too much damage. No, you shouldn't view the body." She asks how long her boy was in the water and how long he was on a train. The detective can't answer, and the mother doesn't know what answer she wants. Perhaps she wants to know the day her boy died. What she was doing on that day.

The mother is going to sue. Her boy never ran away before. It wasn't like him to run away. It took the school half an hour to notice he was missing, and in those minutes her boy traveled miles. The city is on her side, and so the city promises that it will pay but still prepares to mount an impenetrable defense. The mother did not check to see if her boy was in the classroom; she left too quickly. The public school system and the NYPD can do only so much when a woman is a bad mother. The posters are taken down from the subway walls in the night. The city forgets.

Hurricane Preparations

In his office, Nathan is confused by the comments on his blog. Some remarks he made seem to have inspired strange reactions. He's lost control of the tone.

Why'd your wife leave? Were you a bad husband?

He writes, *I mean, I tried my best.*

What if your best wasn't good enough?

You spend a lot of time thinking about home repair. Maybe that got in the way of your best?

I don't know why she left.

>So you weren't paying attention.

This is an article about succulents. Do you

382

have a question about succulents?

>>I don't care about succulents.

Nathan tries to reason with the comments, get them back on track, and responds to Ginny, Chloe, and Rafi, who are on their respective computers, making life hard for him. It's what they are doing to preoccupy themselves as they Gchat about where to meet in real life.

This in-real-life meeting is at Rafi's request. Rafi happens to be in the city for the weekend, visiting for his cousin's bat mitzvah. The bat mitzvah has been canceled because of the hurricane, but Rafi and his family remain because the commuter rails are no longer running. Rafi and Chloe have met up in the park and made out on some benches and then in the 9th Street F station, but now Rafi wants privacy. He also wants Ginny to be there. Chloe types that other girls would be made to feel insecure by this request, but not her. She knows how much Rafi loves her, and only her.

The thing is, they need someplace to hang out. Rafi isn't allowed at any of Chloe's houses, not even her mother's boyfriend's condo in Dumbo, where Chloe and Ginny are currently hanging out, typing on their laptops. Chloe's parents don't think she should be dating yet, she admits verbally, and Ginny is briefly astonished. Chloe not being allowed to date makes her seem young. No restrictions like that have ever been placed on Ginny. Chloe snorts and says, "Well, it's never really been an issue, has it?"

Ginny hides her hurt but both says and types that her house is off-limits as well. Chloe looks put out, whines, "Why?" Ginny explains that her father doesn't leave the house anymore. Chloe says, "Well, tell him we're going to be working on a project for school. A report. Can't you tell him that?" Ginny says no, he would want to know the details of the project, then he'd want to help. He would make them snacks and photograph the snacks and them eating the snacks and using the toilet after the snacks. Ginny and Chloe laugh at the image of Nathan in the bathroom with them with his camera.

Ginny has an idea: what about the school?

"Isn't it locked on the weekends?" Chloe asks.

"Nope," Ginny says. "My mom went there on the weekends all the time. Sometimes they let people rent the chapel. I think the volleyball team practices on Saturdays. I can say I need something from my mom's office and then let you both in through the side door."

"Awesome," Chloe says, and she types the plan to Rafi, and he types back, *Yeah, no, totally, meet you there in an hour.*

Ginny almost texts her father. When she asked to stay over at Chloe's the night before, he said fine, but she had to be home by noon because of the hurricane. He said it could be dangerous out there; it wasn't an irrational rule, it was for her own good. So Ginny should text her father that she'll be home later than planned, but she'd like him to be unsure of where she is.

HURRICANE SUPPLIES

Sveyta's at work in the city for the after-noon, and Marion's ready. She bought a small roller suitcase, and it's the correct size for her new clothes, her Grace Kelly skirt, and $34,000. She's leaving behind the knapsack that belonged to her daughter, as the suitcase is both more efficient and less noticeable. Soon it will also contain the Russian teenager's laptop, but first she needs to do one last task and clean out the account. She reminds herself that the money is hers. She clicks Yes, she approves this transaction. Yes, she is sure.

And it's the same rush, but more luxuri-ous somehow. She should have made this transition to larger sums years ago, but she didn't know she was capable of both the labor and skill of embezzlement and detach-ment in its most elegant and pure form. She is perfect in this moment, and she mourns a little because she could have been perfect all along. She wasted time being imperfect, because she thought she had to be in order to stay human, unnoticeable and unremarkable.

She closes the laptop and has settled it on top of the skirt in the suitcase when the front door opens, and it is Sveyta with three plastic grocery bags.

"There's more in the car — would you help me?" Sveyta calls out from the hallway. "Supplies."

"Supplies for what?" Marion stands in the door frame of her bedroom, blocking Sveyta's view of her packed suitcase with her hip.

"The hurricane. Haven't you looked out the window?"

Marion's window looks at a brick wall, and the weather is indiscernible. Hoping that Sveyta is preoccupied by the weather and therefore won't notice the suitcase, she walks to the kitchen window and sees gray clouds forming over the beach. The wind is strange, and she knows this because the trees are pushed sideways and then go still. The sky is clearly about to break open.

"Oh," Marion says. She could leave the apartment under the pretense of getting the rest of the groceries from Sveyta's car and then make her planned escape. The problem: then she must leave her things behind. Sveyta will question the rolling suitcase. If she returns for it, Sveyta will not let her leave the apartment again. Sveyta will lock the doors. *No one may go outside during a storm,* Sveyta will say.

Marion Palm could leave the suitcase behind and begin again. If she is perfect, this is a possibility. It has to be.

Sveyta hands Marion the keys to her car. "It's parked down the street."

Marion takes the keys and leaves the apartment and her suitcase. As she descends, she feels lighter than ever before, and this convinces her that she doesn't need her suitcase. Besides, $10,000 is waiting for her in an offshore bank account. But how will she get access to the bank account without identification? She's on the street when it begins to rain. Marion could steal Sveyta's car. The keys are in her hand. But the skirt, the money . . .

"What are you doing?" Sveyta must roar from the building entrance to get Marion's attention. "Get inside."

Marion runs for the car, opens the trunk, and lifts out the remaining bags. She closes the trunk and locks it.

"You are going to catch a cold," Sveyta yells, and Marion runs back to her, doing what she is told, fetching.

Sveyta and Marion climb back to the apartment, and Sveyta takes the bags from Marion and instructs her to wait on the doormat. Sveyta returns with a soft pink towel that smells like lavender and drapes it over Marion's head. She helps Marion out of her wet shoes and socks and into a pair of slippers reserved for visitors. Marion rests her hand on Sveyta's shoulder for balance. Sveyta tells Marion to change out of her clothes while she makes tea, and they will tape all the windows, change the batteries in the flashlights, put out candles, and make an inventory of the dry and canned goods. Maybe even have a glass of wine. It's been a stressful day.

Marion is under the spell of Sveyta's care for her. In her bedroom, she opens the suitcase and pulls out fresh dry clothes from under the money and the skirt.

The women act fast and quietly. They make *X*'s on all the windows with duct tape. They unwrap large candles and place them strategically around the apartment. They peer into the fridge and decide what will need to be tossed if the power goes. Once they've made sure everything is in place for the storm, Sveyta opens a bottle of wine. In the kitchen, Marion sits before one of the large glasses that Sveyta has poured. Sveyta stands but picks up her own and clinks it to Marion's glass. "To our safety," she says, and takes a sip. Marion does as well, and tries to hide her wince at the sweetness of the wine.

The two women sit there in silence as the rain falls and enjoy the electricity while it lasts. They drink slowly. And just when Marion is about to tell Sveyta how much she cares for her, Sveyta interrupts her thoughts.

"Marion. I need to know Nathan's last name. I need to make the phone call."

"Palm," Marion says without hesitating. "His name is Nathan Palm."

PROOF

The boy is sitting next to Jane at the kitchen table when she reads in the paper that his body has been found. Her father is in his new office next to the kitchen. Jane traces the outline of the article with her index finger. The missing boy is still beside her, but he's opening and closing his mouth like a fish, and no sound comes out. She asks, *Are you still here with me?* He manages to make a kind of sucking sound with his throat. *What happened to you?* She reads that his arm was found by a girl her own age. *I should have found it,* she says to the missing boy. But she imagines the arm, and she's glad it wasn't her. The guilt of this realization makes her reach out for his hand, but he doesn't respond. He can't move like he used to. He looks to the side of her rather than at her.

Nathan doesn't hear his daughter go out the front door. She leads the missing boy onto the street. She's decided that the body was not the missing boy's after all. The missing boy is still at the beach with her mother, alive and well, and she's taking the train out there to prove it.

THE ABANDONED CHURCH

It's easy to break into the school. Ginny enters first through the main hall, having left Chloe and Rafi on the street, and tells the hall master she needs to retrieve a book from her mom's office. Her dad is waiting for her outside in the car, double-parked, she explains. The explanation is unnecessary, as the hall master is focused entirely on the weather. The hall master says, "Sure, honey," without looking up from her phone. "Just get home soon and safe. It looks like the storm is going to be on top of us in an hour." Ginny says, "Sure, thanks," and goes on her way.

She finds the side door, which is notorious for being broken most of the time. The sign that warns of the alarm is a joke. All she has to do is hold down the latch as soon as the door opens, and the alarm stays quiet. It just takes nimble fingers and maybe a lookout on school days. Ginny Palm finesses the door open as her mother showed her to. Marion said it could be useful.

Chloe and Rafi are on the other side of the door, trying to avoid the rain, which has just begun, and Ginny lets them in. Rafi is shorter than Ginny expected, shorter than Chloe, but taller than Ginny. He wears a lot of gel in his hair and smells like soup or maybe Nilla wafers. He hugged Ginny when he met her, and Ginny didn't know where her arms should go.

"You know what we should do?" Ginny says. "The church."

Chloe coos at the goodness of this idea. "It's like this abandoned church," she says. "It's a structural hazard."

Rafi grins and says, "Let's do it."

Ginny leads the way. The hallways are dark except for the red exit lights. It's only the three teenagers and the worried hall master, who is already packing up her things to go home. The teenagers are intoxicated with the freedom of being alone with each other in a place where they are usually supervised. Rafi has even brought a joint, and they're going to smoke it somewhere, if they can find the best, coolest place.

They must pass Marion's office to reach the church, which is accessible only through the dance studio. Ginny listens for Daniel, who often comes in on weekends. Marion never knew what it was he did. Marion told Ginny that she suspected he was escaping his family, in particular his son. But it's hurricane weekend, and it seems that Daniel must act like a father in the midst of possible natural disaster. The coast is clear.

The doors to the dance studio swing open, and the teenagers are in what looks to be another former church, but the floor is covered in gray plastic sheeting. The ceiling is arched and vaulted with brown beams, and the windows are large and high. There's even a structure that looks like a pulpit: a staircase that leads to a small balcony, which is used often by the modern dancers in their choreography. The teenagers turn and watch themselves in a wall of mirrors. Mesmerized by their own reflections, they pause. Rafi asks, "Is this the church?" But the two girls shake their heads. Their school used to be a religious one. Many spaces were designed with an ecclesiastic aesthetic.

Underneath the pulpit there is a door, a small one, and if it is jimmied just so, it opens. The couple follows Ginny down a dank hallway that opens up into the designated building site of the glorious new science wing. The architect has promised to incorporate some of the original architectural features of the church. Such blending of past and future, faith and knowledge, will please the parents and the alumni. The students will miss the sublime unsafety of the church.

Ginny, Chloe, and Rafi are met with the stale-smelling wet air of a room shut up for too long. The narrow vaulted windows have been covered with plywood, but light edges in where it can. The three teenagers use their cell phones to create more light and pad softly into the church. The pews have been removed here as well. Old desks and bureaus are scattered around. A pigeon flaps its wings in the rafters.

There's a balcony supported by suspect beams, and it sags. The teenagers know not to go up there. It could easily collapse, and that would mean expulsion for the girls, as well as some broken bones.

Rafi whispers that this is fucking awesome. Ginny blushes at the praise. Chloe leans over and mumbles something into Rafi's ear, so Ginny explores on her own. She's on the altar when the two call her back to join them. Rafi has lit the joint, and the smell of the weed fills the room, mixing with the humidity from the storm.

The rain on the roof beats a fast pattern. It's picking up speed. There are holes in the roof, they can see the angry gray afternoon sky, and the rain comes through. They hear a crack of thunder and the church fills with white light. Chloe screams, and Rafi mocks her for screaming, and so she hits him. They stumble, laughing.

Ginny shushes for them to be quiet, but Chloe is up and running away from Rafi. They're playing a game of tag, but it's something more. Ginny wants them to shut up and tells them so, because she's got a bad feeling. Rafi runs up to Ginny and, as in a movie, puts her hair behind her ears and tells her that everything is going to be okay. He licks his lips and leans in as Chloe objects. Ginny is consumed by something emotional and hard and emptying, and she turns from the arguing couple to find her own salvation. The altar of the church is crowded with chairs attached to desks (or desks attached to chairs), but behind is a crucifix. The Jesus nailed to this crucifix is not abstract but also not in pain, and not blond. Ginny begins to climb over the desks and chairs to get to this Jesus, and the doors of the church open wide. The hall master is there, shining a flashlight onto the teenagers. From behind the hall master, a voice in the dark corridor says, "Hello, Ginny."

HURRICANE RENÉ

A tropical cyclone that formed over the Atlantic near Cuba makes landfall in New Jersey. Brooklyn is next, and Nathan is prepared. So is the city. The subway has been shut down, businesses have closed, the mayor has warned the city to stay inside. Stay safe. Nathan finishes his last hurricane-preparation blog post. He tells his readers that he'll check in after. Now he must be with his daughters. Luckily, the unruly comments seem to have lost interest, and it's only the faithful sending him messages of love and hope. Nathan writes back, *And to you as well,* and turns off the machine.

With the noise of the wind of the oncoming storm, he didn't notice that his house had become quiet. Or perhaps he is now more accustomed to the quiet. Jane isn't in the kitchen, where he left her; there's only the open newspaper. He climbs from the first floor, shouting her name, to the second floor, to the third. He opens Ginny's bedroom door to ask if she has seen her sister, and she isn't there. He remembers that Ginny should be home by now. That's what she promised.

Nathan has a panic attack in the hallway and sinks to his knees. He may throw up on the carpet. He opens his mouth and no sounds come out, even though they need to. He must call for his daughters again, because they must be in the house. There is no other option. *Get up,* he thinks, *get up.*

Nathan retraces his steps, looking into each room again, looking for his daughters in impossibly small places. He asks if they are hiding from him deliberately, and if so, can they please not. They're scaring him. He returns to the kitchen and watches the rain stop. The air outside becomes still like the air in the house. Nathan is in a lot of trouble. The phone rings.

"I've got someone here," Anna tells a panting Nathan. "In my car. I'm bringing her home."

"Jane?"

"No, Ginny," Anna says, a little confused. "You've lost Jane too?"

"No, no, but thank you. Why do you have Ginny?"

"We will discuss that later."

399

Nathan places his hand over his chest, but his eyes open wide again.

"You shouldn't be driving," he says. "The hurricane."

"Didn't you hear? They downgraded it to a tropical storm and it's headed for Massachusetts. New York is in paralysis for a little wind and rain. It's quite funny."

Nathan leans over the kitchen table and looks at the open newspaper. It's the article about the body of the missing boy. His daughter has scribbled over the article with a red Sharpie. He reaches for his phone and calls Denise. He hasn't heard from her since his email, but he needs help.

As the phone rings he paces the first floor, and Denise sends his call to voicemail. Nathan hangs up. He stops in front of his family desktop and sees that Jane has sought directions to Coney Island.

Nathan moves to his foyer, heart pounding, and slips his feet into his running shoes, which he has not worn in a long time. He moves to the door but remembers that he told Anna he would wait for Ginny to be returned. He freezes at the door, knowing that a plan is needed. He must act.

QUESTIONS ABOUT GOD

Ginny sits in the front seat of Anna's BMW, still stoned. Anna drops the couple off at Chloe's mother's place, Rafi looking miserable to be joining his girlfriend. Anna assumes that he was having a good time being the oldest, acting as the authority figure to two pubescent girls. With his peers, Rafi is probably not much of an alpha. He plays video games and never speaks to girls his own age. Anna guesses that Rafi won't change and will always seek out younger girls. It's funny to see that sort of behavior in its nascence.

The hall master was the one who called Anna about Ginny. The hall master wanted to go home but couldn't find the teenager. Anna lives close to the school, but also told the hall master to let her know about anything concerning the Palm girls. Anna has made this discreet request to several people in the school, ranging from lunch ladies to deans. The hall master was the only one to come through with something truly helpful, and Anna classifies the hall master in her brain as a competent woman. She'll remember her, possibly at Christmas.

She wants to ask Ginny what she was doing in the church — her church, as she's come to think of it. After all, it was her idea to renovate the decrepit building into the new science wing. She walked up and down the center aisle with an architect, a contractor, and the principal. She wore a hard hat and discussed her vision for the space. The architect and the contractor balked at some of her suggestions, but when the blueprints arrived, they'd mostly accepted them. So this was her church, and there was Ginny Palm at the altar, standing on a desk, her arms stretched out theatrically, and she was laughing. When the flashlight shone into Chloe's and Rafi's faces, all Anna saw was adolescent fear; they didn't want to be in trouble. Ginny, however, looked up at the sky. She lifted her arms as if she were conducting an orchestra, and brought them down again, concluding the concerto. Anna doesn't want to read too much into it, but the rain stopped. She had to pull Ginny off the desk and walk her to the exit.

It occurs to Anna that she is angry with

Ginny on a personal level for desecrating this space. Upon further reflection, she is also angry with Ginny for her mother's behavior, which has put the Wing Initiative in jeopardy. Anna breathes in through her nose and out through her mouth and reminds herself to be generous. She tries to imagine what led Ginny to coerce her friends into joining her in trespass. Anna breathes yogic breaths and empathizes mindfully with young Ginny Palm.

"Ginny. Do you have questions about God?" she asks. "Is that why you were in the church?"

Ginny looks at Anna, confused. "What?"

"God, Ginny. Sometimes in times of trouble, religion, or spirituality, or . . ." Anna trails off because Ginny is looking at her as if she's insane. "Never mind. It doesn't matter."

Ginny plays with her cuticles and says, "No, I have no questions about God."

"That's fine. Is there anything you want to talk about?"

"You mean, do I want to talk about my mother? You mean, do I want to talk about where my mother might be? Or do you mean, should I talk about what my mother did?"

"Do you know where she is?"

Ginny shakes her head. Anna tries to feel sorry for the stoned girl even though she is being so rude. It can be difficult to be high and depressed and thirteen.

"I'm sure she misses you."

Ginny laughs, raises her arms, and cries, "Hallelujah! Hallelujah!" Anna almost swerves into incoming traffic as she avoids Ginny's outstretched left arm. "Praise Jesus!" Ginny cries.

THE DETECTIVE REACHES THE END OF HIS ROPE

The detective gets a call on his cell from Nathan, who stammers that he's sorry to trouble him but his daughter has run away.

The detective asks, "Where do you think Ginny might be?"

Nathan, ashamed, corrects: "Actually, it's Jane, my youngest. But I think I know where she is."

At this moment the detective should tell Nathan to call 911. He should make this official, but he cannot begin the process again. He needs to believe that Nathan knows where his daughter is. The wind has died down. He says, "Why don't I go look for her?"

Nathan says, "Thank you, thank you. I would go look myself, but . . ."

And the detective waits, then finishes the sentence for him. "No, you should stay at the house in case she comes home."

Nathan says, "Right. That's what I thought too."

Nathan Palm says that Jane's trying to go to the beach where they found the missing boy. That takes the detective aback. Nathan admits that Jane has become a little involved with the case. He's seen his daughter talking to someone who's not there. And he found a window on the desktop with subway directions to Coney Island.

The detective says, "Hang on." He puts on a raincoat. Walter makes horrible noises from under the bed. It must be the storm, the detective thinks. That or he's finally dying. Before he leaves, he opens wide the bathroom window, the one without a screen.

The detective jogs outside to his car, clearing branches out of the way. He's had enough of missing children, so he's going to fix this before it begins. He's happy to take this responsibility away from the father, because this father can't keep his kids safe. He can't keep his wife. This is the father's fault, and if Nathan were a better man, none of this would have happened. If the missing boy's mother had been a better mother, her kid wouldn't have died. He's disgusted by parents, and will sort their messes for them. Still, even in his proactive mania, he believes that Jane will be the next one to vanish.

What would the city do for her if she was gone? It would bleed; it would tear its hair out. And what will happen to him? No one can ever learn that he failed to report a missing child. It won't matter, he tells himself, because he is going to find Jane Palm. Jane Palm is not missing. The subway doors close on Marion Palm repeatedly.

The detective drives to the train station closest to the Palm brownstone. Nathan believes this is where Jane would begin her journey, as this is the train station she is most familiar with. The detective parks the car. He locks it, even though he doesn't have to. This is the safest neighborhood in Brooklyn. He jogs down the steps into the dark train station. An odd sight to have this part of the city be still. He calls out Jane's name and explains who he is. He says, "We talked before." He says, "Your father asked me to come get you."

The subway turnstiles are all gated shut, so there's no way she could get into the actual tunnel, he tells himself. She's not in any real danger. He thinks about repostering the city anyway. He thinks, *Don't think about that. It's done now.*

"Jane!" he yells. The name echoes back to him, and even though she couldn't be in the train tunnel, he waves his flashlight

407

beyond the turnstiles into the dark abyss of the nonfunctioning station. He sees movement, but when he focuses the light, he realizes it's the movement of rats crawling out from the tracks. No humans deter them from the platform to scavenge for food. It's also the hurricane. The rats feel it, just like Walter does, even though the storm has passed. He can't look for long because it's a revolting sight. Nothing should move like that. He turns, and the beam of light catches the girl in the face and she holds her hands up.

"Jane? Is that you?" the detective says. "Your father is worried about you."

"I need to go to the beach," she says. "But I couldn't get by all the rats."

"They shut the trains down. It would have been a long walk."

"He's alone."

"Let's take you home."

"I don't want to go back there."

The detective needs to put some distance between himself and the rats, so he picks up the girl and carries her out of the train station. She's kicking and punching, trying to wriggle away from him.

"Christ," he says. "Can I put you down? Will you run away?"

From Jane's silence, he infers that she will.

He huffs to his car and must put her in the back with locked doors, as if she is a suspect. Inside the car, in the front seat, as he catches his breath, he wants to tell her that her mother is safe, but he can't because he's not sure. Instead he asks some mandatory questions: "Is there a reason why you don't want to go home? Has anything bad happened to you?"

"No, nothing bad."

"Do you feel unsafe?"

Jane shakes her head.

"Your father is worried about you — he misses you."

"I don't care," Jane says. "I want to go to the beach. My friend is there."

And the detective has had enough.

"Your friend is not there. Your friend is in the morgue and he's going to be buried soon, so his mother can have some peace."

Jane shakes her head; no, that is not her friend. The detective exhales and starts the car. The stubborn eight-year-old has made up her mind, and why should he try to change it? He'll take her back to her father. It's really not his problem.

HURRICANE DINNER

Sveyta makes her phone call to her friend and gives the name. She says the last name in English and in Russian. Explains, "Like the palm of a hand." From the background, Marion helps: "Like the trees in Hollywood." Sveyta turns to her, surprised that she understood the Russian. Marion is nonchalantly sipping her wine, doesn't know that she's betrayed anything. Sveyta translates Marion's suggested phrase into Russian. Her friend understands.

She hangs up and begins to prepare dinner for herself and Marion. The storm seems to be moving on, but neither woman checks the weather. They both want to watch from the window. Sveyta's making blinis with the good canned caviar she bought and a dollop of sour cream. She makes blini after blini until she hears back from her friend.

"Whatever you do, don't let her leave."

"Why?" Sveyta asks in Russian, though aware that Marion seems to understand.

"There's a problem. Some money is missing."

"From the apartment?"

"No, from one of the daughters' savings account. And other people are looking for her. A private school in Brooklyn Heights. They published an ad in the *Bay News.* We're following up."

Sveyta looks at the frumpy woman in her kitchen, middle-aged too soon, her shoes ugly, her skin sagging where it should not sag.

"Really?"

"Don't let her go anywhere."

Sveyta will make more blini.

MARION'S FATE

Anna receives a phone call from the private investigator while she's driving Ginny back to her father's house. She texts at a stoplight for him to call her in ten minutes. When she pulls up in front of the Palm brownstone, she waves to Nathan, who stands in the door frame. Ginny slinks from the street to the house and disappears inside. The PI calls again, and Anna picks up this time.

"We've got her," the PI says. "Someone called in about the ad." Anna watches Nathan wave a final time and close the front door.

It's Marion's current employer who replied. It seems Marion has kept up her bad habit of taking what does not belong to her, and so this employer would like a face-to-face meeting. Anna wholeheartedly agrees, and is looking forward to working with this new employer. When she gets the address of the midtown penthouse, she asks the PI,

412

"What was Marion doing there?" The PI replies, "The woman wouldn't say. She sounded Russian."

A van honks at Anna, who is double-parked and blocking the street. She gives the van the finger.

"And Marion is still working there? They have an address?"

"They were kind of cagey about that. I think so."

The van driver leans on the horn, and Anna attempts to finish the phone call with the investigator. She compliments him on a job well done.

He says, "One more thing. Did you know the Palms are tapped out?"

"Marion and Nathan?"

"No, the whole family. The trust. It never recovered from the recession. So, the reward. I get a ten percent finder's fee, right?"

The van is able to inch around Anna's car but still knocks off her right side mirror. It speeds away. Anna hangs up on the PI, grips the steering wheel, and attempts to scream in frustration. What comes out is a high-pitched but soft vowel sound.

Inside the brownstone, Nathan is plating spaghetti Bolognese with an arugula salad and focaccia he baked from scratch. His delinquent daughters sit at the table, and

Nathan places the plates in front of them. He grates Parmesan onto the plates. Ginny picks up her fork, but Nathan says, "Wait." He takes pictures of the food. He says, "Go ahead," and Ginny and Jane begin to eat, and Nathan continues to take pictures. "Can you smile?" he says. Jane smiles, but Ginny does not. "My soul, Dad," she says. "What about my soul?"

Nathan takes more and more pictures, because he cannot eat any of the food he prepared. He can't ingest anything; his heart and stomach won't permit it. Also, he must keep moving or his daughters will see his deterioration.

MARION IN CUSTODY

Sveyta and Marion sip white wine until they finish the bottle, and Sveyta tells Marion she knows. Marion asks Sveyta, "Know what?" Sveyta replies that she knows about the money. Marion looks out the window and asks if there are any blini left, and Sveyta shakes her head. There is a knock on the door.

Sveyta opens the door with curt yet elegant Russian greetings, and a short man with broad shoulders and a buzz cut enters carrying a rolled-up magazine. Sveyta leads him into the kitchen, and says, *Eto ona*. Marion translates: *This is her.* The man grunts and sits at the kitchen table and opens the magazine and leafs through a few pages.

"Is he going to take me somewhere?" Marion asks.

"Eventually, but for the time being he's going to make sure you don't leave," Sveyta says. "I have work to do in the morning." She washes the dishes and says goodnight.

The short man reads his magazine, then stretches out on Sveyta's white sofa, kicks off his loafers, and begins to snore. Marion leaves the kitchen table and is walking to her bedroom when the man speaks.

"Don't even think about leaving," he says. "There is no escape scenario for this situation."

"Why not?" Marion asks, genuinely wanting an answer.

"It would not be safe," the man says, and he appears to fall asleep again.

Marion returns to her bedroom and sees that Sveyta has tidied. The skirt was spilling out; her clothes were on the floor. Now the skirt and the clothes are neatly folded on her bed and the suitcase is zipped shut and upright by the door. Marion opens it and finds what she expected. The money is gone. So is the Russian girl's laptop.

She tucks herself under her blanket. She turns off the light. The cross is back above her bed. The air is humid with the hurricane that didn't happen. She listens to the short man snore in the living room.

Anna and the Matriarch

The day after the failed hurricane, Anna drives alone into the city. She hasn't told the board about the Palms' financial situation, or about the reward money she now owes. She has a certified check in her bag from her personal checking account, but it's not the whole amount. It's all she could get her hands on in a day, but she'll come up with the rest. That's what she'll say. And it's better to handle this reward situation on her own. Better to report that action has been taken, rather than ask for permission. Anna's learned a lot in her years of service to the school.

It's occurred to her that this meeting may be pointless. She may find Marion, and the Wing Initiative will still be unfunded. The school will still be missing over $100,000. Anna tells herself that Marion could sort out the taxes, could be of some use. But Anna expected total victory. She has found herself to be, at long last, incompetent.

It's a shiny tall building next to the park. In spite of her anxiety and depression, Anna is able to sneer at the new construction. This ostentatious wealth is both a relic and a beacon, she believes, of a different New York. The New York she knows and loves is vanishing, being replaced by a mausoleum for the financiers of the world and their pampered families. She enters the cavernous, boring lobby and is directed by a suited doorman to the multiple elevators. She takes one to the twenty-sixth floor, and a well-manicured woman is waiting for her when the doors open.

"Ms. Fisher," the woman purrs.

"Oh, Anna's fine."

"Anna, it is a pleasure to meet you." The matriarch leads Anna to the open door down the hallway and into the light-filled apartment. Anna is, like everyone else, astonished by the view. This sort of view does not exist for most. She wants to press her nose and her hands against the window and look down at the magnificent stretch of the autumn park. She will never again have this perspective of the park, but when the matriarch gestures to the leather sofa, she obediently sits.

Anna unhooks her large tote bag and her

purse from her shoulder. She wanted to be prepared for the meeting, so she brought proof of Marion's embezzlement, along with the reward check, but now she feels grace-less and uncoordinated, loaded up and down, truly out of place. The matriarch holds nothing, just her perfect posture, her rib cage in true alignment with her head and her pelvis, and she seats herself ele-gantly on the sofa with Anna.

A pause happens, and then Anna begins to talk and shuffle through her papers, clut-tering up the Russian's coffee table with the proof. She's pointing at columns of spread-sheets, demonstrating the many times Mar-ion fudged the numbers for her own gain. She talks fast, buzzing from one subject to another, not realizing how hurt she sounds. "At first it's twenty dollars here, forty dol-lars there," Anna explains to the matriarch, "but she's stealing more. She's taking it from us. From me. And the worst part is, her girls are on partial tuition because she works for the school. Look, she stole a thousand dollars from me," pointing at her own last donation to the school, which never made it where it was supposed to go. The matriarch rests her hand on Anna's shoulder, and Anna stops with her mouth hanging open. Then she asks, "Well, what did Marion take from you?"

The matriarch looks Anna in the eye. "Nothing that we won't get back."

"What do you mean?"

The matriarch stands and walks to the kitchen. She reaches into the fridge and pours a glass of water for herself from a pitcher that stands on the top shelf. She pours one for Anna too.

"Did you contact the police?" the matriarch asks.

"No, we didn't want the publicity. We still don't."

The matriarch returns with the cold water and places both glasses on coasters next to the papers.

"Good, neither do we. I am willing to make reparations to you and the school if we can handle the Marion Palm situation privately."

"Reparations?"

"How much did Marion embezzle from the school?"

"We think around a hundred and forty thousand dollars."

"Let's call it an even two hundred thousand dollars. I will tell my bank manager to make the transfer to the school as an anonymous donation."

"I don't understand," Anna says.

"It will be over soon," the matriarch says. "We will handle Marion, and you will handle the school. I think that is the most efficient course of action."

"But why would you pay —"

"It's over."

Anna hesitates and then tidies her mess of papers on the coffee table.

THE PALM FAMILY FORTUNE

The Palm Trust financial manager is making a series of somber phone calls to the current generation of Palm artists, volunteers, drug addicts, and socialites to explain that their checks are going to get smaller. The family has been a fruitful one — Nathan has more cousins than he can recall — but has dipped into the capital once too often. The Palm family fortune is finally running out. The financial manager thought he would be all right — he thought he had invested correctly and that the market would replenish the losses — but it didn't happen. He explains this on a loop to increasingly bewildered people. They will all be all right, he assures them, but they must make some changes to their spending habits.

Nathan gets the call the day after the hurricane doesn't happen. He's still feeling hollow from his daughters' disappearance, so he doesn't worry about the money. This is the latest in a series of disasters, and it will be fine. The financial manager thanks Nathan Palm sincerely for his generosity of spirit and kindness. Nathan says, "It's not your fault."

When Nathan hangs up the phone, he wonders why he said that. It *is* the financial manager's fault, but Nathan can't be angry. He pulls up his blog again on his computer. The more intrusive comments have gone quiet, and it's all about window blinds today. He answers questions, gives his opinion assuredly but not fanatically. The individual must decide: *What would look best in your house?* The comments say, *Thank you, and by the way, how are you holding up? How are your girls doing?*

Nathan writes a post about his daughters' reactions to his wife's disappearance. He writes poetically about Jane's connection with the missing boy and Ginny's recent delinquency. He hopes that one day they will be stronger women because of this hard time. At the end, he talks about himself. He invents a moment he and his daughters shared recently, a difficult but frank conversation, and inserts one of the pictures from the hurricane dinner to the post. The spaghetti Bolognese looks red and hearty. The Parmesan shavings are artfully scattered, and the basil leaves at the center of each plate are the perfect shade of green. The table is set with three white plates crowded with pasta on a reclaimed farm-door table with mismatching silverware and checkered napkins. The storm candles are lit, even though the electricity never went out. There's a picture of Jane with sauce at the corners of her mouth, and she's turning to Ginny with a sprig of basil between her index finger and thumb. Ginny looks like she could start laughing. He publishes.

An email pops up in his inbox from a subsidiary of one of the larger publishing houses in New York. Nathan eagerly clicks. It's an editorial assistant or an assistant editor — it's not clear. She's been reading his blog and believes there is a book there: Would he be interested in a meeting?

Nathan knows enough to not write back immediately. He thinks about the meal he will serve the editorial assistant/assistant editor. He's already decided to be forthcoming about his new agoraphobia. It will only make the book more sellable. He'll do webcam readings and radio podcasts, meanwhile serving delicious drinks and meals made from ingredients delivered to his door. He'll make it a mentally handicapped-lifestyle-guide-slash-memoir. He's imagining the book jacket.

MISSING PERSONS

The detective has no children. He has no wife. He used to date a woman, but they broke up when she decided to move to Michigan to be near her family. All he has is Walter, whom he found half starved and fully crazed in his brother's empty apartment. After doing the dishes and writing out a check to the landlord for the owed rent, the detective took Walter home, along with his brother's plasma TV. He left a note for his brother explaining where his cat and his television set could be found, should his brother return. Up till now, the detective has paid his brother's rent and Walter's still alive, but he's had enough of Brooklyn families. This will include his own.

Nathan Palm wouldn't come out to the car to get his daughter. The detective had to take the girl in his arms up the stoop. Nathan expressed a certain amount of helplessness at the door and hung his head.

in shame, but collected the small girl and promised her there would be repercussions for her disobedience but also a hot meal. The edge of the hurricane had downed some trees, tossed some garbage around, and so the prospect of a warm house was a good one. The detective wondered if Nathan would invite him inside.

Nathan did not. Instead he brought his hand up to his forehead and pinched his temple with his thumb and forefinger. The detective watched as Jane Palm disappeared into the house.

A minute or two passed with Nathan and his temple. Finally the detective spoke up.

"Is there anything else I can do for you?"

The detective thinks about why he asked this question. Was it sarcasm? Or did he really feel like he hadn't done enough? Because Nathan let his hand drop, and without looking at the detective he said, "No, that'll be all."

Was it a joke that Nathan Palm made? The detective tells himself yes, yes, it was a joke, even though Nathan stepped back into the house and shut the front door on him, even though he was still waiting on the stoop.

He returns home to find Walter pissing in his hallway. The detective opens every window, lifts every screen. The cat follows,

and as he fumbles with the rusty hardware
of the screens, the cat rubs its lips up and
down the detective's socked toes and ankles.

ANNA GETS HER WAY

The girls are waiting in the anteroom outside the principal's office. Inside, Anna, the principal, and the deans of the middle and lower schools sit around a mahogany conference table with Nathan. Nathan is sweating, but not nearly as much as he thought he would be. It seems he *is* capable of leaving his house. This is not mental illness but preference. Nathan would prefer to be in the safety and security of his house, but he doesn't need to be there. He worries about his house while he's gone.

It's George, the middle-school dean, who's speaking, and he's speaking about adjustments, and how it can be hard for girls Ginny's age. He's trying and failing to make the room laugh or smile. The only one who does is Anna, and it is a tightly controlled response. Only Anna knows that she's having a very good time. Her interaction with the matriarch has left her euphoric, because the universe finally makes some sense. The Wing Initiative will succeed, despite Marion, despite the Palms. Anna has won. The only thing left is the punishment of the Palm family. It's unfortunate that Marion is not here, but it can't be helped. Besides, the Russians will take care of Marion. Anna stifles a giggle.

The middle-school dean explains more about the specific chemistry, the alchemy of a class, and how Ginny is such a great girl. He keeps saying that, and Nathan isn't clear why there are so many people in the room. He's looking confused when Anna interrupts the babbling dean.

"Based on Ginny's behavior two days ago, it's been decided that she will be expelled. Well, not just two days ago, correct? Ginny has been on a kind of probation."

Nathan opens his mouth to defend his daughter, but all that comes out is "For just one joint?"

"And trespass," the principal includes.

"And a few other things," Anna says. "Ginny's behavior has been . . . well, let's simply say erratic." Anna was about to say promiscuous, but she's a feminist. She tries not to comment on the sexual behavior of girls.

"Is this because of Marion?" Nathan asks.

The teachers and administrators look at their laps; Anna does not. She smiles and says, "Can you tell us specifically what you are referring to?"

"Well, the emails said . . . And you said that you thought Marion had been, well . . ." Nathan trails off.

"Please. Continue. What has Marion been doing?" Anna says. "I'm sure everyone would like to know. She is, after all, your wife."

Nathan submits. "Nothing. Nothing. I'll take Ginny home."

"There's more, Nathan," Anna says. "A minute more of your time."

The lower-school dean clears her throat. "We've been having some concerns about Jane."

"Jane? Why?"

The lower-school dean begins to explain that Jane is a wonderful little girl, but developmentally she hasn't been matching her peers. The administration feels that this school is not the appropriate environment for her, because it is not the type of environment in which an imaginative girl like Jane can flourish.

Anna takes particular pride in this speech. Jane's expulsion was more difficult for her to manage, as Jane's teacher seems invested in the youngest Palm staying at the school. Anna had to elucidate to the teacher that the decision was not hers to make.

The lower-school dean concludes with a wave of her hands and leans in; she also wants Nathan to smile. All these teachers and administrators, all they want in their hearts is for Nathan to say, *Yes, you are right. Thank you.*

Nathan slumps in his chair. "You're expelling them both?"

"It's for the best," Anna says, and the teachers and deans bob their heads and repeat, "The very best."

MARION NEGOTIATES A DEAL

Marion spends two days in the apartment with the short man. He mostly sleeps. He finishes his magazine and asks Marion if she has any books he can read. She says no. He spends some time looking at Sveyta's bookshelf, which is filled with classic Russian literature and romance novels. He chooses a romance. When Marion asks why he made that choice, he tells her that his Russian isn't good anymore, and it would depress him to notice the decline of his mother tongue. Marion says, "You don't have an accent." The short man begins to read.

The third day, Marion is woken in her room by a sharp knock on the door, and then, "It's time." Marion wonders if she is going to be killed. She decides that if this is the last day of her life, she's going to try on the Grace Kelly skirt. She steps into the center of the tulle and shimmies it over her hips. She sucks in her stomach and buttons the skirt over the T-shirt she's been wearing as a nightgown. There isn't a full-length mirror in the room, only a small handheld thing, and Marion tries to gather intelligence on how the skirt fits from different angles. She steps into the hallway to ask both the short man and Sveyta, but he's waiting outside for her.

"Let's go."

"I still need to brush my teeth," Marion says.

The short man doesn't care, and holds her arm with a firm grip. He gives her time to step into her shoes, and they are out the door. He's pulling her down the stairs, and Marion clip-clops after him. In the midst of this, she recognizes that she loves the feeling of the skirt around her legs, and believes in herself once more.

Sveyta waits in her car for them, and the short man puts Marion in the backseat. After the door shuts, he sits in the front seat and Sveyta locks all the doors. He reaches into his jacket pocket and pulls out a stick of gum and offers it to Marion, who gratefully accepts.

"Good morning, Sveyta," Marion says. "You must have had an early start."

Sveyta says nothing and pulls out of her

parking spot.

The ride to midtown is stressful for Sveyta. The traffic is terrible, and the short man comments often on her driving, repeating the sentiment that women are bad drivers because of biology. On the Belt Parkway, Marion stands up for Sveyta, says, "You are making her nervous," and the short man turns to slap Marion across the face. It's a small movement, and from his ease with the action, Marion knows it's not the first time he's hit a woman. She asks if he is Ukrainian, and Sveyta says, "No, Marion, this is not him." Marion presses her warm, wet cheek. When the short man slapped her, she began to cry. She remembers: this is her physiological response to being hit, and it has nothing to do with sadness or pain. She chews her now flavorless gum.

They pull up in front of the midtown apartment building, and the short man opens the door for Marion and helps her out. Sveyta drives away. The wind blows through the skirt, and Marion can't help but look down at the beautiful movement. She thinks, *And this will be my last time outside.* It's a fall day in Manhattan. It could be worse.

The man pulls her into the apartment building, past the doorman, and into an elevator. He pushes the button for the twenty-sixth floor, and the doors close.

"Do you have a piece of paper maybe?" Marion asks. "For my gum." The short man lets go of her arm and puts his hands into his pockets. He pulls out a receipt. Marion takes it and spits her gum into it. She crumples up the wad and then discovers that her skirt has no pockets. She drops the wad of gum on the floor of the elevator, discreetly, she thinks, but the short man sees and rolls his eyes.

The doors open, and there is a slow walk down the hallway to the apartment. Marion counts her breaths, her inhalations and her exhalations.

The matriarch opens the door, perfectly coiffed, and visibly registers Marion's outfit. The short man asks if he should stay, and the matriarch says, "Outside." The door is closed, and Marion is instructed to sit on the couch. The matriarch sits in a wing chair facing her.

"You have done an incredibly stupid thing," the matriarch says. "Why?"

"Because I could," Marion says.

"What about your family?"

"I miss them sometimes. But mostly it's fine."

"Why are you wearing that?"

"Do you like it?"

"You are too old for it. And too fat."

"I'm only thirty-eight. Are you going to kill me?" Marion asks. The matriarch says nothing. Marion looks out the window at the park, gestures to it, and says, "May I?"

The matriarch says yes. Marion walks to the window and looks at the orange-and-red park below and the gray buildings and finally the gray sky. She knows the window opens just wide enough to slide her body out. It would be difficult to maneuver, but it might be for the best. However, the matriarch hasn't confirmed whether she is going to be killed, so she'll wait. It would be terrible if she committed suicide when she didn't have to.

The matriarch asks Marion to sit down again, and Marion does as she's told.

"Do you know how we caught you? An associate of ours happened to see an ad in a paper, and then we believed our daughter. Sveyta searched your room and found the laptop. Electronically, you were untraceable."

"That's nice to hear."

"Was it easy for you?"

"It wasn't hard."

"And Sveyta says that you are learning Russian."

Marion flips her hands up to the sky to express that she can't help herself.

"We may have an opportunity for you," the matriarch says. "For a person with your talents." She explains that they are having difficulty with a certain source of income; it would be easier if that income appeared to come from somewhere else. Perhaps even an educational institution. The matriarch feels she should make it clear: the position would require relocation. Would Marion still be interested in this opportunity?

Marion beams. It's good to be recognized.

ANTEROOM

In the anteroom to the principal's office, seated next to her sister, Jane daydreams. She's bored and wishes that her sister would talk to her, but Ginny won't talk to anyone without yelling. Jane doesn't understand her anger, the way it behaves, the way it moves. She gets angry sometimes too, but eventually stops being angry. Her sister stays angry, as if she doesn't want to feel another way.

The missing boy has faded. It had something to do with the rats. He wouldn't help Jane pass them. He had no good ideas, as he did before. He's become quieter, and she keeps thinking of him in parts on the beach. The thought invades her subconscious and shocks her and she wants to think of something else, anything, because then she thinks of herself in parts. She's been dreaming that she has a hole in her arm and can see her own pearly white bone. Her flesh is pink and layered and reminds her of a photo of a canyon from her science textbook. The layers of rock signify different eras in the formation of the earth's crust. The hole in her dream is a neat and perfect circle. In her dream, she knows this peculiar injury will kill her, but not right away.

Jane shuts her eyes to see something besides the hole in her arm, and when she opens them, Beatrice is in the doorway. She has never been more grateful to see a person, this tall, beautiful girl who is always nice to her.

Beatrice asks, "Is my mom still in there?"

Ginny glares at her and won't reply.

Jane fills the silence. "Uh-huh, with my dad."

Beatrice smirks. "So, you guys ready for the wonders of the New York City public school system?"

Ginny tells Beatrice to go fuck herself, and Jane tries to defend Beatrice, but Beatrice doesn't need her help.

"So did you guys, like, have any idea about your mom? Did you, like, know?"

"Know what?" Jane asks. She's baffled that Beatrice is allowed to talk about her mother. It seems that no one is allowed anymore.

"She'd been embezzling for years, my

mom said." When Jane looks confused by the word, Beatrice clarifies. "Stealing. Your momma was stealing."

"No, she wasn't," Jane says, incredulous.

"It's actually kind of cool," Beatrice says. "Your mom is, like, a criminal."

Ginny repeats that Beatrice should go fuck herself.

Beatrice says to Jane, "And you gave her up. Her baby girl. Hilarious. Tell my mom I came by. I need her to sign some form or something. Whatever."

Beatrice leaves and Ginny looks at Jane.

"Is it true? Did you tell them where she was?"

Jane shakes her head. Ginny pinches her arm.

"Did you tell? Did you? How did you know?"

The doors open up, and it's their father, pale, and Anna, victorious. Ginny drops her sister's arm, realizing that it doesn't matter. Their father has lost. Then Ginny does an uncharacteristic thing for a thirteen-year-old girl: she reaches for her little sister's hand, and she holds it, even though everyone can see.

MARION AT THIRTY-EIGHT

Marion at thirty-eight is an expert in women who embezzle. She's an encyclopedia of their fates. Her hero, or her alter ego, is a Virginia spinster, Miss Minnie Magnum, who was dubbed a modern-day Robin Hood by *Life* magazine in 1956. Poor Minnie Magnum embezzled over $3 million from the building-and-loan association where she worked. She gave the money away: she funded businesses, bought cars for her friends, offered down payments so they could own homes. She was sentenced to ten years in prison. Poor Miss Minnie Magnum. She wore a little hat when she was fingerprinted.

A year ago, at thirty-seven, Marion tried to stop. After years of shuffling numbers and funds, of misdirection, and of creating fictitious expense reports and employees, she did not know that she would miss it. To fill her time, she read articles on the Internet about Mason jars and bought them by the dozen and filled them with paper clips, pens, loose change, candles and sand, cotton swabs, and various foodstuffs. The Mason jars weren't meant to make up for the embezzlement. They were meant to distract. It didn't work. After twenty-two days, she charged the school events fund twice for folding-chair rental and pocketed $400. That was how it started, and how it remained, and how it ended. Transferring the money into her online bank account, she went to bed feeling safe and calm.

Nathan at forty-eight has spent weeks throwing away his wife's Mason jars. He finds them overused and uninventive.

Now Marion at thirty-eight returns to her house for the last time. She kept her house keys below the money in the knapsack and transferred them to the suitcase, and she never knew why. Now she does. She's been assured by the matriarch that the family will all be out of the house. Marion doesn't ask how the matriarch knows but believes it to be true.

Marion Palm needs her passport. She will be Marion Palm again. She isn't illegal anymore. The matriarch has fixed her little problem. She said, "You can be once more like a tree in Hollywood."

Marion lets herself into the house that she knows so well. Nathan has made changes. The furniture has been rearranged. The wallpaper's been stripped and the walls painted. There are more plants. The house smells like Nathan and like her daughters. She climbs the staircase, looking for evidence that she once lived here. A few pictures of her hang on the wall, but there were never that many to begin with. She hates the way she looks in photographs. But perhaps she always knew she was going to leave and thought it would be easier if her face was allowed to become unrecognizable to her family. She wonders how her daughters will be affected by her disappearance, but allows the thought to float away like a soap bubble.

On the second floor, in her bedroom, in her closet, Marion retrieves her daughters' birth certificates and Social Security cards from a manila envelope. She places the documents on the bureau for Nathan. The bureau has been moved: it's now against the wall across from the windows, and Marion believes it has been refinished. A large plant hangs in the corner, looking well cared for. The room seems lighter, more open. The bed is made. Her things have been organized but not stored away. Her clothes still hang in the closet; her tooth-brush is in a glass by the sink. Marion brushes her teeth, then puts the toothbrush and a tube of expensive moisturizer in her suitcase.

She hears the whining of the gate in the front yard. She returns to the top of the stairs. The shadow of her husband appears in the frosted windowpane of the front door. Marion is calm as she retreats to the kitchen. She's made this escape before.

Marion at thirty-eight remembers Minnie Magnum. If Marion adjusts for inflation, Minnie stole around $26 million. Marion, in other words, has work to do. She'll do it for the matriarch, or for the matriarch's husband — she isn't sure yet of the organizational hierarchy. But it seems that Marion, with her special skills, may be of some use to this graceful and perfectly poised family. She wonders how long it will last, her usefulness; how long can she be good? Marion Palm hopes the matriarch understands what she is.

In the basement, she retrieves her passport, driver's license, Social Security card, and birth certificate from the pink armoire. When Denise found the documents weeks ago, she thought to herself, *Oh, Marion's dead.* Then she thought, *She killed herself.*

And she thought, *Good.* After that, she struggled with her happiness that Marion was no longer breathing and with the fact that what she was feeling was not relief, it was joy. She should have left the Palm house then and never come back, but she didn't. She allowed Nathan Palm to do what he always does. She found herself sneaking into a house to satisfy and fulfill some need that she doesn't believe should exist. She sat in the living room with her scary shoes on and listened to Nathan with his daughter. She could have introduced herself, and she could have become Marion if she had wanted. She left without saying goodbye.

Marion slips the documents into her purse and listens to the creaking of the floorboards above her as Nathan and the girls move about on the first floor. Ginny calls out.

Marion exits through the basement door, and like the last time, she leaves it unlocked. It didn't concern her then, and it doesn't concern her now. She has a flight to catch.

MARION IS SAFE

The detective is sitting at his desk at the station when he gets the phone call. Marion Palm has resurfaced at JFK. She's leaving the country.

"Where's she headed?" the detective asks.

"Hang on," the voice on the phone says. "Moscow."

"Moscow?" the detective repeats. "Well. That's unexpected."

The detective requests that Marion Palm be detained; he wants to talk to her. He speeds the whole way to JFK, siren blaring, cars pulling out of his way. He makes it to JFK in twenty-four minutes. A new record.

He rushes into the terminal, locates the security office, and flashes his badge. He's led down a hallway to a fluorescent-lit room. There Marion Palm sits with a small suitcase, wearing a gray T-shirt and a bizarre skirt that doesn't fit. It is the woman from the train. The detective was right. Her roots are showing now, a thin stripe of brown down the middle of her scalp. She's patiently sitting at the table, hands folded in her lap. She looks up at the detective and smiles.

"Oh, it's you!" she says brightly.

"Marion Palm?" he says.

"Yes," she answers. Her voice is low, and there's that hint of Brooklyn in the vowel.

"Your family is looking for you," the detective says. Marion Palm looks at him and wrinkles her nose. "Are you in any trouble? Can I take you home?"

"Oh, no, I'm fine," Marion says.

"Can I tell them where you are? Or where you're going?"

Marion appears to think about it, but ultimately shakes her head.

"I think it's better for everyone if you don't. Thanks for asking."

The detective has no choice but to let Marion go on her way, and so he informs the TSA agent standing outside the door that Mrs. Palm is free to leave. He briefly considers doing Nathan Palm a favor and reminding Marion Palm of her daughters, thirteen and eight. But he doesn't feel like doing anything more for Nathan Palm.

Marion pauses before she leaves and turns to the detective. "It's a good thing I came early. I had a feeling this might happen. But it's nice to see you again."

"Yes. Safe flight," the detective says.

She smiles, and she's led back to airport security by the agent. It has occurred to Marion that she could be going to Moscow to be killed. She will be easier to murder in Moscow than in New York, and that's perhaps worth the price of her plane ticket. But why worry, she thinks, and besides, no decision is irreversible. At the gate, her plane is boarding. Marion hands her boarding pass over to be scanned, waits in another line, is corralled and belted into her seat, she's taxied, and then she is officially not on the ground anymore. She's herself and she's flying.

The detective sits where Marion Palm sat. He takes his phone out of his pocket and calls Nathan, who answers on the second ring. "Hello," Nathan says in weary voice. He wants to watch television, update his blog, and drink a glass of wine. He will even allow himself takeout. A day away from his house, though not frightening, was exhausting.

The detective clears his throat. "I wanted to let you know that we have located your wife and she's safe."

Nathan says, "What? Where is she? Put her on the phone."

"Well, she asked me not to tell you. And she's not here anymore."

"But you know? You know where Marion is? Tell me, I need to know. You have to tell me."

"No, I don't," the detective says.

Nathan keeps talking even though it's clear that the detective is no longer on the other end. He wishes he were afraid. He wishes Marion were dead. He turns, and his daughters stand there, looking.

THE PALM WOMEN

In the years to come, the Palm girls will tell the story of their mother often. They will tell it to friends, lovers, therapists, police officers, loan officers, deans of admissions, and salesmen. They will tell it to coworkers at happy hour. They will tell it after sex. They will tell it before sex. There will be a long version and a short version. There will be a funny version. Sometimes Jane Palm calls her father and wants to tell him the story, but she falters. Ginny Palm is the only one who can mention her mother to her father, because she can tolerate Nathan's long silences.

Sometimes the girls tell each other the story. They don't live in the same state, but they call. They talk around Marion Palm for a while but inevitably fall into the same conversation. *Remember the diner? Of course I remember.* And they begin to remember their mother. Sometimes they sympathize. Most times they don't. They try to understand why their mother married their father. They wonder why she had children. They don't wonder why she took the money. They do wonder how. The conversation ends when one Palm girl asks, *Where do you think she is now? What do you think she's doing?* The other Palm girl says, *Probably embezzling. Probably stealing. Maybe in prison. Probably not.*

And each girl silently recognizes within herself the part that belongs to Marion Palm. The Palm girls are unremarkable-looking women. They gain access. They earn trust. They wait for the perfect opportunity, believing that this part, this dark impulse, is common only to themselves and other criminals. They never tell, but the Palm girls think of their mother.

ACKNOWLEDGMENTS

There are many people I need to thank. This book wouldn't have been finished without them.

My incredible agent, Claudia Ballard.

My wonderful editor, Jennifer Jackson.

My deep gratitude to the University of Denver and to Selah Saterstrom, Laird Hunt, and Brian Kiteley.

Many thanks to Marina Romashko for her help with translation.

My dear, thoughtful friends, many of whom were kind early readers: Mona Awad. Mairead Case. Teresa Carmody. Caroline Cabrera. Rebecca Beck. Emily Lamia. Melanie Closs. Emily Klasson. Susan Heyward. Mariel Delghavi. Jessica Carbone. Karen Chau. Johannes and Nicole Van Der Tuin. Gary Tomlin. Lynda Myles. Patty Shay.

My family. I am fortunate to have been born into a family of talented writers. Thank you to my sister, Kathleen, for being one of my first readers and for answering my many questions about city-beat reporting. Thank you to my parents, Carolyn and Richard Culliton, for their generosity, support, and encouragement.

Thank you.

ABOUT THE AUTHOR

Emily Culliton is a PhD candidate in fiction at the University of Denver and earned her MFA from the University of Massachusetts Amherst. She was born and raised in Brooklyn.